Blackflies & Blueberries

by
Sharon Ledwith

Pandamonium Publishing House
Publishing Made Simple.
www.pandamoniumpublishing.com

ISBN: 978-1-998467-24-2
Published by: Pandamonium Publishing House
Publishing Made Simple.
www.pandamoniumpublishing.com
pandapublishing8@gmail.com

Printed in Canada

For permissions, inquiries, or additional rights, please contact Pandamonium Publishing House at the information listed above.

Follow us on social media for giveaways,
contests, and more:
Facebook: Pandamoium Publishing House
Instagram: @Pandamonium_Publishing_House8
YouTube: Pandmonium Publishing House
TikTok: Pandamonium Publishing
Pandamonium Publishing House
Publishing Made Simple.

Prologue

An icy breeze from the kitchen window sliced through Catherine Stewart. Her stomach tensed and she frowned. *Something is about to happen. Something bad.*

She drew her mouth into a straight line and bit her bottom lip, leaning against the kitchen counter. Her coral T-shirt rubbed across the counter's lip and her worn jeans lightly brushed the chestnut cabinet. She drew a deep breath and closed her tired, powder-blue eyes, allowing the ominous energy to consume her. Images filled her head. Images of bone-weary migrant workers harvesting vegetables in a sea of green, of blistered hands and grimy, sweat-stained clothes. Startled by these visions, she opened her eyes and looked into the sink. Her long, thin fingers were immersed in a strainer full of shredded lettuce. A laugh escaped her, allowing the uneasy moment to dissipate. Ever since Catherine was a young girl, her hands had possessed a special sight all of their own.

A shadow crawled across her oval face, like a spider stalking its prey. As a child, Catherine had often been dubbed a freak by her peers. Just because she was different; just because she possessed unusual *powers*. She had found out early in life that objects *talked* to her. Not talked in the same way that two people could carry on a conversation, but talked as in Catherine sometimes received subtle information from holding an object about its history and who had owned it. Personal objects like jewelry could tell her loads about the owner: what he or she did for a living, who they loved or hated, where they lived, and more. Catherine could get a person's whole life history if the object communicated this information to her. Sometimes what she found out was too emotionally overwhelming, too burdensome, so Catherine decided to keep her psychic ability a secret. That is, until she discovered it was possible to make a living using her powers.

Psychometry. That was what the fortune teller at the Toronto Exhibition told then thirteen-year-old Catherine her special power was called. That was over twenty years ago. Nowadays, Catherine preferred to call it her meal ticket. Over the years, she went from skipping classes to dropping out of school completely, choosing to sell her *object-talking* craft on the slick city streets. When her mother found out what she was up to, she went ballistic. So dear sweet mom packed Catherine's bags and sent her up north by bus to live with her aunt and uncle for a while. Catherine swallowed hard, tasting a lump of sour bile. The bus depot was the last time she had seen her mother alive.

Another sharp breeze broke Catherine's concentration. Her skin prickled. She reached over and slammed the window shut, knocking the jagged, purple rock she kept on the window sill into the sink. She scooped up the rock before it could land in the lettuce. A smile spread across her freckled, pale face. The small piece of amethyst had been given to her by her mother's older and only sister, Gertie. Catherine's thumb gently grazed over her childhood memento. *I wonder if Aunt Gertie still lives up in Fairy Falls?* Then she stiffened, thinking how she had no choice but to endure the last few good years of her youth in rustic Fairy Falls after receiving notice that her mom had been killed in a subway accident.

The amethyst cooled Catherine's palm. Her nose flared, picking up the scent of pine needles and fresh country air. She relaxed and half-smiled. *I guess it wasn't all that bad living in Fairy Falls.* There had been morning and evening canoe rides on Blueberry Lake, campfires, toasting marshmallows, and telling ghost stories. There had been swimming lessons in the warm afternoons and cool skinny dips in the hot, sticky evenings. But the best by far was blueberry picking on Aunt Gertie and Uncle Pete's extensive bushes in late July and early August. Blueberries were their main source of income in the summer, and enough had to be picked to fill the orders of local resorts and restaurants. After that, any berries left over were sold at the local Farmer's Market. This was where Catherine had honed her skills as a sharp saleswoman. Skills that had served her well through many years of participating in psychic fairs.

As these memories flooded Catherine's mind, she brushed her straw-blonde hair back behind an ear and brought the crystal up to her face. She rubbed it against her cheek and her smile increased. *No, it hadn't been all that bad in Fairy Falls.*

One particular day at the market fate had intervened in the form of a very handsome, and very sexy, tawny-haired boy named Tony Benton. Her aunt had taken an instant dislike to him. Her uncle, however, had been subtler, pulling out his rifle and cleaning it whenever Tony showed his face on their property. *Tony Trouble.* That's what Aunt Gertie had dubbed him, but Catherine didn't listen to her aunt, and she avoided her uncle like a swarm of blood-sucking blackflies. Soon things got serious between the pair of lovers, and Catherine confided in Tony about her special ability to talk to objects, about her psychic career on the streets of Toronto, and about the incredible amount of money she had made. Soon after that, she became Tony's meal ticket. She also became pregnant.

At seventeen and with only a minimal education, Catherine felt she couldn't tell her aunt and uncle about her pregnancy. They would have had Tony lynched in seconds. So one night, under the cover of the stars, Catherine and Tony hitched a ride to the nearest bus depot, leaving for Toronto. Catherine sighed heavily. She had never told her Aunt Gertie and Uncle Pete about Hart. The only information she had shared was a letter written in haste to let her aunt and uncle know she was safe, and that Tony had been offered a good paying job by a cottager who owned a business in the city. That was it. No mention of her pregnancy. No return address.

Soon, Catherine's dream for a better life turned into a nightmare when Tony broke her legs by pushing her down their apartment building's stairs, because according to him, she hadn't made enough money from her side-street psychic readings. He needed that money to supply him with enough beer and smokes for the week. Catherine winced, reliving the haunting pain of torn muscle and splintered bones, as if it had happened yesterday.

A bead of sweat ran down the side of Catherine's face, thinking back on the effort it took to try to crawl up those same stairs she'd been pushed down when she heard her three-month-old son, Hart, crying for her. A neighbor finally had the sense to call 9-1-1, and all Catherine could remember after that was waking up in the Toronto General Hospital, her legs plastered and in traction. Catherine's chin trembled as she wiped her slick cheek.

Six months of physiotherapy followed, while Hart was placed in a foster home. Catherine was determined to heal her legs and get her son back, at any cost. She was ready for a change in her life and she knew only she could make that happen. And change would have started by pressing charges against that abusive sleazebag she had once loved, but by the time a warrant had been issued for Tony's arrest, he was long gone. It was like he had disappeared off the face of the earth, or at least Catherine's tiny part of it.

Social workers helped her through the tough times, finding her a decent place to live, and a respectable job at a nearby food market. It wasn't much, but it was a new start. Once Catherine got Hart back, she started doing psychic readings at home in the evenings to supplement her income and pay for the extra food and clothing she needed for her growing boy. Her reputation as a psychic grew again, only this time she chose more wisely, deciding to help people the best way she knew through her gift of psychometry. News of her amazing abilities spread and soon she was invited to join the psychic fair circuit. Even the police had asked her to help out in a few baffling cases, getting Catherine to *commune* with articles of clothing from a missing child, or pieces of evidence left at a crime scene. Most of the time, Catherine would shine, but then there were those cases that would simply stump her and leave her in the dark, grasping for answers. Sometimes the object she held remained silent and there was nothing she could do.

A loud crash from Hart's bedroom startled her. Twisting, Catherine smacked the amethyst against the yellowing counter and lost her grip. The rock hit the floor and split in two pieces. Swearing, Catherine took a deep breath and headed toward the hallway.

Damn it. Hart must have left his window open again and another stray cat got in. The last cat that had managed to sneak into his room sprayed everything he owned. Catherine shook her head. She'd told him to lock his window the other day. There had been a rash of burglaries in this area and last week the police had gone door-to-door warning the residents to tighten their security. Her skin prickled. *I have half a mind to wring Hart's freaking neck when he gets home from school!*

Catherine chewed her bottom lip. She wasn't looking forward to another homework session with Hart. His reading and writing skills were appalling, yet he managed to squeak by each grade. Maybe she was partly to blame. Catherine couldn't count the number of times they'd moved. Better chances and better opportunities in her line of psychic work had opened so many doors for her. And with the moves, came new schools. And with the new schools, came the frustration of misplaced records, making new friends, and starting over for Hart. Now an intermediate attending his third high school, she would see to it that this would be his last.

Standing at the entrance of Hart's bedroom, Catherine cautiously peered in. A messy bed, clothes strewn across the floor, scattered video games on the dresser, and a broken lamp under the window greeted her. Catherine wrinkled her nose and grunted. *When is he going to learn that I'm not his maid?* She brought her tongue to the roof of her mouth and clicked, "Here kitty, kitty, kitty. Come out, you flea-bitten hairball."

Catherine caught a moving shadow on her left. Before she could turn around, a pair of hands encircled her thin neck and squeezed hard. Catherine's eyes widened and her mouth went dry. Instinctively, she reached up to grasp her attacker's hands. Even through the latex gloves, she could feel the ugliness of bulging veins, like an anaconda's coils rippling around its prey. She slid her hands up until her right thumb connected with a man's chunky, thick bracelet. Gasping, Catherine begged the bracelet to talk to her, to tell her what this man wanted.

Her stomach tightened. He wasn't here to rob her. He was here to kill her.

1. Welcome to Fairy Falls

The bitter cold snap was unusual for this time of year. At least that's what Hart Stewart had been told by the truck driver who had given him a lift up to this godforsaken area. Now here he stood, in the heart of this rinky-dink town called Fairy Falls. He shivered in his plaid hoodie, and tried to keep warm by stomping up and down on the front porch of the Fairy Falls General Store. His breath billowed another puff of cold air as he continued with his odd dance to keep his circulation going. Hart's faded jeans stiffened against his frozen legs, but he kept moving. In fact, he had been on the move for a year now, ever since the day he'd found his mother's lifeless body in his bedroom.

Hart grimaced. His unshaven face sunk before he hawked a sour-tasting ball of spit onto the porch. Nothing had been taken from their apartment that day. Nothing, except his mother's life. Why? Who would commit such a heinous crime and not take anything? A disgruntled client because his mother hadn't given a good enough psychic reading? A deranged ex-con doling out his revenge because she had helped the police in the investigation that put him away? Hart clenched his jaw. Even the police didn't have any leads. It was a cold case that had left Hart homeless and orphaned until social assistance informed him that he had relations up here in Fairy Falls, something his mother had never told him.

Sighing, Hart pulled a ratty piece of paper out of his pocket. On it, the social worker had scrawled his great-aunt's address. He puckered his mouth to one side. He could pick out some of the words and knew the numbers, but he couldn't read it. Thankfully, the social worker had told him the address, which he had memorized. A little trick he had picked up throughout his elementary school days to help him cope with being basically illiterate. Now school was over for him and life stood in front of Hart like a blurry neon sign he couldn't make out.

Somewhere on Blueberry Lake. That's where Hart was headed. Now all he had to do was wait for the store to open so that he could ask directions there. Hart checked his wrist watch again. *Six a.m. Great. Still another hour to go.* Shuffling his five foot eleven frame around, Hart stuffed the paper with the address back in his coat and continued to stomp off the cold.

Questions bombarded his mind. Questions like, who did his mother's aunt resemble? His mom? Him? Why hadn't mom kept in contact with her aunt? What had happened between them? As these questions surged through Hart's mind, he managed to stomp over to the local bulletin board. He stopped and stared at it.

Letters crashed together in their unrecognizable forms, running as one and colliding until Hart managed to pick out a few words. A bright yellow flyer with the date 'May fourteenth' printed on it captured his eye. The word 'jobs' followed the date. Hart licked his bottom lip, then snatched the flyer from the cork board. If he was going to stay here for a while he'd need a job, unless his great-aunt tossed him out on his ass and sent him packing. Well, at least Hart would know by May fourteenth whether he'd be staying or going. Folding the flyer neatly in three, Hart reached for his tattered khaki backpack and stuck it in one of the pockets. He'd ask someone about the particulars of the flyer later, but for now Hart had to deal with the present.

Then he sneezed. *Damn. Hope I'm not coming down with another cold.* The last one had kept him flat on his back at the shelter in Toronto for over two weeks. He wiped his crooked nose roughly with the back of his hand and winced. His nose still hadn't healed properly from the fight he'd been in four months ago. All because Hart had been on someone else's turf. Someone bigger, stronger, and angrier than he was. In hindsight, Hart had been lucky to get away, especially with his knapsack still on him.

Hart's knapsack held all of his worldly possessions: a few changes of clothing, a tightly packed sleeping bag, and some toiletries. That was it. The rest of his and his mother's belongings had been sold. The sale had given him enough money to buy food and rent a room while he figured out what to do with his life. Then one night, after leaving his dishwashing job at a local tavern, Hart had been blindsided in an alleyway and relieved of his funds. A few weeks later, he was homeless.

After that, Hart had wandered from one shelter to another, still trying to figure out what to do and where to go. He had no job, no roots, and no hope. Then one day, he recognized one of his mother's clients coming toward him on the street. She looked frazzled and desperate. For some reason unbeknownst to Hart, he stopped her to ask if she was all right. Watery, almond-shaped eyes darted back and forth as if looking for someone. Beading perspiration gleamed all over her tight, olive face. In both chubby hands she clenched a rhinestone-encrusted leash. Without a word, Hart reached for it, and brought it up to the middle of his forehead, to a place his mother had referred to as the 'third eye'.

Talk to me, he had asked the leash. That was all. No smoke. No mirrors. Just a simple form of common courtesy to allow Hart access into its world. And as soon as he got the go ahead, he just let it happen.

His eyes rolled back, preparing to move into the realm of super-consciousness. To his *special* dimension. His surroundings began to fade into the background, letting him see in a different way. The same way as his mother saw. Like a movie shown in reverse, Hart allowed the story to unfold. To find out what had taken place. To get to the truth. At first he saw a small brown dog. He wasn't sure of the breed, but it had a fuzzy, curled tail, a cute button nose, and eyes as bright as the rhinestones on the leash. It was running, and it was scared. Down one alley, then another, until it reached a dead end. There it scampered into a cardboard box. Then something clicked. Hart recognized that alley. He knew it because he had spent a night there the other week.

Coming out of his self-induced trance, Hart grabbed the woman's hand and led her down the same alley he had seen in his vision. At first, the woman stiffened and tried to resist, but she relaxed when she saw her little dog, matted and dirty, but alive, shivering in an upturned cardboard box. She squealed, then threw her arms around Hart's waist and hugged him tightly. She was so grateful that she gave Hart two hundred dollars to buy some new clothes, and fed him a generous meal. All this because he had used his psychic ability to help her. An ability he had inherited from his mother and had kept hidden, even from her, ever since he'd discovered it.

Hart stood and rubbed some warmth back into his thighs as he moved toward a garbage can at the end of the porch. He swore aloud, icy breath spirals emitting from his mouth like a dragon's fire. His mother had been too involved with her stupid psychic career to care about him. His stubbled chin trembled as he thought back, even now. Hart hadn't one close friend because of her, because of the constant moving and changing schools, and because of what she could do when she touched objects.

He frowned. *Well, she can stuff her damn psychic ability! All it ever did was drive a wedge in between us!* He snorted indignantly. If his mother had known about his supernatural powers she would have dragged him along with her to every psychic fair she could book. *No thanks. That kind of life isn't for me.* Hart had only used his psychometry skills for survival. Unlike his mother, he never relished the thought of his abilities being used for the purpose of someone else's entertainment. The bitter tang in his mouth returned.

Furiously rubbing his hands together, he looked down at the ground near a green, dented can with the hope of finding some discarded cigarette butts—a recent habit he had picked up, not to poison his lungs, but to warm his hands. He flinched as the ball of his thumb grazed a fresh cigarette burn on his palm. Later, it would end up being one of the many scars that littered Hart's palm. Spying a half-smoked cigarette, he smiled and reached for it only to stop in mid-air and narrow his eyes. There, not six inches away from the butt, lay a gold ring with a large diamond in the middle, flanked by two good-sized rubies. Hart grinned at his new find. *Things are looking brighter already.*

Ignoring the crushed butt, Hart reached for the ring. He whistled. *This must have cost a bundle.* He sneezed again, this time knocking his baseball cap off his head, releasing his shoulder-length, tawny locks. Carefully wiping his nose on the sleeve of his coat, he reached for his cap. As his hand clutched the cap's tattered blue brim, a surge of emotions swept through him. His mom had brought this cap home from one of her psychic fairs. An eye in a triangle was embroidered on the front, and the words 'ALL IS ONE' in black lettering were stitched on the back. At the time, his mom had explained to him what this symbolized, but Hart had long forgotten its meaning. He only remembered that she had been a no-show for most of that weekend.

Standing, Hart brushed the cap against his thigh to remove the dirt, and placed it on his head backwards, so that the brim covered the back of his neck. He banged his worn Nikes hard against the wooden porch in order to get some feeling back in his toes before he returned to examining the ring. *Somebody must be pretty pissed about losing such a nice piece of ice.* Hart rolled it around in the palm of his right hand.

Suddenly, the ring vibrated information to Hart without him asking for it. Even the burn scars on his hand didn't dull the sensitivity of his unique ability. It was here to stay no matter what. No matter if Hart wanted his freaky psychic anomaly or not, it was branded to him like some horrid birthmark. He clenched his teeth. What did he care what this ring wanted to tell him? There was no one around to profit from it. No owner. No one but him. And he wasn't giving the ring back, that was for sure. He'd pawn it as soon as he could. *At least hocking stuff is more respectable than doing stupid psychic readings.*

But the ring wouldn't let up. It kept trying to pull him in. Make him see. *See what?* Hart wondered. *See some old rich lady toss her empty Starbucks cup into the garbage can, while her ring slips off her finger unnoticed? Like that's interesting.* Then, as if the ring wasn't going to take no for an answer, Hart's breathing hastened and his head pounded. He shuddered violently. He'd never experienced anything like this while communing with objects before. Any object. Sweat broke out on his forehead, rolling past his dimples to drip off his strong, square chin. His lower lip trembled. Hart's weakened body collapsed to the porch as he realized that this ring was absorbing his energy, plugging into him.

Hart brought his clenched hand with the ring up to the middle of his forehead, between his eyes, and yelled, "Okay, okay, you win!"

Hart's eyes rolled back, as he surrendered to the ring's strange, unrelenting force, and mentally prepared himself to be thrust into the realm of super-consciousness.

Buildings, trees, cars, everything faded into the background. A thick, soupy fog encompassed Hart while he remained on the ground, his knees pressed to his chest, his breathing raspy and out of control. The feeling of being whisked away, like having an out of body experience made him shudder.

The fog cleared around him. Whoa, where am I? *Hart blinked a few times to gain his bearings, and noticed that he sat about ten feet away from the front end of a big-ass, blue Cadillac in a vacant parking lot. His throat thickened, staring at the car's wide hood ornament leering down at him, the full moon casting an eerie shadow across his face.*

Hart frowned and glanced up at the sky. Wait a second. Something's not right. There was no full moon last night. What's going on? *Then a funky aura surrounded the area, and a sudden noise startled him. His skin prickled. He heard someone approaching him with frantic, hurried steps. He squinted, seeing an attractive, red-headed woman close the gap between them. She looked older than his mom, but not by much. Hart watched her fumble for her car keys while juggling a large parcel in her arms.*

"Do you need any help?" Hart asked, mindful not to spook her.

But she didn't answer him. She didn't even acknowledge his presence. Hart's chest tightened. It was as if he were a ghost.

He heard her mumbling to herself and managed to catch the odd word. Development. Scam. Traitor. *But that's all. He narrowed his eyes. None of it made any sense to him.*

A shadow snaked across Hart's right side. He shivered at the cold, icy feeling. The woman was suddenly ambushed from behind by someone wearing a black ski mask and trench coat. Hart watched helplessly as a pair of gloved hands wrapped around her willowy neck. Instinctively, she dropped the parcel and fought back. Somehow, she managed to use the car as a brace and turned to face her attacker. Her arm defensively swung up and she grabbed for the mask. She desperately pulled it, and as a reward for her efforts, half the mask was torn from her attacker's face. The woman balked. Hart's eyes widened. Without being able to see who the woman saw, Hart knew she knew her attacker. He violently cringed and curled forward, cupping his belly with his hand. How is this possible? He could feel her stomach churning and heating up.

"B-B-Bastard!" escaped from her mouth before she was viciously pinned against the car.

"Leave her alone!" Hart yelled, releasing his stomach, but there was no response. He clenched his jaw. Trying to help this woman is freaking useless. No one can see me and no one can hear me. *His whole body hardened.* Wait, maybe they can feel me? *Rolling to stand, he was instantly pulled back down as if magically shackled to the ground.* What the hell? *He gasped, feeling the muscles and veins in his neck tighten. His eyes bulged, and still clutching the ring, he clawed at the invisible fingers around his throat. He could feel the woman's pain, her anguish, her battle to breathe. Gasping and struggling for air, Hart forced his lungs to work overtime, but it was hopeless. His lips trembled as he watched her face turn purple and her eyes roll back.*

"Please stop, please stop," Hart whispered hoarsely. But it *didn't stop. The woman's body fell to the ground like a rag doll, her head smacked against the door mirror. He flinched at the searing sensation. His head throbbed. He felt a goose egg rising on his forehead.* How is it that I feel what she feels? It's impossible.

Trembling, he closed his eyes, and willed himself back to reality. But it didn't work. It was as if the ring was in total control of this vision, like a movie director calling the shots and setting the tone. In previous visions, he'd been the one to pull back out of a trance at any point and any time he chose. But not this time.

All Hart heard was his own laboured breathing. He opened his eyes to witness the murderer open the passenger's side door and lifting the dead woman into the car, positioning her in the front seat like a soulless mannequin. Then the killer calmly snatched up the parcel on the ground, slid into the driver's seat, and started the car. Hart jerked, blinded by the headlights. Spinning tires devoured gravel, and in a jolt, the car gunned straight for him. Panicking, Hart raised his arms in a useless attempt to shield himself from the oncoming vehicle and as he did this, the diamond and ruby ring jumped out of his hand.

A metallic thud brought Hart out of his vision. Sitting on the porch with his knees pressed tightly to his chest, Hart shivered like a newborn baby. The frigid spring temperature seduced his hot, shaking body. His sweat mingled with the frost, and he was glad of the union. Glad that it was over. Glad to be back.

Hart licked his lips. *What just happened to me? Did I really just witness a murder?* He frowned. If so, what did the ring have to do with it? Was it cursed? Or was it the only witness left to testify to this horrible crime? Confused, sweat-soaked, and a little dazed, Hart reached for the ring, next to his shoe. If what he had seen was true, then something had happened to that red-headed woman.

Something bad.

2. The Three Muskateers

"Where is it? Where is it?" Diana MacGregor muttered, frantically rummaging around her brown suede purse.

"Where's what?"

Startled, Diana looked up to find her best friend, Brook Bennet, leaning against the steel gray locker next to hers. Bright blue eyes held Diana's green ones captive for a moment. Brook's recent nose ring was a distraction, but at least Diana couldn't see her friend's six-month-old tongue piercing. Brook swept her newly-dyed, short, raven hair behind her ears. Thin, but not too thin, Brook loved to dress in black. Diana checked over her friend's attire. Her own low-rider tan pants and long-sleeve plaid blouse paled in comparison to Brook's flashy outfit. Today Brook wore faux leather pants and a thin, short-sleeve lacy T-shirt. Sexy, high-heeled shoes adorned with charms Brook called pentacles twinkled up at Diana. A matching belt accompanied the ensemble. All in all, Brook looked like the modern-day witch she claimed to be.

"Hey, Earth to Diana," Brook said impatiently. "Where is what?"

Diana shook her head. "Honestly, Brook, you're looking more Goth every time I turn around."

Brook raised a thin, dark brow. "Wiccan, my dear. I'm a Wiccan."

Diana shrugged. "Whatever." She passed Brook her purse. "Here, see if you can find it."

"Find what?" Brook asked, dipping a pale hand into the purse.

"My mother's diamond and ruby ring. I can't find it anywhere. You check my purse over and I'll scour my locker again. It's gotta be somewhere."

"Are you sure you put it on this morning?" Brook asked, fishing around the purse's bottom.

Diana glared at her friend. "You know I never take that ring off, Brook. I've been wearing it since...since..." she said, stumbling over the words.

Brook ceased her search and put a hand on Diana's shoulder. "I know. It's hard, today being the first anniversary. You know I'm here for you, girl. Always was, always will be."

Diana smiled weakly, placed a fair, freckled hand over Brook's pale one, and squeezed it gently. "Thanks, Brook. You're definitely the Good Witch of the North."

Brook rolled her eyes. "Wiccan!"

"We can what?" a male voice teased.

The pair of friends turned in unison to face Donovan Johnson, Fairy Falls High School's lacrosse hero. He had also been the third 'Musketeer' in their group since they were children. Diana noted Donovan was wearing his new purple lacrosse team jacket embossed with the Fairy Falls Falcon's logo. He'd been beaming ever since he scored the game winner the other night.

Diana chuckled. "We can all search for my ring now that you're here, *Studmuffin!*"

Donovan's dark face fell. He cupped Diana's small chin and wiggled it. "Being saucy again, *Red?*"

Diana swatted Donovan's large hand away and scowled at him. She hated being reminded of the colour of her hair. It went so well with her face full of freckles and her pert nose. She'd be a shoe-in for that 'Anne of Green Gables' look if it ever came in style, but Diana was forced to keep her fiery mane shoulder length instead of long because it was wickedly wavy and disobeyed even the biggest brush. She sighed. At least Brook could experiment with her fine, thin hair, with whatever style inspired her and whatever colour beckoned.

"Don't force me to break up another one of your famous scraps, children," Brook scolded, passing Diana's purse to Donovan. "Here, make yourself useful and search this for Diana's mother's ring."

Donovan put up his hands. "No way. Guys don't go through chick's purses. It's just not right."

"Fine. Then help Diana go through her locker," Brook said, shrugging.

Donovan cringed. "That's even worse than searching through a purse!"

Diana ignored her bickering friends, and went back to her locker check. Sweaty gym clothes hung lifeless against the cold, steel wall. On the opposite side, her blue hiker jacket swung on a busted hook, pockets stuffed with the rolled yellow flyers she'd have to finish distributing before this weekend. Above her, the well-used textbooks Diana had removed twice to check behind stood erect on the shelf. The bottom was filled with an assortment of shoes, all flat and sturdy. Family pictures decorated the vented door. Pictures of the last Florida vacation during March-break with her family before that horrible day on May 6th. Diana's throat tightened. *The day my life changed forever.* Now there were only the three of them at home on Loon Lake. Her twelve-year-old sister, Nancy, and her dad, Michael MacGregor, who doubled as the town's mayor and practiced law at his firm, as he had done for the past fifteen years.

Diana's chin trembled. She coughed, tasting the sourness that continued to linger there. For the past year, all she had wanted was to find her mother's murderer and get the justice she deserved. Diana moistened her dry lips with her tongue. A real estate agent working for a city development company had found her mother's body slumped in the front seat of her Cadillac on a vacant lot, near one of the lakes north of Fairy Falls. Yet nothing had been stolen from her. Not her purse or her jewelry. Nothing. Only her life had been taken. An extensive investigation had been launched, and some suspects, the real estate agent and a local tree-hugger, were brought in for questioning, but they were later released. No evidence pointed toward them and their alibis were air tight. No other witnesses came forward. The only clue the police had found was that the security cameras at her father's law firm had been suspiciously moved away from the parking lot. Diana's eyes welled, remembering, and she blinked back tears. Only her unanswered questions and her continuing grief kept her going. Kept her fire burning.

Her face heated up. Her nose began to fill, then run. She sniffed. Her chest tightened as if a vise was squeezing her lungs, stealing her breath bit by bit. *Uh-oh. Asthma alert! Gotta get to my puffer!* Diana grabbed her purse from Brook, then dumped the entire contents on the floor. Within seconds she was down and, spying her medication next to her snake-skin wallet, she lunged for it. Startled, Donovan and Brook gaped at Diana while she stuck the inhaler into her mouth and took a few puffs. Her breathing eased and her face, albeit still flushed, cooled a degree or two. Diana pressed her palm to her heart, grateful that her lungs were working and open again. As for her heart, she knew that remained closed, and would continue to be so until her mother's killer was caught.

"Diana!" Brook knelt down and gave Diana a few hard thumps down her spine.

Donovan was more direct. He reached down, plucked Diana off the floor, cupped her oval face with his hands, and proceeded to give her the once over. His chocolate brown eyes searched Diana's face as if he were a concerned physician. All this with Diana's inhaler still shoved in her mouth.

Donovan shook his closely-shaved head. "Crap, Brook, she wasn't choking. It's her asthma."

"I know that, you dumbass! I was trying out this new vibrational technique Natalie Knight's mother taught me to get Diana's chakras back in line," Brook said, standing.

"Does this freaky technique include making Diana swallow her puffer, Witchy-Poo?"

Fed up with their pointless bickering, Diana pulled away from Donovan, yanked out her inhaler, then turned on her flat shoes and violently kicked her locker shut. Both Donovan and Brook slowly backed away. Brook mumbled something incoherent. A spell, Diana guessed, to ward off the evil spirit that seemed to have taken up residence inside her.

Diana wiped the perspiration from her upper lip. "Look, you two aren't helping by arguing in front of me! I need support from my friends, not help in setting off my stupid asthma! If you two insist on killing me, then do it some other day! Got that?"

Ignoring Diana's rant, Brook squatted, picked up the discarded purse, and scooped the dumped articles scattered across the floor back into it. Even Donovan hunkered down to help. Both were silent, as if they didn't know what to make out of Diana's outburst. As if they really didn't know her at all.

Diana sighed, and then took a deep breath. She knew she was being bitchy and wasn't treating her friends with the respect they deserved. She'd allowed her feelings to consume her, boil within her, releasing only in fractions when her body couldn't handle the pressure anymore. She'd had more asthma attacks in the past year, too. Truth be told, it wasn't her friends who had brought on the attack. It was her, and all those corked up, stuffed feelings of anger, hate, and fear. It was emotional baggage tenfold and it was time to unpack.

Diana cleared her throat. "I'm sorry for freaking out on you guys. I've been such a pain in the ass lately."

"Pain in the ass? Try pit bull with an attitude, girl!" Brook stood and handed Diana her purse. "I swear your bite is getting worse than your bark."

"Yeah, me and Brook are thinking about buying you a muzzle before final exams start next month," Donovan teased, passing Diana a couple of lipstick tubes and a silver compact.

Diana stuffed her inhaler, along with the make-up into her purse. She offered her friends a weak, apologetic smile. "The truth is that I feel mom is still around when I've got her ring on. You know what I mean? Like Mom's not quite…" she fumbled with her words.

"Gone?" Brook cut in, and then smiled. "We know what you mean, Diana. But remember, nothing is ever lost, just changed."

Diana huffed. "Didn't I ever tell you that I hate change?"

Donovan chuckled. "I don't know about that, Diana. Change can be a good thing. Underwear, for example."

Before she could laugh, the school bell rang, making all three friends jump. "Oh crap! What time is it?" Diana asked.

"Still the beginning of lunch," Brook replied. "Why?"

Diana rubbed her temples with the tips of her fingers. "I have to get my column done for the Fairy Falls Gazette and hand it in by tonight, so lunch is out for me. I thought I'd have more time to search my car."

"Consider it done, Di," Donovan said. "Hand me your keys."

Diana crinkled her nose, then turned and opened her locker to retrieve the keys from her jacket. She stared at the yellow flyers poking out of her pockets and her stomach rolled. "Double crap!"

"What now?" Brook asked.

"What if I lost my ring sometime this morning while I was posting flyers around town?"

Donovan frowned. "What flyers?"

"These flyers," Diana said, plucking one out of a pocket.

Donovan arched his brows. "The Stagview Resort is hosting another Job-fest?"

"Yeah. They need more staff before tourist season kicks in later this month. And seeing as they handed me a cushy job as restaurant hostess, management asked me to post some flyers around town for them." Diana stuffed the yellow paper into her purse and tossed it in her locker.

Brook smirked. "Oh the joys of kissing butt!"

Diana shrugged. She dipped a hand into her jacket pocket, fished her keys out for Donovan, then slammed the door shut. "Damn it, guys, what if the ring isn't in my car? What if I did drop it somewhere on my route? Or worse, what if someone found it?"

Brook reached out with both hands and gave Diana's shoulders a supportive rub. "Let's just concentrate on the present and go with the flow, girl. If Donovan scores a big fat zero checking inside your ride, then when school cuts we'll comb every place you visited this morning, leaving no stone unturned. And who knows? Maybe some honest person found your ring and handed it into the police station. That's worth a check, too."

Diana shook her head. "You're too positive for your own good, Brook."

"That's my motto," Brook replied with a bewitching smile.

Donovan laughed. "Yeah, and mine is, 'I'm here for a good time, not a long time', so hand over your keys, Red."

Diana let her index finger graze the key's outline, allowing the steel ridges to push into her skin. Finally she nodded and said, "Okay. But please don't forget to lock my baby up when you're done and try not to make a mess."

Donovan rolled his eyes. "You know you're getting too neurotic about that thing. It's only a car."

"*Au contraire, mon ami,*" Brook cut in. "It's not *just* a car. It's a 1970 Chevelle 454 SS to be exact. Or have you been hit with one too many lacrosse balls to remember that?"

Diana saluted Brook, then tossed Donovan her keys. A big hand reached out and swiped the keys in mid-air. They turned to see Brett Bean dangling the keys above Donovan. Diana frowned. *It figures.*

If both Donovan and Brook are my blessings, then Brett is definitely my curse. She wrinkled her nose. All talk, no action, that was what Brett Bean was all about. Since his father had died three years ago, he'd gotten everything on a silver platter, including his deceased daddy's mint 1979 silver Trans Am. His mother, Karen Bean, owned and operated the busiest real estate office in town, so Diana assumed that nothing was off-limits to Brett, with the exception of possibly his mother's attention.

Donovan jumped up for the keys, but it was no use. Hard work may have given him an athletic build, but fate hadn't been kind in the height department. At five foot six, he had no chance against Bean's six foot frame. Brook, however, seemed to have a better idea. She plowed her elbow into Brett's rib cage, making him cave instantly, and she snatched the keys out of his hand.

"Isn't that bad karma for a self-proclaimed witch, Freak?" Brett asked, rubbing his ribs.

"Bad only if I hurt you for selfish reasons, Beanie-brain," Brook cracked, passing Donovan the keys. "Come on, hero, let's go find us a ring to make our girl smile." Brook pushed Donovan past Brett and down the hall.

"I wouldn't trust Johnson with my ride," Brett said in a raised voice. "The only four wheels he's managed to master is his skateboard, and even then he has a hard time making the curves."

A chorus of guffaws erupted behind Brett. Diana peered around him. It was Brett's pit crew of car club jerkies, all sporting the same clothes, same attitudes, and same egos. Brett bent down close to Diana. She could smell cigarettes on his black leather coat and his white T-shirt reeked of strong cologne. She crinkled her nose and tried to step back, but couldn't. Her locker blocked her exit. Bravely, she swallowed hard, tasting the remnants of her medication, and glanced up to look Brett in the eye. His coffee-brown eyes held hers for a split second. He raked his wavy brown hair off his pimply forehead and smiled, showing off his straight, perfect white teeth, his reward for a few years of torture wearing braces during the last grades of elementary school.

Brett parted his wide lips. His tongue darted out to caress them a way a snake would. He moved closer to Diana and craned his head down to her ear to whisper, "Diana, I know it must be hard for you today of all days. I know what it's like to lose a parent. It sucks. I can comfort you, make you forget."

Diana's eyes widened. *Forget?* That did it. Being a pompous jackass was one thing, but openly propositioning her while telling her to forget about her mother was quite another.

In the time it took for her to exhale, Diana planted both hands firmly on Brett's expansive chest. *Brook mentioned that Brett had a nipple pierced the same day she had her nose done.* She braced herself. Then, not knowing which one of his nipples were pierced, she positioned first her left hand and, feeling nothing, seized Brett's left nipple with her right hand and twisted. His face broke out in a sweat, contorting grotesquely with each tweak she delivered. In seconds, he was down on his knees in front of her, his breathing harsh, his skin pallid.

Slowly, Diana bent her head down to Brett's ear, so that only he could hear her whisper, "Your father, unlike my mother, died of a heart attack while doing the nasty with his secretary. So, no, you don't *know* how hard it is for me today. Nor could you, or anyone else, make...me...forget." She released her hold on Brett, and pushed him away.

Brett scrambled to his feet, cupping his chest as though he'd been shot or stabbed, or both. Anger exploded across his face. Diana's eyes darted from the left to the right. There was a crowd around them, holding out their cell phones while waiting for Brett's comeback.

Brett lunged to make his move, but one of his buddies grabbed his shoulder. "Brett, teacher's coming."

Diana looked down the hall. Ms. Fisk was headed their way. Cloaked in an oversized white lab coat, her frizzy brown hair bounced wildly off her thick, black glasses. It made her look more like a frazzled, mad doctor than Diana's grade eleven science teacher. The crowd splintered off into groups; some went down stairs, others went up. The rest fanned out toward their lockers, leaving Diana and Brett alone for the moment. As Ms. Fisk passed by, she nodded a curt 'hello' before entering the classroom closest to Diana's right.

A shadow engulfed Diana's whole body. Brett, now inches away from her, slammed his hand against her locker, making her wince. Diana's stomach hardened. Brett's breathing was shallow, his breath stale. "You sure have the nerve, judging my father, when your mother was probably out screwing around, too. If you ask me, MacGregor, your mother got what she deserved."

3. Gertie Ellis

"Where the hell am I?" Hart muttered.

This can't be right. The store owner must have given me the wrong directions.

Hart adjusted his backpack, which was heavier now as it had warmed up enough for him to strip off a layer of clothing. He welcomed the cooling sensation of sweat trickling at the back of his neck. It was far more appealing than the bitter cold air that had attacked his extremities early this morning. Hart pulled the directions from his jeans pocket for the fifth time. He'd been wandering for hours and was getting tired and hungry.

"Hey, you lost?"

Startled, Hart jumped and turned around. He'd been too busy staring at the directions; he hadn't noticed a small red car pull up beside him. A red-headed guy who looked to be about his age hung out the driver's side window, smiling, with a pretty teenage girl beside him.

Hart swallowed hard. He glanced down at the directions that he couldn't fully comprehend, and then raised his head. "Sort of, I guess. I'm looking for Blueberry Lane. Do you know where that is?"

"We sure do!" the pretty girl with ink-black hair blurted from the passenger seat.

Hart inclined his head, noticing her pink T-shirt imprinted with cartoon cats, and that she possessed eyes as blue as his mother's. He felt a sudden ache in his chest.

The red-headed guy rubbed his ear. "There's no need to yell, Meagan. He's lost, not deaf."

A giggle erupted from the back seat. "Blueberry Lane is about five kilometres as the crow flies, or so Meagan's been told by a few of her feathered friends."

Hart frowned. *Huh?*

He peered into the open back window. Behind the girl named Meagan sat another teenage girl with darker skin, short brown hair, and killer green eyes. A black and white cat was curled up on her lap, its short tail drumming lazily against her indigo jeans. "I…I don't follow you."

"And that's a good thing, according to a couple of dogs I know," Meagan said, pushing over the driver to stick her head out the window. "Why don't you hop in the back with Nat and Oscar, and we'll give you a lift."

"We, Meagan?" the guy grunted, pulling at his creased white T-shirt. "Last time I checked, this was still my car."

Meagan swept her bangs off her forehead and rolled her eyes. "Then why don't you do the right thing and offer him a ride, Reid?"

Reid glanced at Hart and shrugged. "Girlfriends never seem to get tired of bossing us guys around. Right, dude?"

Meagan snorted. "Someone needs to be the pack leader in this relationship." She pushed off of Reid, making him grunt again.

Reid grinned, and then used his chin as a guide to point to the car door behind him. "Get in. Just ignore the mess. It's mostly Meagan's."

"Are…are you sure?" Hart asked, pulling off his knapsack.

"Sure we're sure," Meagan said, buckling her seat belt. "Last time I checked, I still paid for the gas."

"Thanks so much!" Hart opened the back door, set his knapsack on the car's floor littered with candy wrappers, and jumped in. "By the way, my name's Hart."

Reid saluted Hart, then negotiated his car off the gravel shoulder and gunned it up the road. "Did you put an extra bag of cat kibble in the trunk, Meagan?"

"Yup, and some more blankets for those extra shelters you built," Meagan replied, pulling out a red cell phone. "I'll text Aunt Izzy to let her know we'll be a little late meeting her where the lost cats gather."

Hart arched a tawny brow. "Lost…cats?"

"It's a colony of homeless and feral cats living in the forest behind the Fairy Falls Animal Shelter," Nat spoke up as she brushed cat hair from her purple T-shirt. "These cats don't seem to fit in to what humans expect from domestic pets, so we take care of them and see to their needs."

"I know how they feel." Hart gazed out the window seeing nothing but trees and granite rocks. "I'm not sure where I fit in, either."

The black and white cat on Nat's lap stopped flicking its stubby tail to peer up at Hart. It twitched its whiskers, sneezed twice, and then let out a long-winded meow.

"Oscar, that's rude," Meagan said, turning her head. "Some humans sweat more than others."

Nat straightened. "What'd he say, Meagan?"

"Nothing important," Meagan replied, waving a hand. "Something about the way Hart smells."

Hart discreetly sniffed the armpit of his black T-shirt and winced. He glanced at the cat. "Oscar…can talk?"

The three teen friends looked at each other for a split second before Meagan said, "Sure. All animals talk. It's all in the way you interpret them."

Hart narrowed his eyes. *This is getting weird. Why do I feel like I'm with a bunch of my mom's psychic friends?* He cleared his throat and said, "I…I guess you've got a point."

Then Hart reached to stroke Oscar and his fingers brushed across the cat's red collar, making the tiny bells attached to it jingle. His eyes widened. The image of an old white, orange, and black cat flashed through his mind. He sensed this cat was important, special, and very much missed. "Who's Whiskey?"

Meagan gasped. Reid coughed. Nat's mouth dropped open.

"H-How do you know about Whiskey?" Meagan asked, placing a hand on her chest. "She…she died last year."

"She did?" Hart's throat tightened. He instantly regretted opening his mouth. "This is her collar, isn't it?"

"Dude, how'd you know that?" Reid asked, eyeing him in the rearview mirror. "Are you like Meagan?"

Hart removed his hand from the collar and his shook his head. "It's…it's hard to explain."

Natalie patted Hart's arm. Her touch was light and tingly, as if a butterfly had brushed across his skin. She smiled and said, "No it's not, Hart. It's like what Meagan said. If animals can talk, then wouldn't it be logical to assume objects—like Oscar's collar—can talk, too?"

"Right, Nat." Reid chuckled. "Objects are inanimate, not real, like animals. They have no soul."

"The debate is out on whether or not you have a soul, Reid," Meagan said, smirking.

Nat giggled. "What I meant is there are some people who can interpret animal energy, and there are others—" she glanced at Hart and winked at him "—who can interpret object energy."

"Well said, Ms. Knight!" Meagan reached over to high-five Nat.

Oscar meowed again. He rolled off of Nat's lap and rubbed his head into the side of Hart's leg. Hart frowned, noticing that the cat's left eye had been removed and stitched up. This loss didn't seem to bother the cat, though. He continued to roll and stretch his lean, furry body next to Hart. Curious, Hart touched Oscar's collar once more, seeing the white, orange, and black cat again, only as a younger version with a litter of kittens—one with the same black and white markings as Oscar possessed.

Hart's chin trembled. He bent to whisper, "I miss my mom too, Oscar."

A loud grumble coming from Hart's belly made Oscar flinch, but he remained stretched out between Nat and Hart, taking up as much of the back seat as he could. Hart chuckled and stroked Oscar's exposed white tummy. A soft, sedate purr emanated from Oscar, as if the cat was letting Hart know that everything was going to be okay.

"You know, Hart, I do believe you'll fit in here in Fairy Falls," Nat said, passing him a couple of granola bars from her leather purse. "Fit in just fine."

Hart waved goodbye as Reid's car pulled away. He looked down Blueberry Lane. His chest tightened. Trees encroached both sides of the dirt road. Crippled branches hung low, bending as if to pluck up any unwary traveler of their choosing. Hart swore he could make out carved faces in the odd tree. Old, wizened faces that watched your every move. Haunting you. Stalking you. He gulped, feeling a hot lump sink into his belly. Yup. It looked like something right out of a horror flick, with him in the starring role and with no sequel in sight.

Hart shrugged his knapsack back on, and then checked his watch before plunging into the unknown. *Three p.m. Good. At least I'll arrive at my great-aunt's place before supper.* His stomach growled again. He reached in his back pocket for one of the granola bars Nat had given him and tore off the silver wrapper. He devoured it in seconds, tossed the wrapper, and headed down Blueberry Lane. The smell of fresh, pungent leaves teased his senses in a way the thick city air never could. His nostrils flared. The area smelled like a freshly tossed salad. The road looked as if it had been recently graded, so Hart had to mind the loose gravel and sand. His feet and legs ached, but he kept moving, passing thick trunks of looming trees and the protruding girths of weathered boulders that bordered the uneven road. Hart snorted. Give him a wide, flat cement city sidewalk any day, any time.

After half an hour of trudging down Blueberry Lane, Hart gave into his complaining belly pains and pulled out the second granola bar. He ripped off the wrapper, threw it aside, and allowed the concoction of nuts and fruits to swirl inside his mouth before washing it down with the bottle of water Reid had given him. Hart smiled, thinking his mother, a proclaimed health-nut freak, would have been happy that he'd finally gotten some nutritious food into his body today. His smile faded then, knowing she would have killed him if she'd known what kind of crap her son had been consuming in the past year from dumpster diving or side street handouts. *Beggars can't be choosers, Mom.*

As Hart continued his journey, he became aware of a buzzing around his ears. He fanned his hand around both ears in a circular motion, took another gulp of water, and realized the buzzing was still there. Annoyed, Hart whipped his faded baseball cap off, waved it around his head, and put it back on. *There. That should take care of the little bugger.* But it didn't. The buzzing grew louder. Louder and more persistent. Something bit him on the back of his neck.

Hart winced and clenched his teeth. It was as if someone had plunged a sharp needle into him. He reached to slap his sweaty neck a few times. When he pulled back his hand, Hart's blue eyes bulged at the sight of blood smeared across his palm. *What the hell just bit me? A Fairy Falls vampire?*

The buzzing returned, and another creature flew into his ear. Hart freaked. *Maybe it's trying to burrow into my brain? Suck out the fluids? Leave me paralyzed on the road?* His heart raced. He frantically dug a finger into his ear to extract whatever had crawled in there. He winced, hearing a sudden pop, like its body had exploded in his ear canal. Hart's shoulders tensed, as he pulled out his finger. It, too, was smudged with blood. His blood. Sweat blistered across his temples and dripped down his face. *What's going on? What are these strange creatures? And why are they attacking me?*

More buzzing accompanied these thoughts. Biting his bottom lip, Hart wiped the blood from his hand and finger across his jeans, and turned to face the enemy. He dropped his jaw and water bottle at the same time. A flock, no, a herd, no, a swarm of black, buzzing, blood-sucking whatever-they-were, were inches from his face. The black cluster moved in for the kill. Hart promptly closed his mouth, took a step back, then another, and another, but the little beasties followed him every-which-way he went. He broke to the left; they followed. He cut to the right; they pursued. He started to run backward; they kept up with every stride taken. A root snagged Hart's ankle and tripped him. He rolled a short distance down a ravine before smacking into a group of moss-covered boulders.

Disoriented, Hart shook his head, then looked up. That was a mistake. The swarm of flying beasties were now hovering over him. His breathing became shallow, his heartbeat erratic. His mouth went dry. *This is it. I'll be devoured in a matter of minutes by a hoard of vicious, bloodletting demons made of teeth and wings.* Then Hart heard something else to his right. Not buzzing or whining, but a noise that sounded like a nervous-whump, as if someone was thrashing about in the bush. Slowly, Hart glanced to his right. His skin tingled all over. Not more than a metre away, coiled in layers of brown and black, hunched a lone rattlesnake, ready to strike.

In one breath, Hart rolled to his left, stood, and sprinted into the forest. He ran like his life depended on it, cutting his own path, while branches and saplings scraped his face and whipped his legs.

The flying black demons were hot on his trail but Hart soon lost them, and after about fifteen minutes of constant running, looking back, running, and looking back, he sensed it was safe enough to slow down. His lungs protested, his legs screamed their silent pain as Hart, now sweating like a fat man in a sauna, collapsed in a clearing and surrendered to his body's wishes.

Feeling his legs cramp, Hart reached down to rub both his calves briskly. Tired and hot, and now probably lost again, he knew he had to find his way back to the road, wherever that was. Hart swore aloud, angry not only with himself, but with the strange, savage creatures that lived up here. He had thought he had some idea of what to expect. The trucker, whom he'd hitched a ride up here with, had told him about the numerous golf courses that dotted the area, about the million dollar cottages nestled amongst the trees, and about the condominium style resorts that were being built around many of the lakes' shorelines. Hart banged a fist against the spongy forest floor. He thought Fairy Falls would have been more civilized, more developed. But he was wrong. Dead wrong.

Hart heard a growl. His stomach hardened. He looked up. Nothing was in front of him, so he turned left, and then right. *Nope. All clear.* He took a deep breath, and slowly turned his head to look behind him.

He balked. A big, yellow dog, with droopy brown eyes and puffy jowls stood behind him. Two thick lines of drool hung from its mouth. Hart cringed as the dog growled again. Its tail wasn't wagging, so that wasn't a good sign. A horrible thought occurred to him. *Could this dog have rabies? Or is it feral like those lost cats Nat and Meagan were talking about?* Either way, Hart knew that this brute's bite would be worse than the flying beasties that had pursued him in here. He swallowed hard. It just wasn't his day.

"Skoka! Skoka? Oh, bugaboo, show y'ur self, ya dang dog!"

At the sound of a human voice, Hart stiffened. He grabbed the closest stick he could find, jumped up, and took a step back. Now the dog seemed to think Hart was playing and lunged for the rotting birch branch. The stick broke in two, with one piece going into the dog's mouth and the other flying out of his hand and into the bush. Hart stumbled and fell back. His mouth went dry. Before he had time to collect another stick, a black rubber boot pressed Hart's hand into the moist, leafy soil, as if it were nothing more than a worthless, ugly-eyed insect.

"What'er ya doin' trespassin' on me property, boy?"

Hart looked up. He blinked, and then did a double take. An old woman, probably somewhere between the ages of sixty and a hundred, glared down at him. Despite the fact that she appeared intimidating, Hart figured that if he were standing, the situation would be reversed as she looked to be about five feet, if that. Streaks of grey wove their way through her dark brown hair, which had been pulled back into a tight bun. This made her weathered face looked pinched and out of sorts, like someone with constipation. Owlish hazel eyes bore down on him menacingly as if he were a defenseless mouse. Her body was covered by a hooded brown plaid jacket and a pair of baggy beige pants. In one hand, she clenched a sharp-looking long-handled axe. Hart gulped.

"Are ya deaf, boy?"

"Huh?"

"I asked what'er ya doin' on me property?"

Her tone was gruff, her manner, urgent. Hart didn't want to argue with the old woman. Especially since she was wielding that axe around his head. He smiled weakly, and said, "I'm lost, I…I think."

The woman was taken back. She stepped off of Hart's hand. "What do ya mean ya *think* y'ur lost? Ya either are, or y'ur not. Which one is it, boy?"

Hart licked his dry lips. No use arguing with a backwoods hillbilly from Fairy Falls. He cleared his throat, and said, "I guess I'm lost. I'm looking for Gertie Ellis' place. Do you know where she lives?"

The woman screwed up her face, which made her look even scarier than before, and then rubbed her bristly chin, as if she was actually contemplating beheading him. After a few seconds of silence, the old lady grunted. "Then I guess y'ur not lost, boy. Y'ur looking at her."

Hart's mouth fell open. His heartbeat accelerated. *No way. She can't be. Not her. Not this crazy, ancient biddy from the woods.* He felt his face burn. This wasn't who he expected. This whole freaking place wasn't what he expected. Before Hart could reply, a sudden nudge under his right elbow begged for his attention. The dog, with a stick in its jaws and his tail wagging, wanted to play. It dropped the slobbery branch in Hart's lap, then sniffed his bloodied ear and licked it. Hart winced as a gob of doggy drool dripped off his lobe. Gertie Ellis giggled, sounding suddenly like a little girl. He tipped his head to the side. *Maybe there's more to her than her backwoods charm?*

"I see Skoka likes ya," she said in a syrupy voice.

Hart smiled, then carefully patted the dog's big, solid head. He sniffed Hart's face and tried to lick his mouth. Hart ducked in time. "I think Skoka likes granola bars more."

Gertie laughed again. "Ya got that right. So what do ya want with me, boy?"

Using Skoka as a brace, Hart lifted himself off the leafy forest floor, and turned to face Gertie Ellis. He was right about her height—five foot nothing—and noticed she brought the axe up across her stocky body, as if getting ready to defend herself. Hart shook his head.

He stuck out his hand. "My name's Hart. Hart Stewart."

She relaxed, grabbed his hand, and shook it firmly. Hart winced.

"So, Hart, what can I do fer ya, then?"

He frowned. "You don't know who I am?"

She shrugged. "Should I?"

Hart bit his bottom lip. "Does the name Catherine Stewart mean anything to you?"

Gertie balked. "Catherine? Me niece Catherine?" She was silent for a moment, as if downloading old memories. Gertie scratched the bridge of her bulbous nose. "Hmm, yeah. Looked after her a spell when her mom passed. Then one day she just up and left me and Pete. No warning, no note. I only heard from her once in all the years." She paused, as if letting the past catch up, and then looked up at Hart. "So, what of her, boy? Where's she at now?"

A facial tick attacked Hart's left cheek, then moved down to his mouth. *Doesn't she know about my mom? Hasn't anyone contacted her?* Hart wiped his face roughly to halt the twitching. "She's, uh…she's six feet under. She was murdered, a year ago today."

Gertie's leathery face clouded over, as if a shroud had covered her soul. She swooned and dropped her axe. Hart moved his foot before the axe's head embedded itself into the earth. As Gertie fell back, Hart was there in seconds, holding her up, shaking her. She grasped his arm and pulled herself up. He could feel her warm breath on his skin, sense the shaky, unsureness in her touch. Shock, Hart assumed, and he suddenly wished he had informed Gertie of his mother's death in a different way.

"M-murdered," Gertie mumbled.

"It's okay, Aunt Gertie, take a deep breath," Hart said, encouragingly.

Gertie jerked. "A-aunt?"

"Oh, sorry. Great-aunt."

Her face darkened. "What do ya mean? I got no family left. Me Pete's been dead since last winter and now ya tell me Catherine's gone."

"You got me," Hart whispered.

Her face reddened and she pushed Hart away. "And just who are ya?"

"Catherine's son," Hart replied.

Gertie reached down to seize the axe. It made a slow, sucking noise when she yanked it out of the ground. Hart's great-aunt clenched the handle, her knuckles whitening under the pressure. "Liar! Catherine had no kid. She would'ha told me! Y'ur just a scoundrel after me fortune!"

Hart backed away slowly. He put his hands up and said, "Look, I don't know what went on between mom and you, but you gotta believe me, I'm Catherine Stewart's son. Don't you see any resemblance at all?"

She ignored Hart and continued to advance like a zombie hunting for brains. Skoka whined, then barked, but Gertie kept approaching, drawing nearer and nearer, with that big-ass axe in her grasp. Her breathing hardened and her face contorted. Then Gertie tripped over a rock half-hidden in some mossy debris, and the axe flew out of her hands. Hart ducked and fell to his knees, as the axe missed his head by inches. Gertie had managed to catch herself against a skeletal, tree trunk. Hart took a deep, shaky breath. *If this keeps up, I'll lose a body part for sure.*

Hart's mind buzzed, struggling to figure out what to do, how to explain to Gertie that he was who he said he was. A pendulous movement caught his eye. He spied a pair of metal-rimmed glasses, dangling out of her left breast pocket. Hart's eyes widened. He jumped to his feet, lunged for the glasses, and then backed away. The spongy ground slowed his pace as if getting ready to swallow him whole.

Gripping the tree trunk for balance, Gertie clutched at her breast. "Them's me Pete's! Give'm back, ya thief!"

Hart raised his chin. "I'll prove to you that I'm Catherine Stewart's son!"

He glanced at the glasses cradled in his scar-riddled palm, took a deep breath and placed them against the middle of his forehead. "Talk to me."

Hart's super-consciousness kicked in. His eyes rolled back, his surroundings blurred, his body moved in reverse, allowing Gertie's late husband's glasses to take him to another place, another time. A time Hart had no known knowledge of, except what the glasses wanted to share with him.

And share they did.

A billow of steamy breath escaped through Hart's mouth before he caught a man standing in front of a line of tall, drooping pine trees sprinkled with snow. Hart narrowed his eyes. He appeared to be around seventy years old, maybe more, and was about his height, only with a bulkier build. He was clean-shaven, with short silver hair and a hawk-like nose, and Hart noticed that he was dressed warmly, wearing dark blue overalls and a quilted brown jacket. His face was tanned and wrinkled, and perching on the bridge of his nose were the same pair of glasses Hart held to his forehead. The man appeared busy, piling freshly cut wood near an oddly-shaped building. Hart blinked and shook his head to make sure his eyes weren't screwing with him. But they weren't. That's the weirdest looking cottage I've ever seen. Looks like three cement igloos merging into one another, kind of like ghostly humps on a prehistoric monster. *He noticed a light dusting of snow covered the domes, and a chimney stack puffed out spirals of heavy, white smoke. Hart shivered.* I wonder if Mom ever stayed in that thing?

Hart's ears pricked. The man was singing a song. Hart tilted his head and tried to pick up the tune, but he didn't recognize it. The words were broken and sounded off key. "The lake, it is said, never gives up her dead...blah...blah...blah...Edmund Fitzgerald." That's all he got. What kind of song is that? *The man repeated it, over and over. Hart winced at his grating voice.* This was getting annoying. *The man was definitely tone deaf.*

As the man whistled, hummed, and sang, he grabbed another log and lugged it over to a long, green machine sitting on two wheels. Grunting, the man rolled the log onto the machine, placed a pair of orange ear protectors on, and pulled a cord to start it up. It rumbled and coughed out black smoke. The man pulled a lever, making the back half of the machine move forward to slice the log in two. He repeated this procedure by placing another log at the opposite end, and turned to pull the lever again. But this time, something went horribly wrong.

The machine's engine sputtered, then exploded, delivering sparks and smoke into the air. Hart screamed out a warning, which he quickly realized was useless. Crap, I forgot. He can't see or hear me. Just like that red-headed woman couldn't. *The thick log struck the man in the chest with dead-aim accuracy. The ear protectors flew from his head and he crumpled to the ground, clutching his chest. Hart watched in horror, completely helpless to do anything but witness what the glasses wanted him to see, while the man, with his jaw clenched and face rigid, attempted to crawl toward the igloo-like house.*

Hart's muscles jumped under his skin, feeling the old man's anguish, his desperation at being in this helpless situation. Blood trickled from the man's mouth as he coughed and groaned his way over the snowy terrain. Hart's neck stiffened. He wanted to run to him, help him, but knew he couldn't. What the hell is the point of being shown this vision? I feel like a prisoner watching from behind bars. *Then, the man suddenly stopped crawling. His face contorted, as if a heaviness had invaded his upper body, and he cupped his broad chest. Hart watched his face turn a blotchy, purple colour, and after one, long breath, the man screwed his mouth to one side, looking directly up at Hart, as if he could see him. "Please take care of my Gertie fer me. The old gal's a handful at times, but she's got heart," he muttered weakly. As the man struggled to wipe the blood from his mouth, he whispered a strangled 'thank you', and collapsed, his eyes wide open, his breathing suspended, his head rolled to the side.*

That was when Hart was yanked out of his trance and back to the present. Exhausted and shaken, he fumbled with the glasses and numbly dropped them to the ground. His palms were cool and clammy, and he was trembling, not sure why the glasses had chosen to show him that man's horrible death and bring him his last words. *Words that were meant for me.*

Hart swallowed hard. A flood of words came tumbling out of his mouth. "An accident. A terrible accident. A machine exploded. A flying log. Hit his chest hard. He tried to crawl. He was afraid, in pain. Horrible pain. His face turned purple, before..." Hart paused, allowing himself to recover, to gain the strength needed to repeat the man's dying words. "Before he died, he looked at me. Told me to 'take care of my Gertie. Old gal's a handful, but she's got heart.' Then, that was it. The glasses stopped talking."

There. I told her. Hart felt purged, rid of whatever dreadful energy possessed those glasses. He took a sharp, hurried breath, and waited patiently for Gertie's reaction. However, Skoka reacted first, barking and bounding head-on toward him, bowling Hart into his great-aunt. He recovered quickly, and tried to shoe the big dog away, but Gertie gripped his arms firmly, as if he had now become the solid tree trunk she'd been hugging. A slow smile graced her weathered features and she nodded. Her hazel eyes were bright, and her manner now calm, as if a kind of peace had entered into her life.

She took a deep, cleansing breath, and said, "I see ya got the sight, Hart. Just like y'ur mom. Ya got her gift of knowin' things." Her eyes welled. "That was me Pete ya talked of. He was a decent sort, he was. A good man. Came home and found him on the ground, just like ya said. But, I didn't know he spoke 'bout the plans he had in store fer me."

Hart inclined his head. "What plans?"

Gertie squeezed Hart's forearms, her blunt nails digging into him like a shovel piercing the earth, and said, "The reason why y'ur here, boy. Don't'cha see? I got *Hart* ta take care of me. Pete said so 'imself."

Hart's eyes bugged. *No, wait. She misunderstood. I'm not here to babysit some senior citizen. I came here for answers about my mom. And maybe a few hot meals.* Hart gulped. He needed to put this old timer on the same frequency he was on and fast, but before he had a chance to say anything, his great-aunt shook him gruffly and said, "Oh, bugaboo! Welcome home, boy!"

4. Home Sweet Home

Hart sat on the top step of the low-lying deck of the house on Blueberry Lane, and took a long swig of bottled water. He capped the bottle and then sighed deeply. Behind him loomed the greyish, tri-domed structure he had seen in his vision last week. This was Gertie's so-called home. *Home.* The thought of that word, after having no roots for the past year, made his heart beat faster, as if it were dancing to a new drum. *Welcome home,* his great-aunt had said, but Hart knew it would be short-lived. He couldn't stay up here. He didn't belong. He was city born and bred, and knew he couldn't survive the harsh changes of the seasons, the isolation, the boredom, and the voracious bugs that infested the forest. After all, his mother hadn't stayed here. Weren't those some of the reasons why she left in the first place?

Hart grunted. He had learnt a few things about his great-aunt in the past week. Her fortune, being one of them. Blueberries. That was it. No money, no stocks, no bonds, just the little blue fruit that you'd find in a bowl of cereal or mixed in a pie. There were also the litres of maple syrup collected each spring from the countless maple trees that dotted her huge property. Over a hundred and some acres, with fifteen-hundred feet of natural shoreline. Now that's what Hart would have called a fortune. Not some stupid blue fruit or the sticky sweet stuff you pour on pancakes.

Hart unscrewed his water bottle and took another drink. He had decided to make the best of it until he could purchase a bus ticket to take him back to Toronto. The problem was that Hart needed to make enough cash to carry him through until he could land a job in the city and start over. He mentally went over his plan again carefully, leaving nothing to chance. Earlier in the week, he had shown his great-aunt the yellow flyer offering jobs he'd taken from the bulletin board outside the general store. The same place he had found that diamond and ruby ring. The same ring that was tucked down the left breast pocket of his hoodie. The ring he would pawn as soon as he returned to Toronto. Hart smiled. His plans were moving along like a well-oiled piece of machinery. He had decided to work through the tourist season, then vamoose as soon as the first leaf fell in autumn.

Hart gave into a yawn while scheming his great escape. Aunt Gertie was going into town sometime today and had invited Hart along. She seemed pleased that he showed an interest in getting a job in the area, and had promised to take him to the Stagview Resort, where the jobs were being offered. Hart bit his bottom lip. If this was a hotel of some kind, then there would surely be a restaurant, and he'd apply for a dishwashing or busboy position—the only jobs he could manage at this time.

Hart's cheeks burned, as he downed the last mouthful of water and crumpled the plastic bottle. *I'll have to play it smart. Bring the job application home so that Aunt Gertie can help me fill it out. I'll explain to my interviewers that I left my glasses at home and can't read the print. Yeah. That will work.* Hart lowered his chin to his chest. *It's worked all the other times.*

A shrill cry made Hart jump. A blue jay, perched on a long-needle pine tree branch stared down at him, as if it were king around these parts. It swooped down and turned toward the lake. Hart followed its path until it took a sharp turn and flew out of sight. A small crib dock with an overturned canoe on top of it guarded the shoreline. The canoe, once dark green Hart assumed, had faded to a light olive. Moored to its right floated a small aluminum fishing boat with a fifteen horsepower engine. A collection of dents and a dirty waterline told Hart the boat had been there many summers.

Standing, Hart stretched his aching limbs that had been put to work all morning scraping the deck and readying it for a much-needed paint job. He'd swept away the peelings, banged a few nails into some loose boards, and replaced rotting planks. In return for the various jobs his great-aunt had assigned him, Hart had been fed and was given a place to sleep. It wasn't home, didn't feel or look like home, but it would do for now.

A cool trickle of sweat rolled down the back of his neck. The air was getting warmer and he was feeling uncomfortably hot. He peeled off his plaid hoodie, draped it over the deck's railing, and then pulled his black T-shirt away from his damp back to let the air dry it. Hart yawned again, and a cluster of those flying beasties Aunt Gertie called blackflies flew into his mouth and down his throat. Hart coughed, gagged, wheezed, sputtered, and spit. Not one of the little buggers came out. Hart cringed, making a distorted face.

A giggle erupted from behind him. Hart's shoulders slumped. *Great. First I'm her slave, and now I'm the entertainment. When will it end?* Hart twisted to find Gertie trudging across the newly-scraped deck, in what appeared to be a net jacket, pants, and hat. Hart grinned. Old Gertie looked like she had just had a fight with the screen door and lost.

She stopped in her tracks. "Find som'thing funny, Hart?"

"I wasn't the one who was laughing, was I?"

A gentle smile appeared on her face. Or at least Hart thought it was a smile, seeing as most of her face was obscured by all that mesh. She chuckled again.

"Y'ur a lot like y'ur mom, Hart. Only she would'ha listened ta me and put on a bug suit."

At the mention of his mother, Hart's face fell. "Well, I guess I'm not like my mom then, am I?"

Gertie shook her head. "So ya say, boy, so ya say. Are ya ready?"

"Ready? For what?"

She pulled off her bug hat and looked at Hart oddly. "Ta go in'ta town."

Hart relaxed. Yeah, he was ready. More than ready. It would be a nice change to get away from this forest full of hellish blackflies. He nodded and said, "You bet, Aunt Gertie, let's jet."

She threw Hart that strange look again. "Don't have no plane, Hart, just an old Dodge pick-up, and it does me just fine."

Hart rolled his eyes. Oh, how the differences between them were wide. He cleared his throat. "If it's good enough for you, then it's good enough for me, Aunt Gertie."

Her face beamed, and with a mouthful of protruding, stained teeth, she grinned back at Hart. She walked over and patted his shoulder affectionately. "Good. Now git y'urself inside and change yer clothes. We don't want the school thinking y'ur a bum now, do we?"

School? Hart's eyes bugged. *What school? What's the old biddy going on about now?* Hart heard a buzzing noise hovering around his head just before the sharp sting of a blackfly claimed an earlobe. He smacked his ear, but he was too late and the little bugger got away. He wiped away the film of blood from his hand and said, "Funny, I thought I just heard you say *school*."

Gertie nodded. "Ya did."

Hart's mouth dropped open as his great-aunt turned, ambled across the deck, and slid the screened porch door open. As she entered the weird, tri-domed cement structure, Hart swore that he could hear her humming the same song that her husband, Pete, had been singing the day he died.

As they drove, Hart strummed his fingers against the blue door of his great-aunt's Dodge truck, trying to come up with another plan. A plan that would lead to his freedom from this place. He briskly rubbed his other hand up and down his dark jeans until his palm burned. School was definitely out of the question. He lacked the reading and writing skills necessary for enrollment, and he knew it. Hart bit down on his bottom lip.

"Y'ur quiet, Hart. Som'thing upset ya?" Gertie asked, gearing down into second as they approached a steep hill.

Yeah, you and your freakin' meddling in my life, Hart thought, but instead he said, "Nope. Just enjoying the scenery."

Gertie reached to pat his knee fondly. "I knew y'ud like it up here, Hart. Y'ur mom liked it too."

Hart snorted. "Then why did she leave?"

Gertie shrugged. "Wish I knew." She reached into her patchwork handbag lying next to her on the bench, and pulled out a tattered envelope. "Here." She passed it to Hart. "This was the last letter y'ur mom sent ta me."

Hart frowned. "Why are you giving it to me?"

Gertie sighed. "Thought ya might find what y'ur looking fer, that's all."

Hart stared at the ragged, off-white envelope. The address had long since blurred and faded, the stamp rubbed away with age. He heard Gertie clear her throat. "Ya needn't look at it now, Hart. Y'ull know when the timing's best."

Hart's chin trembled and he nodded. She was bang on. Now wasn't the right time. Now wasn't the time to tell his great-aunt he couldn't read, either. Carefully, Hart folded the worn envelope in two, unbuttoned the flap of his hoodie's breast pocket, and eased it inside to share space with the ring.

An unexpected bark made Hart jump and his ears buzz. A big, yellow head pushed its way through the gap in the rear sliding window of the truck. Skoka wanted some attention, and he wanted it now. Hart laughed, reached over and stroked the bulky head, avoiding the white froth lining his lips and the bobbing pink tongue. A whiff of doggy breath made Hart's nose wrinkle, and he shoved Skoka's head back outside before the dog got the idea that he was welcome in the front cab.

Hart's body jerked sharply to the left as Gertie negotiated a curb, then another, until he saw some familiar buildings ahead. They passed the general store, the post office, and what looked like an antique shop. A coffee shop was situated on the river, complete with a cedar painted veranda, and white tables with green market umbrellas. A combination laundromat and pizza parlor, with a small parking lot already filled to capacity, sat opposite the coffee shop. Just down the river and around the bend, Hart spied the local tavern, where a line of straight docks fanned out with the hopes of seducing any thirsty sailor passing by. Hart hooded his eyes with his hand to find a busy marina across the river from the tavern, nestled among giant pine trees.

The truck jolted as Gertie drove over an old swing bridge. To Hart's surprise, a line of stores greeted him. A bakery, a small department store, a flower shop, a restaurant, an ice cream parlor, and a grocery establishment that doubled as a liquor and beer store, dotted the main drag. A little farther up, an old-style cinema was strategically placed on the corner, its white billboards advertising what was now showing in big, block letters. Tall bronze lamp posts lined the street, and from each one proudly hung a multi-coloured banner. Hart was impressed. For a small town, Fairy Falls appeared to embrace 'big-town' thinking.

Then Hart's eyes widened. The high school was coming up on his left. Students were piling in and out of the big red brick building. Most were laden with bulging backpacks. His heart raced. *This is it. D-Day. Do or die day.* He had to think of something and fast. Gertie veered off the road and turned right. Hart sucked in a deep breath. *That was close.*

In the distance, he could make out a big, grey building. Hart nudged his great-aunt and pointed. "Are we going there?"

"Nope," Gertie replied. "That's the arena, wh'ur the locals play hockey and lacrosse."

"Lacrosse?"

"Yah. It's a big sport 'round these parts," Gertie replied.

Hart bit his lip. *Great. I'm trapped in a land of blackflies, blueberries, and some weird sport I've never heard of.* "So where're we going, then?"

"The police station," Gertie replied.

Hart stiffened. Had he heard his great-aunt correctly? Had she said that they were going to the police station? He shook his head, pulled off his faded blue cap, and raked his fingers through his hair. Sweat beaded above his upper lip. The police and Hart had some bad blood between them ever since his mother's death. Caught a couple of times for stealing on the streets, Hart had been released with a slap on the wrist and a warning. Then, in the middle of the coldest winter on record, there was that break and enter down on Queen Street. The shelters were full and all he wanted was a warm place to stay for the night, but the alarm had gone off and Hart was apprehended going out the back door. That time, things were serious. That time he had screwed up big time. On the way to the station, he had begged the arresting officer to stop at the next coffee shop or he'd piss his pants in the back of the cruiser. The officer kindly obliged. Hart dashed out the opposite end of the store as they walked in, and he'd avoided the police ever since.

Until now.

Hart gulped. "So, Aunt Gertie, are you gonna to tell me why we're going to the police station?"

"I think ya know," she muttered, turning down another street.

His heart skipped a beat. No. No, he didn't know. Or maybe he just didn't want to know. Maybe she'd found out about his past life of crime. And maybe there was a reward out for his capture. Hart shoved his cap back on, and then stared at his great-aunt blankly. He shook his head.

Aunt Gertie made an exasperated sound with her lips, as if trying to blow up a skinny balloon. "Oh, bugaboo, Hart! Ya put the box of maple syrup in the back of the truck y'urself."

Hart inclined his head. "Maple syrup?"

Gertie nodded, driving the truck into the Fairy Falls Police Station's parking lot. The sound of grinding gravel grated against Hart's skin. Three black and white cruisers were neatly parked in the front, and at the side, a man wearing navy overalls was washing a long white boat with a large black outboard motor. A couple of well-trimmed evergreens flanked the glass double door entrance in a sentinel-like manner. Perspiration had now pooled around Hart's armpits. His nostrils flared, smelling his own fear, tasting the sourness of his breath.

A uniformed officer emerged from the white brick building waving in the direction of Aunt Gertie's truck. Skoka whined, then barked; the policeman slapped his thigh and gave a hearty whistle. Out of the corner of his eye, Hart caught Skoka leaping out of the truck's box and high-tailing it toward the officer. The truck tilted and he grabbed for the dash as the driver's door slammed.

"Do ya need an invite or what?" Aunt Gertie said, peering through the window.

"Huh?" Hart asked, still a little shaken.

"I need ya ta carry the maple syrup in fer me, Hart. So git a move on!"

Hart nodded, opened the truck's door, and slid out. His legs felt like jelly, his stomach burned like lava. Gripping the edge of the truck's long box, Hart moved at a turtle's pace, around the gate and lifted the latch. It unexpectedly came down with a metallic crash and hit Hart square in the groin. His eyes bulged. He cupped his privates, let out a weak gasp, and he fell to his knees.

A large, warm hand thumped Hart's back, while the other hand gripped his arm. He was lifted in one swift motion. "Are you all right, kid?"

Hart's face burned. Partly from embarrassment, partly from pain. The area between his legs throbbed, and his knees, most likely bruised now, stung as though bits of gravel had pierced his skin. He turned and saw the constable's dark blue uniform. A pulled down Stetson-style hat almost touched Hart's crooked nose, as a pair of serious brown eyes burned into him. Hart's stomach tightened, his mouth went dry, and all he could do was nod.

The officer nodded back. "Good. Believe me, I know how you feel, kid. I've done that before."

Hart half-smiled as Aunt Gertie chuckled. "Ballsa steel, I'd wager me nephew's got, Scotty."

"Nephew?" the officer asked, inclining his head, as if he didn't quite hear her properly.

Gertie scratched her bristly chin. "Er, great-nephew, I mean ta say. His name's Hart. Hart Stewart. Catherine's son."

"Catherine's? I wasn't aware she had a family."

"Me neither," she said, shrugging, then turned toward Hart. "This here's Constable Scotty Wright, Hart. Loves me maple syrup, as much as me blueberries, he does."

Constable Wright reached for Hart's hand and shook it firmly. "Catherine's boy, eh? Man, that name brings back memories. So where's your mom now, Hart?"

Gertie coughed. "She's...she's with me Pete now, Scotty."

"Catherine's dead? But she's about my age!"

"My mom was murdered just over a year ago, Constable Wright," Hart said in a steady, controlled voice.

The officer's face took on an ashen colour, which made his short, light blonde hair stand out underneath his hat. Thin, fair brows knitted together, while a freckled hand wandered to his gun, and strummed the hard leather casing. Hart gulped as the glass doors of the station flew open. A brown-skinned woman ran out, looking frazzled and alarmed. She was in full dress uniform and heading straight for him. Her thick, black ponytail whipped around from shoulder to shoulder, while she held the brim of her blue Stetson-style hat. Her other hand, however, was draped over her sheathed revolver, as if she were preparing to draw it. Hart's throat tightened. *Uh-oh. Maybe she recognizes me from a wanted poster hanging in their station? Or worse. Maybe she shoots first and asks questions later!*

Hart placed his hands behind his neck, then crumpled to the ground. His knees burned as the woman yelled, "Scotty, there's trouble downtown at the mayor's office!"

Constable Wright balked. "Trouble? What kind of trouble, Sara?"

Sara panted. "A crowd of protestors led by that loony Dan Boone are surrounding the building and some of them are getting really nasty. A rock has already been thrown through a window!" She halted about a metre away from Hart and knitted her dark brows. "What's going on, kid?"

Hart looked up. How many times could he screw up in one day? He smiled sheepishly, then took a breath and said, "I-I thought I dropped something."

Constable Wright's face turned flame red. "Damn that friggin' Boone! He's been nothing but trouble since he's heard the rumours about a development coming into town."

Hart's cheek twitched. "Development?"

He hadn't meant to say it aloud, but he had heard the word once before. About a week ago when the diamond and ruby ring took him for the ride of his life. Took him to a place where a woman he'd never seen before said the same word. *'Development'*, hummed through his mind. She had spoken this word just before she was brutally murdered. Hart covered his throat. This was getting too weird, even for him.

"It doesn't concern you, Hart," Constable Wright said, helping him up for the second time. "Look, I suggest you take care of your great-aunt. We'll get the maple syrup another time. Take the back roads home to avoid the mob in town."

"No!" Gertie snapped, making all three wince. "I know Dan better than y'all do. He listens ta me! Let me talk some sense in'ta his stubborn hide before anyone gits hurt!"

Both constables looked at each other, then nodded in unison. Constable Wright cleared his throat, and said, "Okay, Gertie, but you're to use the bullhorn, and stay behind Constable Boyd and me, is that clear?"

Hart's great-aunt scrunched her face, as if giving some thought to what Constable Wright had instructed. Then her hazel eyes lit up, and she tossed him a devilish grin that you'd only come across on one of those scary garden gnomes. She nodded. "Yup."

As both officers turned and ran toward their police car, Hart heard her mutter, "Clear as mud."

5. Rumours

Hart couldn't believe the crowd; half the town must have been here. At least fifty or sixty unruly residents were circling a brown brick building, each holding a home-made sign, and frantically waving it in the air. Steps that gradually ascended to the double main doors acted as platforms for some of the aggravated townspeople. Hart thought the building resembled an old church, but no stained glass windows lined its walls. Instead of a bell, a huge round clock sat vigilantly in its tall, narrow steeple, much like a gargoyle presiding over its domain.

From Hart's position in the back of the pick-up truck with Skoka, he spied a grizzly-looking man, whose age was a mystery, and his manner zealous. His long peppery hair was pulled back into a ponytail, and his unshaven face made him look like an angry bear defending its cubs. He had a commanding presence, strutting around in a long, fringed buckskin coat with his arms continually up in the air, as if trying to touch the sun.

He stopped parading to yell, "Mother Earth can't handle it anymore! Fairy Falls is losing ground, bit by bit, every day! Golf courses! Waterfront condominiums! Fractional ownerships! Resort clubs! When will it stop? Soon we'll lose everything that makes this place a paradise! Are we going to put up with it? Are we going to let big business corporations have their way?"

"No!" the crowd responded, waving their signs, cheering on their scruffy, eccentric leader.

"You tell them, Dan! We're with you all the way!" a few participants screamed. Then they picked up some stones.

"Ya can put the rocks down, all of ya! And do it now!" a voice sounding more grizzled than their leader's voice boomed over a bullhorn.

Hart looked toward the source and then grinned. There stood his great-aunt, gripping the bullhorn and pointing a finger. She took no prisoners, that was for sure. He heard some people grumble, then the distinct sound of rocks hitting the ground and rolling away. Aunt Gertie nodded, switched her gaze to the leader, and said, "Dan, we go back a few years, we do, so ya better listen up. This ain't the right way ta go 'bout doing things. Ya know it. I know it."

The man Aunt Gertie had called Dan waved his hand in the air, as if paying her homage, and said, "Gertie, you and Pete, rest his soul, have always treated me like family and for that, I'm grateful. But you know as well as I do that someone has to stand up for Fairy Falls. Against the developments, and against the big businesses choking the life out of this town! It's not the same anymore, Gertie, and somebody has to do something about the murdering of our land!"

"That's an interesting choice of words, Mr. Boone. Would you care to elaborate for the Fairy Falls Gazette?" a young woman asked point-blank.

Startled, Hart looked around. He leaned across the top of the truck's blue cab to capture the sight of an attractive red-headed teenager, sporting tan cargos and a blue hiker jacket. She held out a silver cell phone and tapped her foot. Hart guessed she was around his age.

"Stay out of this, Diana!" a voice boomed over Dan's head.

Hart jumped. Skoka set his front paws up onto the truck's cab and let out a loud, defensive bark, his big otter tail smacking hard against Hart's already sore knees. Annoyed, Hart pushed Skoka down, gave him the sit signal, and then turned back toward the swelling crowd. A tall man in a navy suit, sporting thick, sandy brown hair with a well-trimmed moustache and goatee, took centre stage next to Dan Boone on the top step. His face was flushed as he placed one of his hands in a tailored pant pocket, while the other stroked his goatee. He shook his head, as if he were more disappointed than angry.

"Dan, take my advice and please listen to Gertie," he advised. "This is not the right way to go about handling your concerns. You can voice your opinion at the next town council meeting like everyone else."

Dan snorted. "Right, Mayor MacGregor, and as always, my voice gets lost in a pile of paperwork and political manure."

The crowd cheered Dan on, but a cluster of jeers and boos caught Hart's attention. He gazed over to witness a group of people gathering around the red-headed girl.

"Stopping progress! That's what Loony Boone's all about!" shouted one man dressed in a business suit.

"Yah, the guy's a loser! A bum! What does he know about what's good for the town?" a male student wearing a black, leather jacket yelled.

"I'm still waiting for a comment, Mr. Boone," the red-headed reporter said, her cell phone waving in the air with practiced flare.

The mayor wagged a finger at her. "Diana, I told you to—"

"Oh bugaboo! Mike, fer Pete's sake, tell Dan and the rest of the town that it's just a rumour 'bout that damn development! Nuthin' more, nuthin' less," Gertie Ellis blared over the bullhorn, exasperation apparent in her rough tone.

The mayor smiled at Hart's great-aunt and nodded toward her, as though he respected her wise counsel. As Mayor MacGregor cleared his throat, his Adam's apple bobbed noticeably. "Look, people," he said with a sigh, "rumours have been circulating that construction on a one hundred million dollar resort development may happen somewhere near Fairy Falls as early as next spring—"

"And when does a rumour become a fact, Mayor?" Dan asked, cutting in.

The mayor glared at Boone. "Fact is, yes, some representatives from the Pleasant Point Corporation have approached the Township with interests of building a resort. But other than talking to a few real estate agents, nothing else has materialized. The truth is I haven't heard from these people for a few months. But, if they do return with a proposal, then everything, and I do mean everything—" the mayor paused, glancing at mixture of people behind the red-headed reporter "—will be done to preserve our environment and ensure positive growth for our town. So, case closed, Mr. Boone."

Dan Boone's broad lips curled into a wry smile and he shook his head. "You can't take the lawyer out of the mayor, can you, MacGregor?"

Hart heard the click of the bullhorn engaging. "Okay, folks, show's over! Let's clear the area!" Constable Wright yelled.

Hart grinned. Aunt Gertie had been relieved of her bullhorn duties and didn't seemed too pleased with Constable Wright. She stood in the shadow of Constable Boyd, with her arms folded over her chest and her lips formed in a pout, as if a favourite toy had been taken away from her.

The back end of the truck lurched and Hart turned to find a man with short, black, curly hair swinging his long legs over the gate and into the box. Hart noted he was no bum. Clean-shaven, and dressed in an olive corduroy sports coat and beige dockers, the man made his presence known by looking Hart in the eye and nodding. There was something about his stone grey eyes that held Hart captive, as if this man could see right through him. He straightened, brushed down his coat, and fixed the collar on his taupe shirt. Hart guessed the man was about his height, maybe an inch or two taller. Skoka greeted him with a wag of his tail and a sniff to his groin.

"Skoka, no, bad boy," the man said, pushing the dog's big head away. His eyes widened, and he pointed at the wooden crate situated in the right corner of the box. "Is that what I think it is?"

Hart shrugged. "I dunno. What do you think it is?"

The man smiled heartily. "Why, the best damn maple syrup north of Toronto."

Hart shook his head. "What is it with you people around here? Maple syrup and blueberries. Does anyone ever talk about anything else?"

The man laughed. "Not when it's Gertie Ellis' maple syrup and blueberries. People have been known to commit felonies for her mouth-watering, homegrown fare."

"Is that so?" Hart said, rubbing his chin. "Then should I be guarding this stuff with my life?"

"And with all your heart," the man said, chuckling. He stuck out his hand. "The name's Sid Molnar."

Hart shook his hand. It felt strong, clammy, and smooth. "Hart Stewart. I'm Gertie Ellis' long-lost great-nephew."

The man's grip tightened, squeezing Hart's hand as if it was in a vise. Then, Sid's face relaxed. He released Hart's hand, and smiled. "Yes. You have Catherine's eyes."

Hart perked up. "You knew my mom?"

Sid nodded. "She used to help Gertie and Pete out at the Farmer's Market every Thursday. I remember that smile of hers to this day. She was a born salesperson, and she knew it. As soon as Catherine would flash her pearly whites, that was it, your wallet was coming out and you'd be buying stuff you'd didn't need." He paused, then chuckled. "Your mom also used to do parlor tricks for the tourists. She dressed up as a gypsy, and did psychic readings and things like that, to get them to buy extra. And they always did. A free reading with every two quarts of blueberries, that was her sales pitch. Man, she was great."

Hart inclined his head. "Did you date my mom?"

The question took Sid by surprise. His body straightened, his hands clenched. "Heavens, no. I'm about nine years her senior, and at the time I was doing my internship as a lawyer." Then he paused, looked at Hart point-blank, and said, "But I wished I did."

Hart leaned against the back of the cab and let his mind wander. He never knew his father, and his mom rarely dated. Now, standing here in the back of the truck talking to a man who had shown some interest in his mother, got him thinking. Were there other men in Fairy Falls who knew his mom? And if so, did she ever date them? As questions bombarded his mind, Hart felt a nudge in his side and turned to see Sid scanning the crowd.

"Where's your mom, Hart? I can't seem to find her. She couldn't have changed that much in eighteen years."

Hart swallowed hard. This would be the third person in Fairy Falls that he would have to spill his guts to. "Dead," he muttered as if no one was there. "She...she was murdered last May."

Sid gripped Hart's shoulder. "Oh, oh Christ, I'm so sorry, Hart. Did they catch who did it?"

Still staring into space, Hart shook his head. "No. Whoever killed her is still out there. It was senseless, too. I still don't understand why it happened."

Sid scoffed. "No one understands the mind of a murderer, Hart. With maybe the exception of a lawyer. That's why I became one. To fight for those who don't have a voice, and to see that they get some form of justice, some peace back in their lives, no matter what."

Hart fell silent for the moment, allowing Sid's noble words to sink in. A string of angry taunts assaulted his ears, and he turned to catch the cute redhead taking a swipe at Dan Boone. Constable Boyd had grabbed her arm in time and started dragging her in the opposite direction. The young woman screamed, "Admit it, Boone! You did it! You murdered my mother because she was a visionary! She was for progress in this town! Admit it, you...you bastard!"

A small crowd cheered her on. Mayor MacGregor lunged down the stairs and parted the crowd, as if he were a charging bull. His face was redder than before, his breathing distraught, as if he'd lost this round. "Please take my daughter home, Constable," he said, not taking his eyes off Boyd. "I'll deal with her later."

Constable Boyd nodded and escorted the hot-headed teen away from the riled crowd. Hart whistled. "What was all that about?"

Sid leaned on the top of the truck and sighed. "That feisty redhead is Diana MacGregor, and as you might have guessed, her father is Michael MacGregor, the newly-elected mayor of Fairy Falls. He also happens to be my partner at our law firm down the street. Last year, around this time, Mike's wife, Joy, was murdered. One of the prime suspects happened to be Dan Boone."

"Oh, so I guess there's a lot of bad blood between them," Hart said, propping his chin with a hand, as he took it all in.

Sid snorted. "That's an understatement! You see, Hart, Boone is our local tree-hugging, dirt-worshipper, who has always had it out for anyone who would tear up or bulldoze 'Mother Earth', if, in his eyes, there wasn't any need to. Joy MacGregor was his ultimate nemesis. She was a damn good counsellor for this town, and in the last few years Joy made some changes to Fairy Falls that Boone didn't particularly like."

"What kind of changes?" Hart asked, inclining his head.

Sid raked his fingers through his curly dark locks, and said, "Joy got the town to purchase a vacant piece of property to build a skateboard park for the kids. Trouble was, Boone felt the land should have been left to the wildlife seeing as it backed onto the river. Then there was the infamous Fairy Falls Trail scandal, where Joy was instrumental in the creation of a wilderness trail through a stretch of crown land. Boone and Joy almost came to blows on that issue."

Hart narrowed his brows. "So if there were so many fingers pointing at that Boone guy, why wasn't he charged with Joy MacGregor's murder?"

Sid licked his lips. "Because his alibi was tighter than a fish's butthole. That alibi being your great-aunt, Gertie Ellis."

Hart held his breath, absorbing all of this. His shoulders slumped forward. Aunt Gertie was on the side of a tree-hugging, scraggly old fart who loved the land and hated progress. Then something occurred to him. Half the town was at odds and torn apart: some wanted growth, while others wanted things to remain the same—to keep that small town mentality. Hart glanced at Sid, whose eyes were riveted on Dan Boone, still ranting over the fact that he'd just been assaulted and no arrest had been made.

He gently nudged Sid's elbow. "So what happens if those development guys come back to Fairy Falls looking to build their resort?"

Turning, Sid Molnar looked Hart straight in the eye. "Then, Hart, I afraid that there will be some winners and some losers."

6. Holding Firm

While peeling the yellow rubber gloves from his hands, Hart sneezed and caught the corner of his orange sleeve in time. Sniffling first, then stuffing the gloves in the front flap of his damp, white apron, Hart surveyed the area for something to sit on during his first afternoon coffee break. With a steaming cup of java in one hand, he pulled up a green plastic patio chair from a corner; the scraping noise grating his ears. Hart draped his plaid hoodie over the back of the chair, pulled off his hair net, and shoved it into his jeans' pocket. Falling into the cool, stiff seat, Hart propped his long legs up on a flat, pinkish boulder, and took a sip from his cup. The coffee burned going down, but the sweet concoction of cream and sugar soothed his disposition and calmed his nerves. After all, busing tables and dishwashing for the Stagview Resort was a highly stressful job.

Hart licked the sugar speckled rim of his cup and closed his eyes to review recent events. He smiled, knowing he had lucked out big-time. The interviewer at this morning's job fair hired him on the spot, no questions asked. All because his great-aunt had tagged along with him. She'd even filled out the application form for him, seeing as he didn't know her exact address. He'd found out that the resort knew Gertie Ellis, not only for the maple syrup and blueberries she supplied to Stagview, but because her late husband, Pete, had helped design and build the resort's dock system. Hart opened his eyes, yawned, and allowed his thoughts to deepen. Yesterday was quite an eye-opener for the young city-slicker. He couldn't believe how split the town was about that development rumour. Even if it were true, why wouldn't Fairy Falls jump at the chance to make lots of money? To better themselves? To live the high life? Hart shook his head, trying to figure out the minds of simple country folks. They just didn't get progress. Either that, or the townspeople who were opposed to change were afraid of it. He took another swig of his hot coffee, swirls of steam curling around his crooked nose, warming him inside and out.

Yesterday was also a day of revelations for him, from learning where his mother had developed her amazing psychic sales skills, to meeting a man who actually knew her, and even wanted to date her at one time. Then there was the letter stuffed inside his hoodie's breast pocket. A letter from his mother to her aunt. Why had Aunt Gertie kept it all these years? What was in it that was so important? Hart took the last mouthful of coffee, then plunked the cup on the flat rock next to his feet. He let the hot brew swim in his mouth a moment before swallowing. Wiping his mouth, Hart couldn't stop thinking about his mother's letter. His shoulders hunched. *A letter that I can't even read.*

With the thought of connecting with his mother through her letter, Hart unbuttoned the breast pocket of his hoodie, stuck two fingers in, and carefully extracted the well-worn letter. As he freed the letter from its confines, out popped the diamond and ruby ring. The ring sailed through the air, bounced off the ground, and then rolled to land under a large boulder that appeared to have the face of a gnome carved into it. He cringed. Touching that cursed ring was the last thing he wanted to do.

Swearing aloud, he tucked his mother's letter back into the pocket, and then jumped out of the chair to retrieve the ring. Kneeling, he peered under the rock. In an uncomfortable position, he searched for his golden, bejeweled meal ticket. He found cigarette butts, chewed gum, and a coffee cup lid, but no ring. Hart's stomach tightened. *Uh oh. I know I saw it go underneath. So where the hell is it?* Stretching and turning his neck in a way no yoga master would dare, Hart cupped his right hand to remove some of the earth and debris away from the base of the sculpted boulder. He looked again, and there, farther back, Hart caught a glimpse of sparkle. The ring was there, all right. The problem was his hands were too big.

"Lose something?"

Caught off guard, Hart straightened so fast that the back of his head smacked into the gnome's granite nose. He grabbed his head and swore aloud.

"Are you okay?"

His head now throbbing, Hart twisted around to sit cross-legged, and stared up at the unwanted company. His eyes widened. The cute, red-headed reporter who had tried to get into a scrap with that scruffy tree-hugger stood over him. She was dressed differently today. A silky, green blouse imprinted with the Stagview logo and black, pressed pants gave Hart the impression she was in management. He nodded, although he knew it was a lie. He hurt, big-time.

Her pert nose wrinkled as if she didn't believe him. She extended her right hand. "Suit yourself, if you'd prefer to play the strong, silent type, but at least give me your hand so I can help you up."

Not waiting for Hart to reach up, the girl lunged for his hand and yanked him to his feet in one swift motion. Her hand felt rough, yet her nails were perfectly manicured, sporting a bronze polish. Her makeup, done subtly in hues of browns, made her watchful green eyes stand out, and held Hart captive for the moment. He heard her clear her throat before she pulled her hand away from his. "Are you sure you're okay? I can take you to the first aid room, if you'd like."

First aid? No. No way. I'd sooner be suspended over the highest cliff upside-down then pay a visit to the local bone setter. He rubbed his head, and said, "No thanks, I'm fine. Sometimes my brain needs a smack now and then to make it work better."

She laughed. "You must be from the city."

Hart tilted his head to one side. "You can tell?"

She grinned. "No doubt. By the way, my name's—"

"Diana MacGregor," Hart said, cutting in. "Hi, I'm Hart Stewart."

Diana frowned. Hart smiled, and said, "I saw you in action yesterday, you know, with that Boone guy. Sid Molnar told me who you were and why you were so pissed."

A curtain of blush swept over Diana's freckled face. She averted her eyes. "Oh. You saw that, did you?"

Hart nodded. "Hey, you shouldn't feel embarrassed about what happened. After all, you stood up for yourself and the town."

Hart noticed he was a good four or five inches taller than Diana, and instantly caught a whiff of tropical scent from her wavy, red hair: it smelled fruity and fresh, like an outside market after a cooling rain on a hot day. He let his eyes rove down the length of her perfectly straight, pert nose, to rest on her full, glossy lips. Lips that matched the colour of her nail polish. His face burned and he gulped. *Crap. What the hell am I doing?* Before things got awkward, Hart was back on his knees searching for the elusive diamond and ruby ring.

The sudden presence of a warm body on the ground next to Hart made him feel uncomfortable. He tightened his hands into fists, then loosened them. Diana's silky shoulder rubbed up against him. "What did you lose, Hart?" Diana asked, searching the ground. "Maybe I can help you find it."

"Oh, thanks, but don't worry about it, Diana, I've got it covered."

"Come on, two sets of eyes are better than one."

Hart sighed. There was no way he could squeeze his big hand under the rock. He'd need a shovel for sure. He glanced at Diana's fair, dainty hands, and figured maybe she could reach the ring for him. He nodded, and said, "Okay, but don't blame me if you chip your nail polish. I lost a ring and it's lying underneath this rock, way back. Do you think you could—"

Before Hart rattled off his next word, Diana slid her hand under the boulder. Her scrunched face told him that she'd encountered some nasty stuff before touching the ring. "I...I think I've got it," Diana said, her voice strained, but seemingly victorious.

"Great! Thanks for doing this for me," Hart said, smiling.

Diana blushed, and yanked out her clenched hand. A wad of pink gum stuck to her knuckle and a cigarette butt claimed the inside of her thumbnail. She cringed and flicked away the grungy cling-ons.

Then, Hart narrowed his eyes. *Wait, I'd better take some precautions.* He slipped one of the rubber gloves out of his apron pocket, put it on, and held out his hand.

"Do you have an allergy to jewelry?" Diana asked, depositing the ring into Hart's gloved hand.

Hart smiled sheepishly. He carefully rolled the ring between his index finger and thumb to blow away the dirt and debris caught between the gems, before revealing it to Diana. "With this ring, I do."

Diana made an odd, strangled sound, as if something heavy was trapped inside her throat. *That's mom's ring. No, correction, my ring.*

"Is something wrong,?" Hart asked in a concerned manner.

The sound of his voice jarred Diana, and while still on her knees, she looked up at Hart and stared at him blankly. Her chest tightened and her breathing became harsh and erratic, as if her lungs were working overtime. She coughed and sputtered, and her nose started to run. *Great. This will be the fifth asthma attack this week.* Diana quickly dove into her pocket and pulled out her inhaler. Calmly, she brought it up to her mouth and squeezed hard, breathing in, breathing out. She repeated these actions. Her heavy breathing eased up, her face relaxed. Satisfied, she stowed the puffer back into her pocket, took a deep breath, and looked up at Hart with renewed strength.

Diana pointed to her ring. "Where did you get that?"

Hart choked the ring with his gloved hand and backed off a little. "Whoa, what's up with you?"

"I'll tell you what's up, you…you slimy douchebag!" Diana struggled to stand. "I've been looking everywhere for that ring for over a week! I've checked the police station at least five times a day, posted a reward all over town, got the local radio station to mention my ring on their lost and found segment every day, and had my friends search the entire town with me, not to mention them having to listen to me bitch and cry all week long!" She stopped her tirade long enough to take a few deep breaths. "And…and all this time you've had it! Didn't it occur to you that this ring *belonged* to somebody? What's the matter with you? Don't you bother checking the local newspaper or bulletin boards, or listening to the radio or local gossip around town?"

Hart pursed his lips. "Actually, no."

Diana's face reddened. Her fair brows narrowed in on her quarry, like a cougar eyeing a coyote. She clenched her teeth and her claws came out. She lunged at him. Hart was knocked to the mosaic-style patio, his head smacked against the bricks. Diana heard the 'whump' of his skull connecting with stone, but she didn't give a crap. All she wanted was her ring back on her finger, and as sure as damn, she was going to get it.

She straddled him, reaching for the hand that held her prize. The rubber glove he was wearing made it awkward, almost impossible, and her fingers kept slipping away. Diana braced her hand on Hart's chest and tried to reach for her ring again, but this time he anticipated her move and rolled to the side, pushing Diana off. Still clenching the ring, Hart rolled away from her and jumped to his feet. He held his head, pain evident in his features. His crooked nose flared and his blue eyes raged like a swelling river. Diana swallowed hard. *Maybe I should have taken another approach.*

Hart's breathing turned turbulent. "A-a-are you crazy?"

Diana got up. She balled her hands at her sides. "You'd be crazy too if you'd been looking all over town for something that was so important to you, that—"

"That you'd go ballistic enough to attempt cold-blooded murder on a five-star resort's patio?" Hart yelled, cutting in.

Diana took a deep breath, unclenched her hands and crossed her arms over her chest. "Okay, maybe I overreacted, but—"

"But nothing!" Hart sliced in, moving closer to Diana. He grabbed the back of her neck with his ungloved hand and squeezed hard, making her wince.

"What's going on here?" a male voice boomed.

Hart dropped his hand and backed away. Diana twisted to catch Donovan Johnson staring daggers at Hart. Donovan's green polo shirt was pulled out of his tan cargo pants, and his chest was moving up and down as if he had just run the hundred metre. Diana's cheeks burned. Donovan must have heard them fighting all the way from the resort's Pro Shop on the other side of the restaurant. In one of his hands was a golf club and it appeared as if he wasn't afraid to show Hart a swing or two.

Brook Bennet dashed through the back gate of the patio. She, too, was breathless, her hair askew. Brook tucked her green blouse back into her knee-length black skirt and made an attempt to adjust her hair. "What's the matter, Diana? I heard you yelling at someone from the lobby."

Diana put up her hands. "It's all right, you guys, just a misunderstanding, that's all."

"That's all?" Hart asked, frowning.

She turned around, her lips set, eyes wide. "Ix-nay on the ight-fay."

Hart arched his brows. "Huh?"

Diana rolled her eyes. *Men. Thick-headed and oh-so-not-there.* She sighed. "Look, I want to keep my job and I'm sure you want to keep yours, so let's settle this in an adult manner. Now, I'm going to hold out my hand and you're going to give me back my ring like the gentleman I'm sure you are."

"Ring? Oh, Diana, did you find your ring?" Brook asked, still fidgeting with her hair.

"It's my ring," Hart broke in.

"I beg to differ, it's mine. It belonged to my mother. I can describe it if you like," Diana said, her hands now on her hips.

"Of course you can describe it, I've just shown it to you!" Hart argued.

Donovan snorted. "Then allow me to describe it. It's gold and has a big diamond in the middle, possibly a .75 carat, with two marquis shaped rubies on either side of it. My guess is they're about .50 carats a piece, give or take. Oh yeah, and inscribed on the inside, it says, *To the Love of my Life. Forever and Always.* Is that enough info for you, Dude?"

Hart shuddered, and opened his gloved hand to reveal the ring. He swallowed, prodding it with a finger, as if looking for the inscription. Hart stared at her ring a good minute. Diana narrowed her eyes. *This guy is off-the-chart weird. First the rubber glove, now this?*

"Well?" Diana asked, in the hopes of bringing Hart back from his trance. "Is that a good enough description for you?"

All Hart did was nod. Then, without even blinking, he tossed Diana's ring to her. She caught it in mid-air and held it to her chest for a brief second. Her mouth went dry as she searched for the right words to express herself, but nothing came to mind, so all she managed to mouth was a silent 'thank you'.

Before Diana had a chance to put her ring back on, Hart grabbed her elbow, squeezed it gently, and said, "By the way, your mother *knew* her murderer."

7. A Reason for Everything

Diana's mouth fell open. Dumbfounded, she shook her head. "What...what did you just say?"

Donovan growled. "Look, fruitcake, I'm warning you—"

Hart held up a hand toward Donovan, halting what he was about to say, and then looked into Diana's wide, green eyes. He said, "I know I sound crazy, but believe me, I'm not."

Brook snorted. "And just why should we believe you, anyway? You were about to steal Diana's ring if we hadn't come to her rescue."

Diana swallowed hard. How did this stranger even know about her mother's fate? Surely he couldn't have witnessed her murder. Up until today, Diana had never laid eyes on this guy, and she basically knew everyone in and around Fairy Falls. No. Things just didn't make sense. Her journalistic mind kicked in. She wanted answers and she wanted them now.

"Who the hell are you?" Diana demanded. "And what do you know about my mother?"

Hart rubbed the back of his head, wincing from her patio assault of a moment ago. A pang of guilt seeped through Diana, but she immediately shrugged it off. She looked down into her hand, to where her ring lay between the etched lines of her palm, and brushed it with her thumb. The feeling of emptiness was still within her, still haunting her. And now this...this bozo had blurted out that he knew her mother *knew* her killer. Her fair brows furrowed. There was no way that this freak-a-zoid was getting out of explaining himself. She reached over and poked Hart in the stomach. It felt hard, as if he kept in shape.

"Hey, watch it!" Hart covered his stomach with both hands. "That hurt!"

"That's nothing compared to what I'm gonna do to you if you don't answer the lady's questions," Donovan said in a no-nonsense tone. He slapped the head of the golf club hard against his palm.

Hart took a step back. "Look—" he said, pointing to the ring in Diana's hand, "—all I know is what that ring told me."

Donovan scoffed. "Oh, that makes perfect sense. The ring says, 'To the Love of my Life. Forever and Always'. Now does that sound like anything you just told her?"

Hart rolled his eyes and raked his hair. "No. You don't get it. I...I can read objects, and understand what they want to tell me, just like you can read a book or a text."

In the corner of her eye, Diana caught Donovan advancing upon Hart. However, Brook squealed, as if she understood Hart's obscure garble. "I get it! You're a psychometrist!"

"Psycho is right," Donovan said sarcastically, cutting the distance between Hart and himself by half.

But Brook jumped into Donovan's path and placed her hands flat against his heaving chest. She shook her head and said, "Can the macho crap and listen to me, Donovan. The guy's a psychometrist. It means he can receive a certain energy or vibration from an object he holds and it tells him something important about its owner. Get it?"

Donovan stared blankly at Brook. "No. Now move out of my way, Witchy-Poo, before you get hurt."

Diana frowned. She looked down at her ring again. Did what Brook just say hold any water? Was Hart a psycho-whatever? Could he receive certain information regarding her mother's murder through this ring? Or was the ring a channel, like Brook's silly Ouija board game, that allowed dead spirits to communicate with the living? Diana's mouth went dry. Nothing made sense to her. Maybe her pagan friend believed in all that psychic babble, but Diana didn't. She was studying to be a journalist. She believed in cold, hard facts that were founded on logic and truth. Not some freaky, out-of-this-world belief system that didn't have a firm foundation to stand on.

Diana took a giant step over to Hart and shoved the ring in his face. "Are you telling me that this ring, my mother's ring, *told* you what happened to my mother?"

"Sort of." Hart took a deep breath. "Actually, that ring showed me what really happened to your mother on the night of her murder."

"Okay, cut the crap, psycho-boy!" Donovan pushed Brook aside and advanced on Hart.

This time Diana came in between them. She looked Hart in his eyes, as if searching for a shred of sincerity. "H-How did you know my mother was murdered at night? Those details were never released."

Hart pulled the rubber glove off his hand and shoved it in his apron. He sighed and said, "I told you. I was there, in a sense. That ring took me to where your mother was murdered. It's...it's cursed or something. It's gotta be, because nothing like that has ever happened to me before."

Brook walked over and placed one of her slim hands on Diana's shoulder. She felt the warmth of her friend's breath on her face, as Brook said, "Nothing like what, exactly?"

"Yeah, and what do you mean you 'you were there'?" Donovan asked, flanking Diana's other side.

Hart's face told Diana he was fighting with some kind of demon, struggling to get it out. He cleared his throat. "There was a full moon that night, the night of your mother's murder. Right?"

Diana nodded. Hart nodded back, then continued, "Your mom had red hair just like you, and owned a dark blue Cadillac. While she was trying to get into it, she was mumbling something to herself. Something about a development, a scam, and a traitor—"

"You could hear her talk?" Diana said, her voice strained, as her heart raced.

Hart licked his lips. "Yes. And more."

"More? What do you mean by that?" Donovan asked.

"I—" Hart looked away for a moment "—I could feel what she felt. Her pain, her desperation, her...the way she died. And I was helpless to do anything but watch until the ring was ready to release me."

"But—" Brook broke in "—how could you possibly feel anything Mrs. MacGregor felt? I didn't think that was the way psychometry works."

Hart shook his head. "It isn't. Like I said, this has *never* happened to me before. It was like a 3-D movie, and I paid the price to sit in the front seat and watch the show, whether I liked it or not."

"So who killed my mother, then?" Diana asked, her tone demanding and abrupt. Every cell in her body prickled with anticipation, thrilling in the ride Hart Stewart was giving her.

Hart shrugged. "I…I don't know. He was covered from head to toe, wearing a black ski mask, gloves, and dark trench coat."

Diana's face fell. She could feel her spirits sink as if a lead weight was pulling her under. Then, Hart grabbed her chin and pulled it up so that his powder blue eyes pierced her green ones. He half-smiled and said, "You're a lot like your mom, Diana. She was a fighter. She managed to rip part of her murderer's mask away. The problem was that only your mom got a good look at him because his back was toward me. Her last words were, 'You bastard', so I knew she recognized him. She had to have. She had something on him, and he was willing to kill for it."

For over a year now, Diana had wondered, prayed, and longed for any information regarding her mother's murder. *And now this guy shows up, who claims he has these psychic powers that can communicate with objects. Objects like mom's ring.* Diana pressed her lips together. An object that had been there, at the scene of the crime, a viable witness to a heinous act. It all seemed so far-fetched, so out there. Yet what did Hart have to gain from all this? This wasn't a fortune telling session, this was real. So was Hart for real?

"Who are you, anyway?" Brook asked. "The sorcerer's apprentice?"

Hart threw her a strange look. "No. My name's Hart Stewart. I'm Gertie Ellis's great-nephew."

Diana snapped out of her self-induced trance. *Gertie Ellis? Not the same Gertie Ellis who was Dan Boone's only alibi? No. This is all too much.* It was information overload to the power of ten. Diana thought she heard Donovan mumble 'Uh-oh' as he took a step back. He swung the golf club behind his back, as if anticipating her next move, but Donovan would have never have guessed what was about to happen next, because what came out of her mouth shocked even

Diana. "Name your price, I'll pay you whatever you ask. You can even have my car, if you want it."

Donovan dropped the golf club.

Brook gasped.

Hart snapped his head back. "Pay me? Pay me for what?"

"To find my mother's killer," Diana replied. "Let's face facts. You're the only person who has these special psychic connections and no one else has been able to solve her murder. Look, I've got all the information on my mother's murder, I've kept impeccable files, know the suspects, and can help you get anything you'd need. What do you say?"

"Your...your car?" Donovan muttered.

"Are you sure you want to do this?" Brook asked, concerned.

Diana held her hand out toward Hart. "Do we have a deal?"

Dumbfounded, Hart looked at Diana's offered hand, then glanced back to her face, searching for a hint of sincerity. He nodded. "I'll help you, if you help me."

Startled, Diana arched her thin, fair brows. "Help you? How?"

Hart took a deep breath. "My mother was murdered too. In Toronto, just over a year ago, in our apartment. Nothing was taken. She had no enemies to speak of and we weren't rich. All I have is a letter my great-aunt kept from when mom was my age. Maybe it will help answer some questions, maybe it won't."

Diana nodded. "So what does it say?"

Hart cast his eyes to the ground. His face reddened, his hands balled at his sides. He took another deep breath. "I...I don't know," he replied, his voice cracking. "I can't—"

Diana inclined her head. "Can't what?"

Hart's eyes locked with Diana's. His chin trembled as he whispered, "Read."

Silence, except for the sudden, chilly gust of wind coming off of the lake.

Donovan broke it. "Dude, did you just that say you can't—"

"Donovan!" Brook elbowed him in the ribs. "Don't be so insensitive!"

Donovan rubbed his side, and nodded. "Dude, you're illiterate?"

Brook rolled her eyes. "That's not what I meant, you bonehead."

Diana ignored her friends and got straight to the heart of the matter. "Then I'll teach you to read. We'll help each other. That way, I'll get what I want, and you'll get what you want."

Brook made an odd sound at the back of her throat. "I don't know, Diana, you should always be careful what you want or wish for. It could backfire into something unrealistic or unforeseen."

Diana glared at Brook. "Don't you want justice for my mother, Brook?"

Brook stiffened. "Yes, of course I do, but not if it means screwing around with the laws of the universe. It's just not right."

Donovan laughed. "This advice from somebody who worships some lame Egyptian god named Thoth."

Brook whirled on her high heels to face Donovan. Before she could spew a curse at him, Hart reached for Brook's elbow and spun her to face him. Speechless, Brook stared up at Hart, her mouth agape, her breathing heavy. Hart shook his head, and said, "I promise, no one's going to screw around with the universe, Brook. If anything, it's the universe that's screwing around with me. And like my mom always said, 'there's a reason for everything'."

Brook, still speechless, nodded. Hart smiled, and then stuck out his hand toward Diana. "You've got yourself a deal."

While Diana shook Hart's hand, she felt several raised rough spots along the inside of his palm, as if he'd suffered an injury. His handshake was firm, and engulfed her entire hand as if it were a lion's mouth.

Donovan stifled a chuckle.

Diana knit her brows. "Is something funny, Johnson?"

Donovan grinned mischievously at Hart. "Dude, you should have taken the car!"

8. New Boyfriend

"**D**onovan was right," Hart said, scanning the inside of Diana's car.

Diana settled into the driver's seat and arched a brow. "How so?"

He grinned. "I should have taken you up on your offer. It's a sweet ride!"

She laughed heartily, stuck a key into the ignition, and then turned it. The sound of the engine pulsed through Hart's entire body, as if the car had a soul.

"So, how'd you score this classic?" Hart asked, buckling his seat belt.

"I inherited it, actually." Diana drooped her shoulders slightly. "From my grandpa. He died about seven years ago." Then she straightened and smiled. "When I was a little girl, I was always around grandpa when he worked on this car, and I went to every car show I could with him. Mom never understood it and thought I should be playing with kids my own age, but I'd rather hang with my grandpa. I guess he figured I was the best choice to take care of his baby."

"Seems like he made the right one to me," Hart said, giving Diana a thumbs up sign.

She beamed. Her fingers grazed the top of the black steering wheel and followed it around until both hands met at the bottom. Her thumbs stroked the wheel one last time before she stepped on the clutch and reached over to throw the car into first gear. The tires spun and Hart braced himself.

His stomach rolled. They were on their way to Diana's house. She had said she lived somewhere on Loon Lake, which was connected to Blueberry Lake by a river at the top end. Diana had invited Hart to supper so that she could go over the file she kept on her mother's case with him. Apparently she wanted Hart to be well informed before he did any more of his psychic mumbo-jumbo on any other objects that belonged to her mother. Hart yawned and checked his wrist-watch. It clicked onto five o'clock. It had been a long day, and from where he sat, it wasn't about to end.

Diana swung her 1970 Chevelle SS around and out of the Stagview Resort's parking lot, negotiating the turn, then shoved it into second gear. With the window down, Hart stuck his arm out and gripped the side of the dark green door, his fingers connecting with the white stripe that ran along its side. He clenched his teeth, thankful that he'd buckled himself in before Diana gunned the engine.

A movement from the rear-view mirror caught Hart's attention. He adjusted his eyes from the road to what was dangling from the mirror and his eyes widened. Strange, he hadn't noticed it before. It wasn't your typical fuzzy dice or dreamcatcher you'd usually find hanging from such a place. It was, well, it looked like a whittled stick with an assortment of coloured crystals wound around it using a thin piece of copper wiring to secure them. What appeared to be a few bird's feathers attached to beaded leather thongs swayed from the end. Then, the decorative stick twisted around and Hart's eyes bugged. A mummified bird's foot was strapped onto the stick in such a manner that it looked like it was emerging from a coffin. He blinked. *What the hell is that thing?*

Without realizing it, Hart reached over to touch the dangling stick. Diana giggled and he pulled back his hand. "That's okay," she said, shifting to third. "I know it looks weird, but Brook made it for me last year, after my mom was killed. She calls it a healing wand."

"Is...is that real?" Hart asked, pointing to the bird's foot.

Diana bit her bottom lip and then nodded. "It's a crow's foot. Brook said the bird hit the window while she was creating the wand.

It died instantly, and Brook took it as a sign to honour the bird and incorporate its soul into the wand. She says I possess crow medicine."

Hart snorted. "And I'd say Brook needs some medicine of her own. Preferably something that doesn't induce hallucinations."

The car hit a rough spot in the road and Hart gripped the dashboard. The Chevelle fishtailed, then straightened and went on, as if nothing happened.

"Uh-oh," Diana muttered. "Now you've done it."

Hart straightened. He was white-knuckling the vinyl dashboard now. "Done what?"

"You've upset the crow spirit of the wand. Brook warned me about that."

Bullets of sweat broke through Hart's brow. He gulped. He knew his mother hung out with people who believed everything possessed a spirit. Crap, she even knew a few people who could talk to spirits. He thought he'd left that life behind, but now this: a practicing sorceress in the middle of Hicksville and a red-headed bumpkin who encouraged her. His scalp prickled. Maybe he shouldn't have jumped on board with Diana's personal quest for justice. Maybe he should've just given her the ring back and kept his mouth shut. A burst of giggles and snorts interrupted his thoughts. He looked over to watch Diana slap her steering wheel and shake her head.

"Are all city-boys as naive as you?" she asked, chuckling.

Hart rolled his eyes and sunk deeper into the black vinyl bucket seat. He was about to defend himself when something swooped down and slammed into Hart's side of the windshield. Diana swerved instantly. No one was behind or in front of them, so that was a plus. As soon as she got the car under control, Diana stomped on the brakes, her fingers wrapped tightly around the steering wheel, her face red. She glanced over at Hart with wide eyes and an open mouth.

"Oh...oh my God, I think a bird just hit us. Are you okay?" she asked in one quick breath.

Hart nodded slowly. "My guess is that the crow spirit wants its foot back."

Diana rolled her eyes. "That was no crow, it was too big."

Hart undid his seatbelt, then opened the heavy green door and swung his long legs out. He looked down the gravel road. A set of tire tracks burrowed into the gravelly earth, and off to the side Hart caught sight of a feathered lump, lying still. Diana saw it too, and she sprinted toward the injured bird. The sound of crunching gravel accompanied her as she ran toward the spot, and she skidded to a halt. She knelt by the bird and gently poked it.

"Ah, that's a shame. It was a red-tailed hawk," Diana announced, as if it had been a member of her family. She sighed. "Well, at least she didn't suffer. Her neck must have broken instantly when she hit the windshield."

By now, Hart had covered the distance to reach Diana. He looked down at the still hawk, and quirked a brow. "She?"

Diana shrugged. "Just a figure of speech."

"So what now?" he asked, hunkering down to Diana's level.

"We bury her. Go into my trunk, there's a collapsible shovel at the side. That should do the trick."

Hart knew he hadn't heard her right. *Bury her?* No. She hadn't said that, had she? *Didn't you just leave roadkill? Wouldn't she be taking away some government worker's job?* Hart shoved his cap up off his forehead and narrowed his eyes. "Tell me you're kidding around with me again. Tell me you're not seriously considering burying this wild animal."

Diana frowned and scratched her chin. "You're right. Let's wrap it up and bring it to Brook. I bet she'd be able to make a nice accessory for you, like a hawk hat, or hey, maybe a hawk foot necklace with a matching bracelet."

Hart's mouth screwed up to the side. "Next you'll be telling me I possess 'hawk' medicine."

Diana smiled. "Well, the hawk was aiming for you. If Brook was here she'd definitely insist—"

"Never mind," Hart said, cutting in. "Let's get this over with before anyone sees us."

As Hart walked toward the car, he ignored the fact that he saw Diana score a few loose feathers from under the dead hawk and slip them into her coat pocket. He shook his head. *And I thought my mom's world was weird and wacky. Crow medicine? Hawk medicine? What next? Blackfly medicine?* He'd take a can of bug spray and a simple dose of cold medicine over that freaky stuff, any time, any day.

It took all of fifteen minutes to dig a shallow grave and bury the bird, before they were off again. Diana seemed more careful on the road now, watching the sky, then the roadside, as if anticipating more bird or animal 'medicine' to dart out at them. But the rest of the journey was uneventful, until Diana pulled her car into a slightly sloped driveway, and slammed on the brakes. Hart put his hand up in time to catch himself from sailing into the dashboard. He instinctively unlatched his seatbelt and turned to give Diana the evil eye and a few choice words on her lousy driving skills. Then he looked up past Diana's head and his jaw dropped.

Hart's eyes widened, and a sharp, staggering intake of breath followed. *Beautiful.* This place and the house held him captive. It was nothing like the simple geometric clusters Aunt Gertie called home; this was a house where a movie star would live. Done entirely in logs, the middle portion of the house towered above the two side sections, as if it were a look-out for the entire area. Slanted windows were set into it, like cat's eyes, watchful and waiting. In fact, there were more windows than he could count. A screened-in porch on top of a deck was on the right side, while the left part of the house dipped down, allowing for the building to merge with a cluster of tall pines. Carefully placed rocks surrounded the property, creating a fortress within the forest. If this was the back of the house, then Hart could only imagine what the front facing the lake looked like. *Just as beautiful,* he thought.

"What the hell is *she* doing here?" Diana hissed under her breath, like a fire breathing dragon.

Hart jumped from his trance-like state and glanced over at Diana. Her knuckles were white and she strangled the steering wheel, as if it were a chicken's neck ready to be snapped. He arched a brow. "Diana? Are you okay?"

Her cheeks, now red, puffed out like an indignant chipmunk protecting its territory. She set her jaw, then stomped on the accelerator, knocking Hart back into his seat, then onto the floor. Clutching for the dashboard, Hart managed to pull himself up half-way, even with the car in motion. He felt every bump, as Diana careened her car in front of a large, double door garage, also fashioned entirely of logs. She promptly slammed on the brakes. This time Hart's head smacked into the glove compartment. He winced, rubbing his forehead briskly, and before he had a chance to ask Diana what the hell her problem was, she shut the engine off again and jumped out of the car.

Hart's cheeks burned as he finally pulled himself up and swung open the door. Shaking his head, then adjusting his faded ball cap,

Hart stepped out of Diana's big green monster, muttering four-letter words his mother would have never have approved of. Turning, he set his sights on his target; a reckless red-headed driver, who was standing by a gleaming white Jeep Cherokee, and peering through the driver's side window. By now, Hart's emotions were maxed out, and his body felt like a crash test dummy that had failed miserably.

"What's your problem, MacGregor?" Hart asked, looming over her.

Diana didn't turn around. Her head was pressed up against the jeep's window, her nose poking through a ten-inch gap, while her hands lay flat against the glass. Hart thought this odd. He squinted, checking out the jeep's interior. A black briefcase, opened and lying sideways on the beige leather passenger seat was filled with professionally typed legal papers, all stapled together. A row of pens, some business cards, sunglasses, and a calculator were neatly stuffed in its upper pockets, like some obsessive-compulsive owned it. As with the briefcase, Hart noted the vehicle's entire inside was neat and tidy to a fault. He glanced at the SUV's side, and recognized a popular real estate logo stuck on the back white panel. Underneath was a name. He mentally read off the letters. K.A.R.E.N. B.E.A.N. Then Hart, without even realizing what he was doing, tried to pronounce the name, as if he'd forgotten he wasn't alone.

"It says Karen Bean. She owns a real estate company in town," Diana said in a low, beaten voice.

He nudged her, and said, "So why does she piss you off?"

Diana sighed, and pushed away from the window. "It's a long, drawn out story, Hart."

He inclined his head. "I'm not going anywhere. That is, unless you've already fired me?"

She smiled and then looked down at the ground. "Well, for starters, I can't stand her son Brett. He's a jackass and a half, and that's being generous."

Hart laughed. "Guys can be such jerks sometimes." Then he smiled and winked. "But, hey, you can't live without us!"

Diana shook her head. "I'll get back to you on that one, smartass."

Hart heard a porch door slam and he looked up. A young girl, wearing a pink floral print top and indigo pants with wide, flared legs, raced across the deck in her bare feet and slid down the cedar railing. Her curly, light brown hair bobbed wildly from side to side as she made her way to where they were standing. Wire-rim glasses set onto a round face made her look older than Hart thought she might be. Possibly ten, maybe twelve. She skidded to a halt when she saw Hart.

"Hey, Nance," Diana said, with a wave. "Hart, this is my little sis, Nancy. Nance, this is Hart Stewart. He's joining us for supper tonight."

Nancy puckered her lips and glanced up at Diana, who had a good seven or eight inches on her. "Is he your *new* boyfriend?"

Hart caught the emphasis Nancy put on the word 'new'.

Diana's eyes bugged and her face turned crimson. Hart stifled a chuckle, then cleared his throat. "New boyfriend, eh? How many boyfriends has your sister gone through?"

Nancy smiled, then screwed up her face in contemplation. Her big sister intervened first, though, pulling the brim of Hart's baseball cap down over his face. "Do you want supper or not, Stewart?" she asked in a haughty tone.

"Depends." Hart adjusted his hat and smiled wickedly. "What'cha serving?"

"Mac'n cheese," Nancy said, rubbing her bulging belly. "I've got it on the stove, all ready to go. I'll just add another box."

Diana rolled her eyes. "I thought we discussed salad and chicken fingers."

Nancy shrugged. "That was before I knew Dad was going out for dinner with Ms. Bean tonight."

Diana's face turned the colour of greyish-green granite. She mouthed the words 'out', 'dinner', and 'tonight', slowly, deliberately, as if she were chewing something bitter. Or something with antennae. Hart reached for her elbow and gave it a squeeze. "Are you okay, Diana? You look like you're about to puke."

Diana heaved, turned, and hurled all over Karen Bean's pristine, white Jeep Cherokee. Nancy jumped back to avoid the splash, and Hart did likewise in the opposite direction. A portion of vomit managed to sail through the partially open driver's window, splattering all over the leather seats and landing in the briefcase.

"Does that mean you don't want Mac'n cheese, Diana?" Nancy asked, plugging her nose.

"Oh...my...good...God! What the devil is going on here?" a woman screamed from the deck.

Hart twisted on his rubber soles in time to see a tall woman gliding down the wooden steps. A gust of wind teased her perfectly coiffed short chestnut hair, but it hardly moved, thanks to the amount of hair spray she must have used. Her soft pink lips were set in a thin line, while her high cheekbones were pulled tight, as if the woman had just had an extreme makeover. Her stylish, black high-heeled shoes were no match for the uneven ground, but she somehow managed to maneuver the terrain, as she strutted over to where Diana was hunched over the Jeep's hood, still pale and heaving.

The woman smoothed her hands down her straight-cut grey skirt, flecked with pink, then folded her arms over the sleeves of her matching jacket, glaring at Diana. "Couldn't you have done that elsewhere, Diana?" she asked, condescension evident in her tone.

Hart furrowed his brows. "Hey, lady, the girl's just been sick! Why don't you have a little compassion?"

The woman's sculpted chestnut brows rose, while clear brown eyes swept the length of Hart's frame. He gulped. *Uh-oh. Now I've done it. I pushed her 'I'm gonna wail on you so bad' button.* She parted her wide lips, allowing for a curl of a smile to appear in one corner, like that of a jackal looking down on a carcass.

"Compassion? Hmm, let me see—" She tapped a long, pink polished nail against one of her sharp, white incisors. "Isn't that something like when you have to tell your clients that you have no choice but to cancel their appointment to finalize their offer on a new house that they desperately need by the end of this month, all because someone's tossed her cookies all over the inside of my car?"

Hart recouped, then smiled back. "Yeah, sort of, but I wouldn't exactly call it 'tossing cookies'."

The woman's eyes widened and she inclined her head. Still, not a hair moved out of place. "Then what would you call it?"

He smirked. "Good aim."

Hart heard Diana giggle between heaves. Nancy slapped a hand over her mouth. The woman, however, was not amused. She narrowed her brows until they almost met in the middle, and took a step toward Hart. He took a step back. Then she took another step forward. Hart repeated, and so did she. Hart moved to the left and she followed his lead. Hart moved to the right, and the woman kept up to him, as if they were doing an odd backwoods waltz. Nancy burst into laughter.

The woman balked, just as the screen door of the house slammed. "Are you ready to go, Karen?"

Hart bit his lip. It was Diana's dad. The mayor. The lawyer. The big guy who took no crap from the locals, or any huge corporation that would corrupt his small town. Hart rubbed the back of his neck. *Great. Talk about first impressions. I just pissed off Mr. MacGregor's date, and I'm sure I'm gonna go down for it.* The woman threw Hart an indignant look, then turned on her high-heels, and said, "I'm afraid I'll have to take a raincheck on our date, Mike. It appears that somebody doesn't approve of our relationship."

"Relationship? What relationship? There is no damn relationship!" Diana yelled, leaning against the jeep, wiping her mouth.

Mr. MacGregor stopped in his tracks. He'd been trying to do up his charcoal tie. Now it hung loosely around his neck, against the light grey shirt he wore. He glared at his daughter while slowly buttoning the cuffs on his sleeves, and then stuffed his hands in the pockets of his pleated black pants. He cleared his throat, and said, "If you have something to say to me, Diana, then by all means say it."

Suddenly, the phone rang from inside the house. "Oh, I'll get that!" Nancy yelled, bolting across the uneven ground and up the stained porch stairs. Hart winced at the screen door slamming shut, its heavy vibrations going through him as if a board had hit him broadside. He silently wished he could have followed her in.

Diana took a step toward her father. "It's only been just over a year, Dad. One. Year. And now you want to forget about mom?"

Mr. MacGregor's green eyes narrowed. "Now look here, young lady, how dare you insinuate that I would ever forget your mother!"

"Then what's *she* doing here? Mom would turn over in her grave if she knew you were dating *her*!"

Mr. MacGregor clenched his teeth, then took a few steps closer to his daughter, so that he leered down at her like an intimidating gargoyle. "*She* has a name. It's Karen Bean. Ms. Bean to you!"

Hart's eyes darted from Mr. MacGregor to Karen Bean. Her smooth, ivory face had turned whiter, but her mouth curled up at the corners, as if pleased at Diana's father's show of chivalry. With one hand on her hip, she glided over to Mr. MacGregor and placed her free hand on his sculpted shoulder. She slowly squeezed it. "It's all right, Mike. I understand. Diana is obviously still grieving over the loss of Joy. She just needs to realize that life goes on, that's all."

Hart's brows arched. *That's all?* To him, Ms. Bean had said it as if Diana were a voodoo doll and she were the pin. Diana winced. She grabbed her stomach once again, her face pallid and twisting, as if she didn't like what she was hearing. Hart bit his bottom lip. He didn't blame her. He didn't like what he was hearing either. Sure, life did go on. It was expected. But sometimes it was hard to get going. Especially when there were so many roadblocks in the way. Then, without warning, Diana did it again. She vomited. This time she hit her mark with precision and accuracy, before she fell to her knees. Karen Bean never saw it coming.

"Aughh!" Ms. Bean screamed as a mouthful of watery puke splattered across her finely woven suit and silky, pink blouse.

"Diana!" both Hart and Mr. MacGregor yelled in unison.

Hart was down on the ground next to Diana in a flash. He grabbed both her shoulders and hiked her up. What he hadn't counted on was the strong pair of hands that landed on his shoulders seconds later. Hart was wrenched away from Diana and propelled backward. He tripped on an upturned root, twisted, and then fell, landing on his side. Disoriented, Hart tried pushing himself up, but his hands sunk into the soft, damp earth, as if it were swallowing him whole. Shaking off this bizarre sensation, Hart looked up in time to catch the hulking form of Mr. MacGregor looming down at him, as if anticipating his next move. So Hart decided to play it safe, and play 'possum'.

"Leave him alone!" Diana bellowed between heaves.

Mr. MacGregor swung around, his eyes now fixed upon his daughter. He snorted like a bull about to charge. "Since I've never seen this boy before, do you mind telling me who he is?" It wasn't a request. It was a demand.

Diana calmly wiped her mouth before she said, "Hart Stewart. He's my *new boyfriend,* Daddy. I assume that since you can date who you want, without any family discussion what-so-ever, then the same logic applies to me."

Hart's eyes bugged. *Boyfriend? Date?* Crap, he'd just met the girl today. What the hell was she doing, and more importantly, where was this heading? Hart's belly twisted. *Now I feel like I'm gonna puke.* He wished Mr. MacGregor wasn't standing so close to him, as he sensed vomit rising in the back of his throat.

The screen door creaked and then slammed. Hart winced, thankful for the interruption. Quickly, he swallowed, wiped his mouth and sweaty forehead, and then looked up toward the house. Something seemed wrong. Seriously wrong. Nancy's face was pale, and she walked down the stairs one at a time instead of sliding down the wooden bannister. Her round face was set rigidly, and her glasses were pushed down her nose. She stopped dead in her tracks as soon as she saw her father. Her mouth fell open, but no words tumbled out.

Mr. MacGregor, face still flushed, stared at his youngest daughter for a moment. Then, as if he'd finally lost whatever patience he had left from arguing with Diana, he raised his arms and blared, "Well? Who was on the damn phone, Nancy?"

Nancy slowly pushed her glasses up off her nose. "Constable Wright," she muttered. "A body has been found up at Blueberry Lake."

9. All is One

"**D**id you know Archie Avery very well, Diana?" Hart asked softly. His shoulder barely nudged hers as they sat next to each other at a round table in a small enclave in the high school library.

Startled, Diana looked up from the open book she'd been staring into, trying to figure out what to teach Hart for his next reading lesson. She sighed and shook her head. No, she hadn't known Archie Avery well. The old man seemed more like the town hermit than anything else. Avery, who barely got past elementary school, was quiet, and to most people around Fairy Falls, a ghost, wanting neither to been seen nor bothered. A man on the opposite end of the spectrum from Dan Boone.

Avery's death had been a shock to the town. His body was discovered by a local handyman who had stopped by to put Avery's docks in for him. He'd reported that he'd found Archie Avery's broken body, splayed and twisted over a group of boulders jutting out from underneath the high deck of his rustic home, overlooking Blueberry Lake. The railing had been busted through, as if it had rotted away without Avery's knowledge.

Diana had overheard her father talking on the phone that the scene looked like it might have been an accident, but the police still had to investigate before any more information could be released. Her father had explicitly stressed to those in charge of the investigation that he didn't want them to get ahead of themselves or to make a wrong guess. After all, next weekend would be the Victoria Day holiday, which marked the beginning of tourist season for Fairy Falls. News of a mysterious death would permeate fast and furious, and hurt the local businesses tenfold, just as her mother's murder had done the year before.

That all happened yesterday. Today was Monday. It had been decided that Diana would tutor Hart during her spare before lunch. That way, if the lesson went past the allotted time, she wouldn't have to rush off to her next class. This arrangement suited Hart fine. Unfortunately, the bell had already sounded ten minutes ago, so lesson number one was now officially over. Diana sighed. There was so much to cover in so little time.

She glanced at Hart, whose eyes were buried in the driver's handbook she'd given him. His tongue stuck out in deep concentration, his sweatshirt's red sleeves rolled up past his elbows. One of the first things Hart wanted to do, besides read his mother's letter, was get his license. A goal, Diana felt this was attainable, and number one with many teens their age.

Hart groaned.

"What's the matter?"

He hung his head. "This reading stuff's gonna be tough."

Diana smiled. She reached over and patted his shoulder. He felt tense and tight as if burdened by the world. "Tough, but worth it. At least you know your vowels and consonants, and the sounds they make individually, as well as blended. That's a great beginning, Hart. We just have to put them together in an order that makes sense for you."

"That's easy for you to say, you're a newspaper reporter."

Diana laughed. "A weekly column about the comings and goings-on at a northern high school does not make a reporter."

Hart looked at her with a fleck of devilry in his eyes. "Okay, then you're taking your gift of gab to the next level."

Diana pulled up the white sleeves on her tight-fitting shirt and fanned her flushed face. "So you want to talk about gifts, do you?" She puckered her mouth to one side. "I'd say you've got me beat hands down in that department."

"What do you mean?" Hart asked, straightening.

Hart seemed defensive and his tone abrupt. Diana imagined that if he was a porcupine she would have received a face full of quills by now. She licked her lips. "You know what I mean, Mr. *Time Machine*. You can hold an object in your hand and it transports you into the past. I *dare* you to name anyone else who can do that?"

Hart perked up. "So you like to play truth or dare, do you? Okay, truth or dare—do you actually have a boyfriend?"

Diana's face fell. She sat back and stuck her thumbs in the top of her belted, green cargo pants. "Look, I already apologized about the infamous 'boyfriend' incident, so could you just drop it?"

Hart half-smiled and then nodded. "Fine. As long as you stop asking me questions about talking to objects. Okay?"

Diana furrowed her red brows. "What's up with that? Are you embarrassed about your gift?"

Hart closed the handbook and sighed. "Embarrassed, no. Ignorant, yes."

"Ignorant?" Diana inclined her head. "How so?"

"It's like reading, I guess," Hart replied, shrugging. "I don't understand this weird *gift*, as you like to call it, enough to make it work properly. I don't *get* it." Diana threw Hart a strange look. He rolled his eyes and said, "What I mean is that you know what you have to do in order to write whatever it is you're reporting for the paper. You know the steps. You know the procedure. Right?"

Diana nodded. *What is he getting at?*

Hart leaned back and placed his hands on top of his jeans. He rubbed hard, as if trying to bring feeling back into his legs. "Up until now, I was the one who was always in control of what object I wanted to *talk* to. And I usually did it for profit, you know, when I needed some fast cash. But—" he licked his lips and cleared his throat "—your mother's ring was the first object that overrode my ability to choose. It was like...like—"

"The ring was in the driver's seat and not you," Diana blurted, as if knowing the correct answer on a game show.

Hart nodded. "Exactly."

Diana sat in silence for the moment, mulling over what Hart had confessed. Somehow, part of what he told her made sense, although it still seemed foggy. She frowned. "Maybe the time has come to try to harness your gift. To understand it, and use it for something other than a quick cash fix."

Hart's brows furrowed. His mouth twisted as if he'd ingested a handful of sour candies. "Why should I? I never wanted it in the first place."

Diana sighed. "My mom used to say that we're always given what we need, not what we want. I think there's a lot of truth to that."

Hart snorted. "Truth, smuth! I need this gift like I need a hole in my head."

Out of the corner of her eye, Diana spied a balled-up paper fly through the air to smack Hart in the forehead. She giggled. "In the future, you'd best be careful what you say."

"How's it going?" Donovan asked between the bookshelves, waving his lacrosse stick at Diana.

"Put that thing down before you poke someone's eye out," Brook said, pushing her way past Donovan, "or before I stick it somewhere dark and dingy."

Donovan saluted Brook. "Ya voldt, Herr Witchy-Poo!"

Diana laughed. "I see taking German this semester hasn't helped your grasp of the language yet."

Donovan shrugged. "Hey, I'm a lover, not a linguist, Red."

Brook dropped her purse and swung around, her long black skirt wrapping around her shapely legs. A lacy, practically see-through blouse draped her as if she were a Goddess, while the silver pentagram hanging from a black, leather thong skitted across her ample chest. Brook gingerly placed her hands on her round hips, eyed Donovan like he was a toad, and then pursed her dark-coloured lips. She raised a hand and took a step back. *"With the fool no season spend or be counted on as a friend."*

Donovan balked. "Huh?"

Hart guffawed and slapped the desk. "Dude, I think the girl just insulted you."

Diana quirked a brow. "You actually understood Brook's garble?"

Hart grinned. "Go figure. My mom hung out with some unusual people, not your typical bunch of palm and tea leaf readers." He rubbed his chin. "I believe some of them were witches, I guess. Growing up around them, you get to know some of their weird phrases."

Brook, turned on her high, black heels, curtsied, then applauded Hart.

Donovan shrunk into his purple leather lacrosse jacket, stuck one hand in his jeans' pocket, and frowned. "So, what'd she say then, smart-guy?"

Hart picked up the balled paper Donovan had thrown earlier, and whipped it back at him. "Well, Brook basically called you a goof, and made it clear she didn't want to hang out with one."

Donovan threw Brook a look that would shatter a crystal ball. "Hey, that's not funny, Bennet!"

Brook laughed. "It wasn't meant to be, bozo."

There was a shush from the front of the library letting them know that things were getting too loud. A few dirty looks from some other students hovering around their area confirmed this. Diana motioned for her two friends to sit at their round table. As soon as Donovan and Brook were seated, Brook pulled out a small package from her black purse, and gently slid it in front of Hart.

"What's this for?" Hart asked, arching his brows.

"Nothing and something," she replied.

Donovan bent closer to Hart. "Just humour her. Or she'll spew some dumb-ass curse at you."

Brook elbowed Donovan. Hart shook his head, and sat back. He pulled off his cap, raked his tawny hair with one hand, then placed the hat on backwards. Brook made a low-key squealing sound. She pointed to Hart's cap and said, "'All is One!' That's so tribal!"

All three stared at Brook with blank expressions on their faces.

"Oh crap, Witchy-Poo's blown another gasket in her broomstick," Donovan said, smirking.

Brook glared at him. "FYI, Johnson, 'All is One' is a sacred truth. It has to do with honour, loyalty, bonding, and identity. This reminds us that we're all connected, and every choice we make, every belief we hold, influences the whole of life. Get it?"

"No," all three answered in unison.

Brook rolled her eyes. "Forget it."

Diana nudged Hart. "Open your present."

"Yeah, before Witchy-Poo decides to talk about chakras and crystals."

The table vibrated. Diana stifled a giggle, knowing that Brook must have kicked Donovan for that crack. Hart unwrapped his gift carefully, as if he wanted to make the moment last. When he pulled the purple wrapping paper away, Diana's eyes widened. Then her cheeks grew hot.

"My, my, what have we here? Bird feathers attached to a funky, home-made pen. But could they be hawk feathers, by chance?" Hart asked, grinning at Diana, who by now, had sunk into her chair.

Brook beamed. "That's exactly what they are! Diana told me what happened to the poor hawk that hit her windshield, but I know it was karma. That bird came into your life for a reason. So since you're beginning a new journey, I thought it appropriate to fashion you a pen with your totem's energy attached."

Hart gave Brook an uneasy look. "Totem?"

Brook nodded. "The hawk is your totem and represents the medicine that you carry. The hawk teaches you to be a true messenger, as well as to be observant."

Diana smirked. Hart's mouth was now opened, as if trying to figure out what made Brook tick. *Good luck,* she thought. *I've been trying for years.*

Donovan chuckled. "Dude, be thankful Brook didn't stick its beak on it."

Smiling, Hart gently wrapped his gift back in the purple paper and stashed it in his knapsack, under the table. "So if Diana has a crow for her totem and I have a hawk, what's yours, Donovan?"

Before Donovan had a chance to answer Hart, Brook said, "Jackass."

Both Diana and Hart howled with laughter.

Another shush was delivered. This time, it was longer and harsher.

"I'd better go," Hart said, smiling, "before I get you guys kicked out."

Brook lunged for one of Hart's hands. Diana frowned. A sudden, raw, burning sensation surged through her body and settled in her chest. She shook it off as Brook said, "Wait, Hart, I've got one more thing to give you."

Brook dove into her black purse again to retrieve what looked like a deck of cards. Diana squinted. *Uh-oh. Those're Brook's famous tarot cards.*

Hart slammed his hand over the deck. Diana jumped, but Brook remained calm. "No thanks, Brook. When my mom died, so did everything that represented her way of life for me."

Brook shrugged. "Humour me. Cut the deck, and see what comes up."

Donovan snorted. "You don't take no for an answer, do you, Witchy-Poo?"

Hart bit his bottom lip. He looked over at Diana. "What do you think, Miss 'Eat Crow'?"

There was a hint of amusement in his voice, yet there was also something else. *Discretion? Discomfort?* She wasn't sure. Diana shrugged. "No harm, no fowl."

"Bad pun, Red," Donovan said, winking.

Hart sighed and cut the deck. He raised a tawny brow. "The Hanged Man? Great. Does that go well with my hawk medicine, Brook?"

Now Hart was being sarcastic. His voice sounded cutting, abrupt.

Brook, however, remained serene. She sat back and folded her arms over her chest. "Depends." She cleared her throat. "Seems to me you're caught between two different worlds, just as a hawk is."

Donovan rolled his eyes. "Stop speaking in tongues and cut to the chase. Explain in a language we can actually understand."

Brook pursed her lips. "He needs to make a sacrifice to achieve greater good."

Donovan jerked. "What, like cutting off a chicken's head?"

Diana giggled, but Hart remained silent, reserved, almost disconnected.

Brook unfolded her arms and swung a hand around to clip Donovan across the back of his head. "Honestly, I swear your totem really is a jackass! No, I mean Hart is in the midst of a major transition in his life right now. What he needs to do is give up the old to make way for the new."

"And how do you suggest I do that?" Hart asked through clenched teeth.

Brook looked from Hart to Diana, and then back to Hart again. Diana wondered where she was going with this reading. Brook sighed. "You need to reconnect with the spiritual dimension of life in order to get a new perspective."

Hart flung the deck of cards down, and stood up so fast he knocked the white plastic chair to the floor. It clattered against the beige tiles, grating Diana's ears and making her wince. Brook's tarot cards scattered across the table, with some landing on the floor. He planted his hands firmly on the table and eyed Brook the way a hawk would a rabbit. Diana stood, reached over, and grabbed both Hart's shoulders. They were rock hard, unmoving.

"Take it easy, Hart," Diana said in a hushed manner. "Brook means well."

Hart's nostrils flared. He straightened, shrugged Diana away, nodded to Donovan, and plucked his backpack from under the table. He turned to leave, then stopped and glared at Brook, now pale, and breathing hard. He sneered. "And you need to be hooked up with some shock therapy," he whispered, before taking his leave through the back of the library.

10. Hawk Medicine

"Reconnect with the freaking spiritual dimension, my ass!" Hart shrugged on his plaid hoodie and kicked open the back entrance door of the high school.

He crossed the overcrowded parking lot, searching for his wheels. There it was, an old moped, chained to one of the steel posts. The motorized bike had once been dark blue, but time had faded it to a lighter shade. Hart had found it the other day while cleaning Aunt Gertie's bunkie behind the tri-domed house after they returned home from the uprising in town. She said he could have the thing if he wanted to put some elbow grease into it. He jumped at the offer and tinkered with it until he got it running. Now the moped was his ride. It wasn't much, but it provided a basic necessity Hart had missed—his freedom.

Strapping his knapsack to the back of the moped, Hart bent down to unlock the chain and roughly stuffed it into his pack's top pocket. He swung a long leg over the bike and pushed off, peddling down an uneven slope before engaging the moped's small engine. It sputtered once, as if thinking over Hart's request, then popped on with a jerk. Leaving a smoky trail behind, Hart guided the old motorized bike onto the connecting main road, then opened it up as fast as it would go—a crawl compared to a seasoned skateboarder going downhill.

Hart knew he'd have to take the backroads until he got out of town. With no helmet or license, there'd be the risk of a ticket, something he couldn't afford at the moment. Passing a few parked cars, Hart drove up a road, then down another, going by a solitary variety store, until he came to a crossroad. The engine grumbled, hinting to Hart that it wasn't used to this kind of abuse. He gave it some gas, as if coercing the moped into a better mood, and proceeded on his journey back to Blueberry Lake where his great-aunt had undoubtedly lined up another job for him to complete before supper. Hart sighed as the wind whipped his cheeks. *I can hardly wait to blow this place and get back to the city!*

A guilty pang twisted at his innards, as if a vulture was pecking away at him, disemboweling him bit by bit. Maybe he'd acted too harshly with Brook. True, Brook Bennet was a first-class looney-toon. A little too eccentric for his tastes. Even his mother's friends weren't as open as Brook was when it came to her blatant, in-your-face witchy ways. Diana had explained to him that this was Brook's outlet, her way of expression, and perhaps even an escape. Five years ago, her parents had gone through a nasty divorce, and Brook was still trying to cope. Hart snorted, collecting a nose full of dust in the process. Maybe Brook had gotten it wrong. Maybe, instead of the hawk, he had a turkey for a totem.

As Hart leaned into a curve, he braced for teeth chattering contact as the moped's tires hit the gravel road that would eventually offshoot onto Blueberry Lane. His stomach twisted again with thoughts of Diana's off-beat, freaky friend. Hart knew he'd have to apologize to Brook. It wasn't her problem he shied away from supernatural mumbo-jumbo. His nostrils flared. *This is all your fault, Mom!* It wasn't enough he'd inherited his mom's occult ability, but now he had no idea how to control it and no one to ask. Hart squeezed the moped's handles, feeling in the dark about his psychic skill, as if he'd been given a hammer, saw, some wood, and nails, and been asked to build something of importance without any plans to go by. He frowned. *Thanks for nothing, Mom!*

An urgent skid behind Hart made him check the rear-view mirror perched on the pitted handle bar. A black truck, possibly a Ford or Chevy, with a faded cap on its box, swerved onto the road in an awkward motion. He switched his view back to the road in front of him, knowing he was getting closer to his turn off. The sound of the truck's engine revved up, causing Hart to check his blind spot. The truck was only a few feet behind him on his left, and too close for his liking. Then the truck moved closer. Hart's mouth went dry. *That douche is trying to run me off the road!*

Panicking, he squeezed the brakes, hoping to back off and let the truck take the lead. That was the plan, but unfortunately, the driver also slowed down, continuing to move in closer to Hart. He tensed. *What the hell is this bozo's problem? The road isn't that narrow! There's plenty of room for both of us!* Hart stood on the moped's pedals and craned his neck to get a look at the driver. A burly man with broad shoulders, bushy dark hair, and a beard was hunched in the driver's seat, sipping on a long-necked brown bottle. Hart snorted. *Figures! He's probably too drunk to realize I'm sharing the road with him.*

Waving with one hand, Hart tried to get the inebriated jerk's attention. When that failed, he banged the side of the truck hard, which proved useless. As the road climbed around a wall of granite, Hart noticed a wicked turn coming up fast. If he wasn't careful, he'd be pinned between the truck and the guard rails on the edge of the road. Slowing down didn't help, so Hart sped up, thinking the truck would slack off to negotiate the turn.

Unfortunately, that didn't happen.

Crunching gravel and spinning tires made Hart clench his teeth. He checked over his shoulder and his eyes widened. The driver wasn't letting up. He was inches away from the moped's back tire, as if getting ready to ram Hart into the guard rails ahead. The heat from the engine felt like the inside of a lion's mouth as reality sank into his bones. Hart's lips trembled. *What is this guy's game? I don't know him and he doesn't know me. So this can't be personal. Maybe he's too smashed to know what he's doing?* Suddenly, the truck's massive tires dug in like teeth sinking into flesh, and the driver veered his truck around to flank Hart, trapping him.

Hart grasped the black truck's silver door handle, intending to open it to scream obscenities at the psychopath and get him off his ass. But Hart's hopes were dashed. The door was locked. He could hear a heavy bass sound thumping from inside the cab; the radio was turned up full blast. Hart's head spun and his guts clenched with nausea. A rapping on the window made Hart look up to find a black glove pressed against the window, giving him the finger. Hart swore just as the truck bumped his moped into the first guard rail. He lifted his right leg in time, hearing metal on metal scrape across the side of his moped.

Hart swung his leg over to ride side-saddle, then planted his left foot on the truck's rusting running board. His left hand continued to grip the door handle, while his right held onto the handle bars. The moped wobbled violently, but Hart held on tight. The incessant vibes of the truck's radio pounded through his body and continued to torture him. He had no choice, and continued to white-knuckle the handle. The truck careened back and forth like a drunken snake, in an attempt to knock Hart off. His head bounced off the side of the door and his muscles, now stretched beyond their limits, seemed ready to tear away from his body. He clenched his teeth. He had had enough of this twisted cat and mouse game. It was time to declaw this sick son-of-a-bitch.

Raising his right leg, Hart's foot connected with the side view mirror of the truck and broke it off. Plastic and mirror smashed onto the road under the truck. He smirked. *There. At least this sick bastard can't check on me.* Carefully, he reached to flip off his moped's engine, huddled his body as tight as he could to the door with both feet on the running board, and then he shoved the moped into the next guard rail post. Hart winced, watching his moped twist around the post, causing the headlight to shatter and front tire to bend, as it came to rest on the steel cable.

What Hart hadn't counted on was the maniac driver slamming the brakes, causing the truck to fish-tail, and Hart to lose his grip on the door handle. The skin on his palm burned, and with terror suspended in his wide eyes, Hart let out a solitary scream, before he plummeted over the edge of the ravine and into complete darkness.

A searing pain originating from the middle of his back charged up Hart's neck to settle in the base of his skull. This sensation stirred him to consciousness. *W-w-what happened?* He grappled with his senses. A sudden wave of nausea swept over him, and his head ached as if a hatchet was embedded there.

Hart slowly opened his eyes. Everything was blurry at first, so he closed them, feeling the intensity of light scorch through him.

Focusing within, he took a deep breath, ignoring the ravaging aches that consumed his body, and listened.

Running water, wind whistling, and birds chirping. Hart's skin tingled. *Where am I?* As his hazy mind cleared somewhat, he remembered being chased. A black truck. A stocky, bushy-haired, bearded man. Loud music. A crash. Blurriness, then blackness, as if a single light bulb had popped in a dark room with no windows or doors. Complete darkness. A prison where shadows crawled over your body to devour whatever light was left. Startled at this vision, Hart snapped his eyes open.

Panic surged through him. "H-h-help!"

There was no response.

"Please, somebody, help me! Help me!" he pleaded, until his head throbbed like it was about to explode.

Still hearing no answer, Hart lifted a hand to wipe the pooling sweat from his brow. His hand touched the brim of his hat. A slow smile erupted from the side of his mouth. It was a plus that he hadn't lost it in the crash. The smile vanished as Hart winced, feeling an oozy, slick substance caked on his left temple. Pulling his hand back, Hart's eyes bugged at the sight of blood smeared across his fingers. Its coppery perfume mixed with perspiration made him heave, and he coughed up a wad of burning bile.

Hart swam in dizziness and agony, but he concentrated this time, not wanting to return to the dark place and go beyond its borders. He took another breath, his body drunk with pain, and tried to move but couldn't. His heart rate accelerated in warning as he felt a numbness run through his legs.

Damn, my legs are pinned, his murky mind realized, *but by what?* Trying to pull himself up, weakness took hold and sent Hart back. His head grazed a boulder and he twisted. It was then Hart figured out why he couldn't stand up. He was hanging upside-down in the deep, rocky ravine.

Hart freaked and his mind reeled. *How the hell did this happen?* Struggling, he grasped for a branch jutting out from the face of a rock. He hiked himself enough to find out what kept his legs imprisoned, sore fingers finding the leverage they needed, until he finally discovered the source. Two thick branches sprouting from a mother trunk emerging out of the sheer granite wall were cradling his legs within their crooked embrace. A piercing trill made Hart jump and almost lose his grip.

Swallowing, and tasting the harsh bile that swam in his mouth, Hart spat and searched for the cause of that odd noise. His eyes followed the branches that supported him until there, settled in the dense green foliage was a nest. *Great. That's all I need. To piss off a mother bird and get my eyes pecked out.*

A large bird swooped down near to where Hart hung and made a pass at him. Hart tensed his body. Pain attacked him in the shoulders and neck, and he lost his grip, suspending his body once again over the ravine. The bird, either deciding Hart was no threat or no fun, landed on one of the outstretched branches and peered down at him. Shaken by its presence, Hart reached for any rocks jutting from the wall and held fast, not taking his eyes off the bird. Then he frowned. This was not just any bird. This was a hawk. *My totem,* he thought, as he licked his cracked lips.

To be a messenger. To be observant. So what was this hawk trying to tell him? Hart's head throbbed. Being suspended over a rocky drop had weakened his body and dulled his mind, and at this point he couldn't give a crap. Then something occurred to him. It was something Brook had said, and now it was starting to make sense. Just like the hawk he was caught between two different worlds—the earth and the sky. Hart sneered as the image of the Hanged Man card loomed in the back of his mind. What if Brook had thrown a curse on him for the way he treated her? He scoffed then, recalling the tarot card's meaning: a sacrifice must be made to achieve greater good. So what did that mean? Hart had already sacrificed his smashed-up moped.

Hart's eyes widened and his mouth went dry. *This could be it for me,* he realized. It was possible that no one would find him. That he would die here, forgotten, abandoned, alone.

Trembling, Hart knew of only one way to beat this fate. He could use his psychic ability one last time and slip into the past, where at least the companionship of spectral images would keep him company during his final hours. And he knew just the object to use. Groping for his hoodie's breast pocket, he pulled out a tattered envelope, its address long smeared away, its colour now yellowed. Carefully opening the envelope, he extracted the letter, mindful not to get any blood on it. Slipping the envelope back into his pocket, Hart wedged his body up so that he felt hugged by the rugged walls, and safe like a bat in its cave. He knew he couldn't read his mother's written words, but he could comprehend her letter in another way. The only way he knew how.

Taking a deep breath, Hart gently placed the folded letter in the middle of his forehead, directly upon his third eye. His voice, parched and hoarse from yelling, allowed him to whisper, "Talk to me."

Hart stilled himself and simply let it happen.

Hart's eyes rolled back. His pain instantly vanished, as he was transported deep into the realm of super-consciousness. At first, everything seemed fuzzy, like a television in search of a signal. Then, as the channel opened, his surroundings cleared. Hart rubbed his eyes and blinked to confirm that he was indeed standing in the middle of a bus station filled with countless people coming and going. His nostrils flared, picking up the scent of burnt coffee and stale sweat. People shouting, luggage dragging across the floor, and babies crying all competed for Hart's attention. His ears pricked at the screechy speaker announcing which bus was leaving for where. Hart furrowed his brows. Why am I here?

Searching around the station, Hart spied a young girl about his age, sitting on a bench. She appeared to be writing a letter. Drawn to her for some reason, Hart moved closer to the girl. She was upset, and amazingly he could feel what she felt. A dread. An ominous anticipation of what-may-come. Tears streamed down her face, and she roughly wiped them away with the sleeve of her oversized green sweatshirt. Sighing, the girl pushed her straw-coloured hair out of her eyes, and placed her pad of paper and pen on the bench. She sat back, lifted the heavy shirt, undid her jeans, and rubbed her bloated belly as if it ached. Hart inclined his head. Maybe she's sick?

"She's not ill, Hart, she's pregnant," a strong, soothing voice announced from behind him.

Hart jumped. He turned a little too fast, almost stumbling, and peered into a set of powder blue eyes. He shook his head, as if seeing a ghost. His mouth fell open. Wait...I am seeing a ghost! My mother's ghost! She's wearing the same outfit she wore the day she was murdered. A coral T-shirt and faded blue denims. *Hart shivered. The image of her lying on the cold morgue drawer haunted him to this day. Everything about her was the same. Her blond hair. Her freckles. Her smile. Even that look she used to give him if he didn't clean his room or make his bed.*

Panicking, Hart backed away. "H-h-how is this possible?"

His ghostly mother held up her hand. "It's possible because my energy is still locked within the letter you possess, Hart. This is how you called my spirit back. It was your intention that brought me here to help you."

"Help me?" Hart stopped, and edged closer. "How?"

"To understand, and to make the necessary sacrifice you've asked of the universal collective consciousness."

Hart narrowed his eyes. His chest tightened and he found the courage to blurt, "Necessary sacrifice! W-what the hell does that mean?"

"Take a breath, Hart. Breathe as if it were as precious as the freedom you seek."

Obeying his mother, Hart took a deep breath through his nose, the air filling his belly until he was ready to burst, and then exhaled out his mouth. There. He felt better, a little more centred.

Hart's mother nodded approvingly. She swept a ghostly hand in the direction of the girl on the bench. "The young girl you see on the bench is me, Hart. At the time, I was pregnant with you and was feeling…well, a little under the weather."

"You were also feeling scared? Why?"

"Because I was facing my greatest fear."

"Greatest fear?" Hart glanced at the image of his youthful mother on the bench, then turned to face his phantom mom. "What was that?"

Her pale skin rippled as she cried, "Having you!"

Hart stiffened. He opened his mouth, but his mother's apparition didn't allow him have the next word. "Understand, I was ill-prepared for life, Hart. At seventeen, I took the easier road, especially with my abilities. It was selfish, and I was selfish. What I foresaw was my freedom being taken from me."

His skin prickled. "Then why didn't you just give me up for adoption!" he screamed, knowing that the images of the walking ghosts in the depot could neither see nor hear him.

"That would have been too easy, Hart, and not an option if I wanted to make positive changes in my life. Your birth got the ball rolling for me. Although it was a little bumpy at first, I figured out what had to be changed, and found the courage within to do it. You

grounded me, and made the doubt dwelling inside of me disappear. Do you see?"

Hart's lips quivered. Then, mustering up every shred of anger within him, he shouted, "You scare me! You and these stupid psychic powers you gave me! You said I grounded you! Even changed you! What about me, huh? You were the one who left me! How in the hell am I supposed to embrace the ability to talk to objects, when I don't even understand it?"

"Don't ignore who you are, Hart. You've been running away from that for a long time. You possess powers people can't even comprehend. You have a gift that can serve and help others. To be a messenger to those in need. Trust that everything you seek will appear in the right moment and the right place. Open up your heart and allow yourself the freedom to be who you are, son. Your bed is made and all you have to do is sleep in it."

Shuddering, Hart allowed his mother's words to pierce him like daggers of truth, slowly bleeding the lies and uncertainty out of him, until he was cleansed of any self-doubt lying within. Hart's eyes widened. His gift of psychometry was his ticket to freedom, not the burden he had envisioned and ignored all these years. A gift, for the most part, he had used for self-satisfaction. With these thoughts firmly planted, Hart now knew what must be sacrificed.

He took a deep breath. "I...I must stay. Aunt Gertie needs me. Diana needs me. And I won't abandon them."

A sudden glow encompassed Hart's mother, as if a light shone underneath her. She reached out to touch Hart's cheek with the back of her ashen hand, grazing it gently like a butterfly's wing. "Now, you see, Hart. Now, I must go."

"B-but, Mom—" Hart hesitated for a split second, fighting back tears "—w-will I ever see you again?"

Catherine Stewart smiled at her son. An amazing aura of pink and green now radiated from her. She nodded. "Yes, Hart, you'll see me every time you look into a mirror."

Sobbing now, Hart fell to his knees. The sudden sensation of being wrenched from the past gripped his entire body. Helplessly, he felt himself growing stiff and cold, as if he were dying. Then, Hart sensed a brilliant white light surrounding him. He closed his eyes, surrendered, and stilled his mind, just as his mother's calming voice whispered, "Breathe, Hart. Breathe."

11. Search Party

The piercing ring of her cell phone ripped Diana out of dreamland. Disoriented, she fumbled for her silver phone lying on the bedside table.

Falling back on the pillow, she glanced at her digital alarm clock before cupping the phone to her ear. Diana's eyes widened. *Six a.m.? Who the hell would call at this hour?* She knew her father was probably at the gym and Nancy was likely still huddled in bed. Her eyes narrowed. It had better not be Brook again. She'd been on the phone with her pagan friend for hours last night, listening to her whine and complain about how people took her the wrong way when all she had for them was good intentions. Brook's case and point: Hart Stewart. Diana had reminded Brook about the 'road to hell' being paved with millions of so-called good intentions. *Let it be*, Diana had finally counseled at the stroke of midnight.

"Er...sum'one there?" a gravelly voice asked.

Jolted back from her thoughts, Diana blinked her dry eyes. "Yes, hello?"

"Er, sorry 'bout phoning ya so early, but I was wondering...do ya know where Hart might be at?"

Foggy with sleep, Diana shook her head, then pushed up to rest her shoulders against the bleached oak headboard. She only knew of one person who could slaughter the English language with such newborn innocence and get away with it—Gertie Ellis.

Diana pulled at the worn Toronto Maple Leaf hockey sweater she had slept in, and roughly rubbed her pert, freckled nose. "Hart? No. He left after class yesterday. Why? Didn't he come home?"

Silence. Then Diane heard Hart's great-aunt clear her throat. She cringed. It sounded like two chainsaws engaging in battle. "No. I thought maybe—" she stalled for an instant "—er, well Hart seems fond of ya, so I thought he might'ha—"

Diana's eyes widened with Gertie Ellis' accusation. "Now wait one minute, Mrs. Ellis, we're just friends," she broke in before Gertie got to the lurid details.

"Er, course, course ya are, dear, no harm meant. It's just, well y'ur his only friend 'round here, and I thought ya two maybe stud'ing for a test, or sum'hing like that. I waited up fer Hart ta come home, but must'a fell asleep in me chair. The next thing I know, it was nearing six in the morning, and Hart still wasn't here. Got yer number from off me fridge, seeing as Hart left it fer me."

As Diana listened to Gertie Ellis's quirky story, her gut began to contract. She knew Hart had been on his way home yesterday, unless he decided to take a detour and cool down after losing it with Brook. Then something occurred to her. Maybe after Brook had confronted Hart with his future plans, he really didn't like what he'd heard, and just took off. Left. Vamoosed. Ran away. It wasn't a long shot. After all, he'd left the city to come up here. A sudden hot flush surged up Diana's cheeks with this realization, and it saddened and angered her at the same time.

Diana licked her lips. "Mrs. Ellis, do you think Hart…" she paused. *How can I put this gently?* "Umm, do you think Hart might have gone back home?"

She heard Gertie snort. "Oh, bugaboo! I told ya, gal, he's not here, that's why I phoned ya."

Okay, that went well. Diana sighed. "No. I mean to his former home, in the city."

Gertie grumbled, and said, "Hart don't belong in no city. His home's here, with me'n Skoka, where he gits food'n shelter'n company. Why would Hart go back to nuthin'?"

Diana raised her fair brows. Gertie Ellis had a point. But first there was something she needed to know. "Are Hart's clothes still there?"

There was a brief pause, and Diana heard a few grunts and some shuffling before Gertie said, "Yup. Nuthin' taken, 'cept fer what he was wearing yesterday."

Diana's stomach rolled. *Where can Hart be?* Surely he couldn't have gotten lost, could he? Unless, he'd taken another route to do some much needed anger management and, unable to read the road signs, he strayed off course. Or worse, his moped could have broken down on some rural back road. Diana frowned and shook her head. Even then, he could've flagged someone down to help him. *This makes no sense.* Hart might be illiterate, but the guy wasn't stupid. After all, he was a survivor first and foremost. Her shoulders curled forward. *Something has happened to Hart. Something bad.*

Diana cleared her throat. "Look, Mrs. Ellis, you call the police and tell them that Hart's been missing since yesterday afternoon. Meanwhile, I'll do a drive around town, and then go over his normal route home. He has to be somewhere. Maybe his moped broke down and he decided to camp out, or he's gotten lost. Either way, we'll find him."

There was a lingering silence on the other end of the phone. Diana swore she heard Gertie sniff. A dog whined, then barked in the background, just as Hart's great-aunt said, "Down, Skoka, down! Sorry 'bout that, he's worried too."

Diana nodded. So was she, but worry was pointless and wouldn't help find Hart. She swallowed hard and said, "I've always got my cell phone with me, Mrs. Ellis, so stay put and I'll call you if I find anything out."

Gertie grunted and then hung up in response, as if not wanting to waste any more time. Diana placed her cell back on the table, and with a sudden burst of energy she whipped back her plaid duvet and swung her smooth, pale legs out of bed. Standing, she allowed herself the luxury of a stretch, and then bolted for the closet.

"Who was on the phone?"

Diana slid to a stop and looked over her shoulder. Standing in her bedroom doorway stood her sleepy-eyed, tousled-haired sister. The flannel green and yellow pajamas, now almost faded to a limey-puke colour, made her belly and hips bulge in an uncomplimentary way. Diana sighed.

Since their mother's death, Nancy had added at least twenty pounds to her five foot frame, while Diana herself had lost weight. Grief appeared to have its own way of peeling back the layers of the psyche, forcing people to deal with loss on their own level, and in their own time. Diana had dealt with it through writing, exercise, and working on her car. Nancy, however, had become a couch and computer potato, watching only detective or forensic shows, and endlessly surfing the net in search of links for criminal investigative procedures. It was this obsession that worried Diana the most.

"Diana? Was...was that Dad?"

The worried tremor in Nancy's voice broke through Diana's thoughts. "Uh, no it wasn't Dad, Nance, now go back to bed. You don't need to get up for another hour," Diana replied, as she pulled open her closet door.

Nancy rubbed her eyes, walked in, and threw herself on Diana's bed with such force it pushed the headboard into the wall. "Then, if it was no one, why are you getting dressed? Was it *Hart*?"

Diana cringed as she yanked off her hockey sweater. Nancy said Hart's name as if she were attempting to sing a slow and sweet Shania Twain ballad. Snorting, Diana tossed her worn jersey on the floor, then reached for a pair of khaki cargos and a beige brushed pullover. She quickly pulled on the pants, then tossed the sweater over her head, allowing for its softness to caress her bare shoulders and back, and adjusted her wavy, red hair accordingly. Grabbing for a pair of thick socks on her dresser, Diana turned to face her sister, who was now making herself comfortable in her plush double bed.

"Go back to bed," Diana said in a no-nonsense tone.

Nancy grinned at her. "Does *Dad* know where you're going?"

Diana frowned. *That little...* she thought, as she crossed her arms and glared at her sister. "I'll text him on my way out, now if you don't mind—"

"I'll do it for you," Nancy cut in. She lunged for Diana's cell phone on the bed stand and started texting. Diana's eyes widened. She charged toward her bed and wrestled her cell from Nancy's grip. Shock lit up Nancy's eyes and she scooted to the far end of Diana's unmade bed, like a scared puppy awaiting certain punishment.

Nancy brought her knees to her budding chest, and then gripped her ankles and rocked. Diana sighed, and calmly sat down at the opposite end of the rumpled bed. "Look, Nance, I've got to take care of something for someone. That's all."

Nancy shrugged, as if she couldn't care less now.

Diana rolled her eyes. "Hart never came home last night. That was his great-aunt on the phone. She's worried, so I told her I'd look around town for him. I'm sure he's fine." *At least, I hope he is.*

Nancy perked up. "Well, did she call the police to file a missing person's report?"

Diana smiled. *Once an amateur sleuth and CSI wannabe, always one.* "She's doing it as we speak, now please go back to bed, I've got to—"

"I want to come too!" Nancy jumped up and bounced on the bed, her body jiggling with newfound purpose.

Diana set her jaw. "Absolutely not! Dad would lynch me if he found out you were late for school."

"But I can help! Two pairs of eyes are better than one," Nancy pleaded. "Besides, what about my keen powers of observation, my heightened sense of awareness, my ability to put myself in another person's head, my—"

Diana held up her hand, halting Nancy's verbal resume of sleuthing skills. "Nance?"

Nancy inclined her head. "Yeah?"

"Get dressed."

Twenty minutes later, the MacGregor sisters, each armed with a cereal bar and juice box, were racing down the rural road in Diana's car. The sun was peeking its fiery head over the tree-lined, rolling hills, creating the eerie effect of a forest fire gone wild. The air, although still chilly, had at least one positive attribute—it kept the blackfly population to a minimum. Stuffing the end of the oatmeal bar into her mouth, Diana took the last swig of grape juice from her drinking box, and tossed it in the small, black garbage container that straddled the transmission hump behind her. Nancy followed suit, though dribbling some of the juice on her pink hoodie in the process. She belched exuberantly as she attempted to soak up the purple stain with a paper napkin.

Diana winced. "Either your manners are deteriorating, or you're striving for that sloppy *'Columbo'* look."

Nancy glared at her sister. "Hey, I like that show, it's a classic. Even if it is old, it's taught me a lot about how to approach suspects and—"

"And piss them off enough to confess," Diana cut in, giggling.

Nancy rolled her eyes. "Say what you want, but I've learned a lot about my intended craft just from watching old detective reruns. Besides, it's time better spent than sticking your head under a car's greasy hood for hours."

Diana's furrowed her brows. "What good is a super sleuth if her car breaks down in the middle of nowhere and she can't change a tire, spark plug, or fan belt?"

Nancy slid her glasses down her nose to stare at Diana. "Isn't that what roadside assistance is for?"

Diana screwed her mouth to one side. "Touché."

Fifteen minutes of silence followed, as Diana drove by the town's three local parks, while Nancy scanned the area with her mini binoculars. Nothing. Just the skeletal outline of playground equipment, barren park benches, and picnic tables to attest to the time of day. It was passing quarter after seven. Frustrated, Diana thought it'd be best to go over Hart's usual route home, and if there was no sign of him, then after she dropped Nancy off at her school, she'd check the local restaurants that opened early for breakfast. Someone in town must have to have seen him at some point between yesterday and today. Diana squeezed her steering wheel until her knuckles whitened. *Where the hell are you, Hart?*

Heading out toward Blueberry Lake, Diana reached for the radio's knob and turned it on to catch the local news at 7:30. Perhaps the station would announce that the police had already found Hart, or maybe inform the public of his disappearance. Instead, the static voice of the morning newsman broke through to broadcast, *"Pleasant Point Corporation ups the ante with town council! The resort development group doesn't seem to want to take no for an answer. Plans are underway to meet with various town representatives to—"*

"Di?" Nancy broke in, turning down the volume.

"What!" Diana snapped, annoyed with her sister's untimely interruption.

"What's gonna happen to Fairy Falls if that development goes through as planned? Will it change our town?"

As Diana negotiated a curve, turning her Chevelle onto Tucker Road, she shrugged and said, "Who knows? Things change. Places change. Towns grow. Who's to say what's good or bad growth.

Certainly it would be good for the local businesses to cash in on the influx of visitors."

Nancy inclined her head. "Not if other bigger businesses take their place, and the true heart of Fairy Falls becomes lost forever."

Diana glanced over at her younger sister, not sure who she was looking at. "Nance, where is this coming from?"

Nancy shrugged. "From...from mom, I guess. She always wanted what was best for Fairy Falls, no matter what."

Diana's shoulders sagged. True, their mother had loved Fairy Falls and all its nostalgic qualities. And Nancy had a point, progress could hurt, but it could also help as well. More jobs. Better pay. Improved medical care. Increased town services. The list could go on. Then Diana looked at the other side of the coin. Too much growth could be devastating to the environment. Pollution. Loss of wildlife. Stress on lakes. An imbalance all around. Diana shook her head. Whether you were a tree-hugging environmentalist or a Bay Street economist, it was catch-22.

Suddenly Nancy grabbed Diana's arm and pointed. "Look! Over there, by that post at the curve in the road!"

Startled, Diana almost lost control on the gravel road, and slammed on the brakes. Strangling the steering wheel, her nostrils flared indignantly as she felt her face blister with heat. "You little twit! Don't you ever do that again!"

But Nancy hadn't heard her sister's rant. She'd already opened the door and was halfway to what she had pointed at a few seconds ago. Diana wiped the perspiration from around her mouth, shut off her car, and got out. *A thick ear would go good right about now,* she thought. *That and a clip across the back of her head.* As Diana trudged over to where Nancy squatted, it occurred to her that an accident had taken place here, and recently, by the look of things.

Shattered bits of mirror and plastic were strewn all over the gravel road. Embedded in the earth were a set of tire tracks, snaking in and out, marking the road in a hazardous manner. Diana scanned the area for blood, but there was none. Well, that at least was a good sign. Most likely, it had been a drunk driver that had come a little too close to the guard rail and promptly turned sober.

"Relax, Nance, it was probably some poor dude who'd spent most of his money at the Court Jester last night."

Nancy shook her head. "You're not looking at the evidence in the same way I am, Diana. A crime scene tells its own story."

Evidence? Crime scene? Since when did her sister become Nancy Drew instead of MacGregor? And what the hell was she looking at to formulate in her delusionary mind that a crime had been committed here? Diana scoped the area again. Broken mirror. Shattered plastic. Tire tracks. Nope. All she saw was a good-old Fairy Falls boy's night of misfortune. Nothing more, nothing less.

"There's another set of tires here, Di. A smaller set. Like you'd see on a scooter or—"

"—a moped!" Diana cut in.

Nancy nodded and stood. She wiped the dirt away from her hands on her too-tight jeans and checked up the road. Diana looked, too. A wicked curve sliced around the granite wall, while ahead a 'Watch Out for Falling Rocks' sign warned anyone who dared to travel the winding route. A sudden jerk to Nancy's portly frame told Diana that something was indeed amiss.

"Look, Diana, something struck that guard post!" She sprinted for it.

Diana squinted. There was a gouge out of the wooden post, as if something had rammed into it and circling the ground were shattered pieces of glass. Moving closer, Diana could see that whatever had hit the guard post had done so with quite some force. By this time, Nancy had pulled some rubber latex gloves out of her pocket, put them on, and proceeded to inspect the area. Diana shook her head. *Does this girl ever give it a rest?*

"Hmm. What colour is Hart's moped, Di?" Nancy asked, as she poked at the gash in the post.

"Blue. Why?" Diana replied, catching up to Nancy's hunkered form.

Nancy slowly stood to face her sister with a blank look in her eyes. Diana's scalp prickled. "Nance? What is it?"

Nancy didn't answer. Instead, she turned, grasped the wire cable that strung along the guard posts, and peered down into the ravine. Diana clamped her hands on top of her sister's shoulders and glimpsed down with her. They both stiffened. A light blue moped, with its headlight shattered, lay on top of a jutting, pink boulder, its frame twisted beyond repair, and both tires blown.

Diana's chest tightened. Her nose stuffed up. Shuddering, she reached for the inhaler in her jacket pocket and shot it into her mouth. Feeling the medicated affects instantly, Diana was about to take another puff when the shrill sound of a hawk made her jump and drop her puffer. It bounced off the wire cable and sailed down into the mouth of the cavernous raven, missing Hart's moped by inches. Diana swore aloud as the hawk swooped down upon the unsuspecting sisters and then glided back up into the air.

Nancy covered her head. "What's up with that bird?"

Numbed from the swirling assumptions about Hart's fate, Diana offered Nancy a meagre shrug. The soaring hawk attacked them again. They both cringed, covering their heads, as it flew up in time and then proceeded to circle them to strike again. Diana wrinkled her nose. *Maybe we're standing near the hawk's nest and this is her way of protecting it? I guess there's one way to find out.* With her sister in tow, Diana pulled Nancy up the road and away from the gouged post. This strategy didn't work, however, as the hawk continued with its dive-bombing routine.

Another dive, this one the closest, made Diana push Nancy to the ground. The hawk's gnarled talons clutched onto a wavy tendril of Diana's red hair and pulled her into the wire cable strewn between the posts. The hawk released its grip, and Diana swung her body over the cable, her legs now pointing down into mouth of the deep ravine.

"Diana!" Nancy screamed, lunging for her sister's hands.

Diana's chest tightened again, its vise-like grip squeezing every bit of breath out of her. A light-headedness was taking hold and Diana fought this with everything she had. Feeling Nancy's hands attempting to pull her up was reassuring, and she obliged her sister by kicking at the granite wall, trying to find a crevice to stick a foot in. Diana thought she heard a curdled, choking sound coming from directly below her, and she looked down.

Her green eyes widened, her body stiffened. "Oh...oh my, God! Nancy pull me up fast!"

Nancy, with her tongue stuck out to one side, heaved up, until she was able to grip Diana's shoulders and pull her over the thick, wire cable. Speechless, Diana fumbled for the cell phone in her coat pocket. She held her breath and proceeded to lick her dry lips, anticipating what she would say next, as her shaking fingers punched in the numbers 9-1-1.

12. Facing the Music

Spying her target, Diana's eyes crinkled with mischief, as she snuck up behind her intended quarry and poked him in the ribs.

Hart jumped. He twisted, took a sharp intake of breath, and glared down at her. "Crap, Diana, don't do that!"

Normally, Diana, being the restaurant hostess, would have had no choice but to reprimand Hart for his outburst, but seeing as the restaurant sported only a couple of patrons, she let him off the hook. It had been one busy morning seating and feeding people, most of whom were here to kick off the Victoria Day holiday, Fairy Falls' first long weekend of the tourist season, and the tips proved to be worth the wait.

Diana adjusted the collar on her green polo-style shirt, monogrammed with the Stagview's logo, before straightening the cotton shirt down over the top of her pleated black dress pants. Her wavy, flame hair, usually brushing the top of her shoulders, was pulled back in a professional manner today and her black shoes flaunted an inch and a half thick heel, instead of her favoured normal flats. Diana slowly batted her eyelids, then pouted.

Hart shot her a lop-sided scowl. "Look, I'm still bruised from a week and a half ago, so play nice, okay?"

Diana's red brows rose and she grinned. "I guess I can cut you some slack, Stewart, seeing as I saved your ass, and all."

Hart rolled his eyes while he juggled a grey plastic tub full of dirty breakfast dishes he'd collected from the neighbouring tables. With his free hand, he pulled at the off-white apron that clung to his green Stagview shirt and dark blue jeans, and then grunted. "You're never gonna let me live that down, are you, MacGregor?"

Diana screwed her mouth to one side. "Depends."

"On what?" he asked, reaching over Diana's shoulder to snatch a couple of coffee cups left on the table behind her.

She stiffened. Overlooking the fact that she could feel the heat coming off of Hart's body, she was having a hard time ignoring the smell of him. It was the heady, crisp scent of outdoors that entranced her—pine mixed with brush, shrubs, and earth. Not like the scents some of the other guys her age wore—the expensive colognes that set her asthma off the moment she got a whiff of them. No, Hart emanated the pure scent of Fairy Falls in the spring—fresh, and full of life.

Scanning his face, Diana observed the lingering traces left by that fateful day she and her sister Nancy had found Hart hanging upside-down in the ravine, close to death. A jagged scar—plagued with the remnants of a flaking scab—was half-hidden in the hairline of Hart's left temple, and a minor scalp wound had been responsible for a few stitches. He had also suffered a concussion, along with some scrapes and bruising to his torso. Doctor Rich Bennet, Brook's father, had ordered an arsenal of tests and scans, and was relieved when he found no signs of a brain contusion. Hart had been lucky to be alive, Doctor Bennet had informed Gertie.

"Diana?" Hart asked, looking down at her with an odd look plastered on his face.

"Huh?" she replied, shaking her head. Diana took a step back.

Hart discreetly sniffed his armpits. He took a step back as well. "Is...is there a problem?"

The tone of boyish solicitation in his voice jolted Diana back. "Uh, no, no, Hart, I was just thinking what a lucky guy you are, that's all."

Hart snorted. "You mean loony, don't you? Face it, Diana, how many people do you know get paid a visit from their dead mother?"

Diana bit her lip. Hart had shared his paranormal experience of seeing his mother's ghost with her. A sudden, jealous pang invaded

Diana's thoughts. She furrowed her brows and said, "At least you got to see your mom again. Talk to her, touch her. At least she tied up a few loose ends for you. Explained stuff. Put things in perspective." Diana paused to shake her head "No, you face it, Hart. You survived being suspended in that ravine, but I'm the one who's still left hanging with no answers or understanding about my mom's death."

Hart's powder blue eyes widened. He placed a hand on her shoulder and gently squeezed it. "Look, I promised I'd help you deal with your mom's murder, and I will. I just have to gain enough strength before I do any more object readings." Then Hart smirked. "Even Aunt Gertie's taking pity on me lately by cutting back on my jobs around her place."

Diana smiled. "Well, if Gertie can cut you some slack, then I guess I can."

Suddenly the piercing, guttural sound of heavy metal music coming from outside made both of them cringe. The boom, boom resonance of bass was sickening. The intense vibes penetrated through Diana, but what was more interesting was Hart's reaction. He released her shoulder, practically threw the tub of dishes onto the closest table, grabbed for an adjacent chair, and plopped himself down. Hart cradled his face into his palms and rocked back and forth in the chair, as if distressed.

Concerned, Diana draped an arm around his shoulder and frowned. *Maybe Hart's suffering from post-traumatic stress disorder? Or worse, maybe Doctor Bennet missed something on the x-rays?* Whatever it was, Diana didn't like the looks of Hart—now ashen and trembling. She rubbed his shoulder. "Hart, you don't look so good. Do you want me to take you to the hospital?"

Hart, with his face buried in his hands, shook his head. "It's that music. It's loud. Too loud. I-I feel sick. Stop it. Please, just go stop it, Diana."

Nodding, Diana patted his shoulders. "Okay, but you stay here. It could be that music has triggered something and you're suffering from post-traumatic stress from your accident."

Hart shrugged, still rocking in the chair with his eyes closed tight. Diana could see beads of sweat blister across his forehead. She reached for an unused glass and water pitcher left on one of the tables, and poured Hart a drink.

"Here." She held out the glass. "Drink this. It'll cool you down."

Shaky, Hart removed one hand from his face, grasped the glass, and sipped at it slowly, refusing to take his other hand away. "Mmm...thanks," he mumbled between gulps.

Diana nodded before she moved toward a succession of screened patio doors, opened the first set, and stepped outside in search of the booming music. It sounded as if it was coming from the back entrance of the pub portion on the other side of the restaurant, where large beer and liquor trucks usually parked to deliver their supplies. Crossing the outdoor patio, the hot, humid air of late May danced across Diana's arms, warning her of the unbearable heat to come. She passed a few of the Stagview's signature green market umbrellas and tables, then rounded the corner of the building; the music leading her like a punked-out version of the Pied Piper on crack.

Walking in between two blue dumpsters, Diana stopped, then scanned the area. Spotting a long silver beer truck, she cocked an ear and figured the whumping sound must be coming from behind it. As Diana got closer, the loud music engulfed her, as if being swallowed by a heavy, chaotic fog. Now she was getting pissed. Didn't the idiot have any consideration for the resort and their guests? Well, she'd put a stop to it, that was for sure. Rounding the rig, Diana spied an old, black Ford Bronco. Rust had eaten away half of the lettering, which now read 'od Bono'.

Diana approached the vehicle. The doors looked as if they were about to vibrate off any second, while the half-opened windows might shatter. The faded cap on the box directed the music toward the open tailgate, allowing for the heavy music to escape out the back. Beyond angry now, Diana stomped toward the truck, stepped on the running board, then reached over with one hand and cranked the radio off with a hard twist. Her shoulders relaxed. *There. That's better. Much better.*

"Hey!"

Diana jerked. She jumped off the rusting running board and turned to face another kind of too-loud music—verbal backlash from the truck's owner. Surprise lit up in her eyes as a tall, slim-figured woman approached her. Her long raven hair bounced with each step like a practiced runway model and her voluptuous assets bulged indiscreetly from the pink tank top she wore. Black, faux-leather pants graced her rounded hips and shapely legs, while pink strapped high-heel sandals allowed her to cover the distance between them. Diana smiled. This could only be one person—Vonnie Shipton, co-owner of the Court Jester—Fairy Falls' popular pub and dance club for locals and tourists alike.

"You don't go turning off a girl's favourite music, that just ain't right!" Vonnie shouted.

"I do if the music offends the employees and patrons of the resort," Diana said with all the calmness of a sunny summer's day. She knew Vonnie Shipton was all bark and no bite. In fact, she kind of liked her. Vonnie was her own kind of rebel. A one-time popular movie make-up artist, now turned entrepreneur, she'd rubbed elbows with some famous Hollywood Stars, and had the pictures posted all over the Court Jester to prove it.

Vonnie balked, and then appeared to squint as if the blaring sunshine blurred her vision. "Diana? Diana MacGregor, girl is that you?"

Diana smiled, then nodded. "Hey, Vonnie! What's up with the Satanic music? I thought you let the seventies go a long time ago?"

Vonnie laughed, sounding haughty and explicit, as if she defied authority. "Give me Black Sabbath or AC/DC any day over that Much Music crap I'm forced to play in my bar for the customers. I'm just a good ol' girl who knows what she wants and goes for it!"

Diana laughed. "You're a character, Vonnie, that's for sure. But seriously, in the future, could you keep the music down a few decibels when you park here?"

"Sure thing, Sweetie," Vonnie said, then winked at Diana before she pulled down stylish black sunglasses over her piercing mauve eyes.

The tattooed Celtic band around Vonnie's toned right bicep rippled at her in an unnerving manner. Diana's eyes narrowed. *Wait, what's Vonnie doing here anyway? She's the Stagview's bar and dance club's biggest competition.* Diana inclined her head. "What brings you out to the Stagview, Vonnie?"

Vonnie raked wisps of dark hair off her forehead with one hand. "Funny thing about a long weekend. Seems to bring out the savage in the best of us. Last night, I must have gone through a couple of cases of beer and wine glasses, some either smashed or stolen, so I phoned here hoping the resort would sell me some extras. Let me tell you, Diana, it's nice to see businesses banding together and helping each other out in times like these. I was desperate!"

Diana arched her brows. "Times like these?"

Vonnie nodded. "You know, talk about that huge resort development that may be coming in, and such. I know damn well if it gets built there'll be at least two new restaurants and bars going up with it. Then I might as well kiss the Court Jester bye-bye, swallow my pride, and go beg for a job at the new place."

Diana sighed. This proposed development was affecting everyone she knew. It didn't seem fair, businesses being here for years only to be ousted by the Goliaths of the resort world. An ache lodged in Diana's throat for Vonnie, a woman whom Diana knew was in her early forties, but didn't look it, who could never return to powdering the faces of the rich and famous. All because a well-known actress Vonnie worked on had a serious allergic reaction to the make-up she had applied to the actress's face and neck. Apparently, Vonnie Shipton had been accused of being hungover at the time, a mistake that had cost Vonnie her career.

A man, whom Diana recognized as one of the bartenders at the restaurant, walked up to Vonnie with two big boxes clutched to his burly chest. "Where do you want these glasses, Vonnie?"

"In the back of the truck, Earl. Most appreciated."

Earl nodded. His slick, brown hair pulled back into a small ponytail, made his jowls more prominent as they jiggled. Diana raised a red brow. *I wonder if Earl knows he looks like a throwback from the eighties?* At least his clothes—a dark green Stagview polo and pressed black pants, somewhat saved his reputation. Carefully placing the boxes in the truck, Earl turned and presented Vonnie with a form to sign. A sudden gust of wind whipped the paper out of Earl's hand. It flew over the Bronco's cap and slid down the right side of the truck.

"I'll get it, Vonnie," Diana offered as she rounded the front of the vehicle. Stomping on the form, she reached down to pick it up. As she rose, her heels sunk into a pothole and she lost her balance. Grabbing for the side-view mirror, Diana found out a little too late that it wasn't there. Stumbling, a strong hand gripped Diana's forearm and steadied her.

"You okay?" Vonnie asked, snatching the form from Diana.

"Yeah, just lost my footing. It's these stupid heels the manager insists I wear," Diana gushed. "I swear I need extra insurance when I wear them."

Vonnie smiled, nodding in silence as she scrawled her signature on the order, ripped the white copy away, and handed Earl his yellow one. "Thanks again, Earl. Come by the Jester for a drink on me sometime, eh?"

Earl threw Vonnie the thumbs up sign. "You can count on it, gorgeous."

As Earl's large, bulky body trundled away, something dawned on Diana. From Hart's description, the truck that ran him off the road bore quite a resemblance to Vonnie's truck. She picked her brain for the moment. *What did Hart tell the police? A black truck. Loud music playing. A knocked off, right-hand side-view mirror. That's three for three.* She rubbed her chin. But what about the stocky, bearded man with dark bushy hair, who Hart claimed had been at the wheel? Diana's eyes widened, and her journalist instincts kicked into first gear.

"Um, Vonnie?"

Vonnie stopped stuffing the order into the front pocket of her tight leather pants and looked up. "Yes?"

"Is this *your* truck?" she asked.

Vonnie's thin, dark brows arched above her sunglasses. "Well, technically, it's the Jester's. Why?"

Diana licked her lips, formulating in her mind a selection of questions that would help her get to the truth. "Have you lent this truck out to anyone, say in the past two weeks?"

Vonnie shrugged. "All my employees have the use of it. If someone needs to go to the beer store to return empties, or go pick up some mix or supplies, then they grab it and go. What'cha getting at, Diana?"

"Well, have you lent it to anyone stocky with dark bushy hair and a beard, lately?"

Vonnie whinnied playfully. "That sounds like most of my clientele, girl!"

Diana's jaw dropped.

Vonnie smiled, shaking her head. "But to narrow it down a smidgen, I do have a new employee that started working for me as a bouncer about two weeks ago who fits that description. Why? What'd he do?"

Diana stared blankly at Vonnie. "I'm not sure. At least not yet. One more question, if you don't mind. What happened to your side-view mirror?"

Vonnie set her lips into a thin line, and said, "You know how it says on every side-view mirror, 'OBJECTS IN MIRROR ARE CLOSER THAN THEY APPEAR'?"

Diana shrugged. "Yeah."

Vonnie threw Diana a full blown grin. "Well, never try to prove that wrong, especially when you're parking too close to a big ass tree in the dark. I swear, a damn branch came out of nowhere and tore my mirror off before I knew it!"

Diana laughed along with Vonnie, but her mind was busy with visions of the stocky, bearded, bushy-haired man who now works at the Court Jester. Was he the man who had tried to kill Hart? If so, did he know Hart was still alive? There was only one way to find out. Tonight, after work, Diana would gather the troops—namely Brook, Donovan, and Hart—to take a drive over to Vonnie's bar and check out her newest employee. If Hart fingered him as the lunatic who ran him down, then a simple call to the police would be in order. Diana smiled. *Yes. That sounds like a sensible plan.*

"Thinking happy thoughts?"

Diana jumped. "Huh?"

Vonnie guffawed in her own throaty way. "You were smiling. To me, that can only mean one thing for a girl your age, coming from this town."

A hot flash rose through Diana's cheeks. She could only imagine what Vonnie Shipton's definition of 'happy thoughts' were. *Sex? Boys? Booze? Drugs? Parties till dawn? All of the above?* Diana cleared her throat. "And that is?"

Vonnie pulled down her shades so that they were resting on the bridge of her perfectly narrow nose. Her mauve stare was intense, her manner recluse, as she curled a corner of her mouth and said, "Getting the hell of this place before it kills you."

13. Fishing for Evidence

Hart sat in the front passenger seat of Diana's car, tapping nervously on the black dashboard. He stared blankly out the windshield, waiting for Diana to return with Brook; the last pick up of the night. Hart sighed. It had been almost two weeks and still Brook Bennet hadn't spoken to him. He didn't blame her really. He'd treated her like crap. Worse than crap. Hart had treated her, a person who understood and even admired what he could do, like the freak he thought other people would call him if they knew of his ability. Hart sunk deeper into the black bucket seat. *At least Brook isn't afraid of who she is.*

"Maybe she doesn't want to come," Hart mumbled.

"Don't sweat it, Hart, Brook's not one to hold a grudge," Donovan blurted from the back seat, as he fiddled with a thin flashlight.

Hart's shoulders sagged. "Then why has she been avoiding me?"

Donovan flicked on the flashlight, bent forward, and shined it under his chin, as if preparing to tell a macabre ghost story. Hart squinted as Donovan threw him an eerie grin. "Because," he moaned like a demented apparition, "Brook's been casting spells to heal the rift between you two."

"Spells?" Hart perked up. "What kind of spells?"

Laughing, Donovan switched off his flashlight. "Dude, all I know is that the spells involve the use of apples. Lots of 'em."

Hart inclined his head and grinned. "Well, as long as they're not poisoned ones!"

Donovan guffawed at the same time the driver's side door creaked open.

"Did I miss a good joke?" Brook asked, as her pale hand reached in and pushed the front bucket seat forward. She settled her slim body into the back seat next to Donovan.

The lacy black tank top and pair of charcoal hip-hugging pants Brook wore attested to the humidity of this evening. Hart fanned his face. He could already feel sweat pool around his armpits. He cleared his throat and said, "Uh, no, Donovan was just being…you know a—"

"—a jackass?" Brook cut in. Then she dove into her black leather purse decorated with astral symbols and pulled out a shiny, red apple. She blew on it three times before reaching over the front seat. "Want one, Hart?"

From the back seat, Donovan made a strange sound. Hart pursed his lips and then nodded. A peace offering was a peace offering. He reached over, and instead of taking the apple, he swallowed her whole hand within his and said, "I'm…I'm sorry, Brook, you know, about slamming you and your beliefs. You didn't deserve my crap. It was all about me, not you. Forgive me?"

Brook screwed up the side of her mouth, as if mulling it over, then smiled. "Forgiven and forgotten. So let's start fresh. I won't push my beliefs on you and you don't judge me. Deal?"

Hart squeezed her hand, gave it a shake, and released it with the apple in tow. "Deal," he said, taking a big bite out of the apple. He immediately stopped chewing and cringed. There was a bitter sweet aftertaste to it that he'd never experienced before, and never wanted to again—like eating a caramel candy doused in vinegar.

Suddenly, Donovan flicked on his flashlight and shone it in Hart's face. Donovan's eyes bugged.

"Holy Mother of God! What's up with your face, Hart? It's…it's turning green!"

Both Brook and Donovan snorted in unison, the back seat filling with sudden hysteria.

"Did you get him?" Diana asked, pushing back the driver's seat, and sliding in.

"Oh yeah!" Donovan chuckled. "That's one for Witchy-Poo, nada for the Hanged Man."

Hart frowned and looked over at Diana, who was pulling down her dark grey T-shirt over the top of her black cargo pants. It was planned that everyone was to wear dark clothing this evening. To be like shadows and blend into the night. Both Hart and Donovan had opted for jeans and plain black T-shirts. Now, they all blended in with the smooth ebony upholstery of Diana's car, like an elite teen surveillance squad awaiting their orders.

Hart eyed Diana suspiciously while she did up her seat belt. As if sensing his eyes burning into her, she stopped, and turned toward Hart. "What?"

"You were in on this poisoned apple joke?" Hart asked, wagging the acrid fruit at her.

Diana smiled. "In on it? *Oh contraire, mon ami,* it was *my* idea," she said, starting the car.

Fifteen minutes later, Hart heard the pounding sound of raucous music fill the air. The Court Jester was nearing. As Diana took another curve in the road, Hart could now see the illuminated bar on his right, set back on the river, in all its glorious blends of reds, blues, whites, and greens. The whole vicinity looked like a freaky display of aurora borealis gone mad. The parking lot was filled to capacity, the outside patio bulging with intoxicated customers screaming in off-key lyrics to the heated music. Hart cringed as a sudden twinge of nausea slammed through him. *Maybe I should have brought some ear plugs.*

"Wow, Vonnie's sure got a rowdy bunch tonight," Donovan said, as he poked his head over Hart's seat and peered out the windshield.

"They're mostly *cidiots*, Donovan," Brook added, "here to act like the wild animals they drove away."

Hart furrowed his brows. "Cidiots?"

Diana giggled. "Brook's pet name for idiotic people visiting from the city."

A finger lightly poked Hart's left shoulder. "Don't worry, Hart, I'm not referring to you. You're one of us now."

Donovan chuckled. "There's no need to freak him out, Brook, the poor guy's been through enough!"

Hart shook his head, a subtle smile breaking across his face. *I'm one of them.* A sudden gush to his heart warmed him all over as he realized he'd never really been a part of anything in his life before, just a wanderer—going from school to school, place to place. Suddenly an uneasy swirling emotion swamped him and he reached for his faded ball cap. Had he made the right decision to stay in Fairy Falls? Or, would things just bottom out like they always did when he got close to someone or something? Hart sighed. Only time would give him the answers.

Diana turned into a parking lot across the street from the noisy bar, prompting Hart to toss her a sideways look. "Why are you parking here?"

"Are you kidding?" Diana blurted, gearing down. "There's no room on this car for scratches or dents, so the farther away from drunk and disorderly humans, the better."

While Diana parked, Hart allowed his mind to wander back through the day's events. After hearing the news that Diana might have found the truck responsible for the attempt on his life, Hart had rushed outside to the shipping area. The truck was long gone, but Diana assured him she knew where they could find it, and who might have been at the wheel—Vonnie Shipton's newest employee. So after work, both Diana and Hart drove back to her place, polished off a quick meal, then proceeded to make plans on how to apprehend his would-be killer. Unfortunately, Diana's younger sister, Nancy, caught most of their conversation and begged them to tag along. Diana's answer had been an adamant 'No!', to which Nancy responded by stomping off into her room. Hart took a long, deep breath. Now, it was showtime.

Pulling up in front of a closed realtor shop, Diana killed the engine, and then the headlights. Hart let his eyes scope the store front, whose decor resembled a cheesy log cabin, complete with a couple of white cottage chairs. Pictures of homes and cottages adorned one side of the front window, while the other side posted a large portrait of a smiling woman, whose name was boldly written underneath in big black letters. Hart's eyes bugged.

"Uh, Diana, isn't that the lady you puked on?" Hart asked, pointing to the picture.

Diana looked up, and grinned. "The one and only."

"Hmm, I wonder if Ms. Bean knows that picture makes her look older," Brook said, cutting in.

Diana giggled. "You think it would be hanging there if she did?"

Donovan snorted. "Now, ladies, put your claws back in, and let's go join the festivities across the street. The night's not getting any younger!"

"Yeah, let's get this over with," Hart muttered.

"Oh come on, Hart, where's your sense of adventure?" Brook asked.

"I'm guessing that he lost it somewhere in the ravine, along with the desire to take up rock climbing," Donovan blurted, as he smacked the back of Hart's seat.

Hart rolled his eyes as both the girls giggled at Donovan's lame comeback. He opened the car door and slid his lean frame outside. Donovan followed him, while Brook went out Diana's side. Suddenly, Diana stopped at the edge of the road, swore out loud, and turned to face Hart, who was two-thirds the way across the parking lot. She held up her keys and said, "Hart, could you bring my camera? It's in a blue case in the trunk."

Hart nodded just as she tossed the keys to him and turned toward the wide green trunk. Jimmying the key, Hart popped the trunk open. His mouth dropped and he jumped back, finding Nancy MacGregor's wide brown eyes staring back at him.

Hart set his jaw. "What are you doing here?"

She brought a finger to her lips. "Please, don't tell Diana."

"Let's motor, Hart!" Donovan yelled from across the street.

Hart sighed. He turned and waved them on. "You guys go on ahead. I'll catch up!"

Diana and Brook crossed the road to meet up with Donovan, while Hart produced his best scowl, twisted back, and glared down at Nancy. He frowned. *Where'd she go?* Grunting, he looked around to the right of the car, and then to the left. *Nope. No sign of her. It's like she disappeared into thin air.* Hart rubbed his eyes.

"I'm under here," Nancy whispered.

Clenching his teeth, Hart grabbed Diana's blue camera case, slung it over a shoulder, slammed the trunk, and hunkered down to peer under the car. There, grinning like a gnome, was Nancy. A small tackle box was clutched to her side. Hart's brows rose. "Are you going fishing?"

Nancy laughed. She wiggled out from under the car, stood, and adjusted her glasses. "Sort of. I'm fishing for evidence."

"Evidence?" Hart twisted his mouth to one side. "For what?"

"To help put the dirtbag who tried to kill you away for a very long time. I know why you guys are here, so I thought I'd help." Nancy raised her tackle box. "This is my forensic kit. It's got stuff like dusting powder for fingerprints, rubber latex gloves, a digital camera, lint remover, some tools, baggies, and small envelopes in it."

Hart rolled his eyes. *This kid needs to get a life*. He shook his head. "Your sister said no, and no means no. Now go sit in the car and wait for us. Diana can deal with you later."

Nancy put a hand on her hip. "No."

Taken back, Hart inclined his head. "No?"

Nancy nodded. "No." Then she reached for the set of keys inserted in the trunk, and dropped them down the front of her navy T-shirt.

This is getting ridiculous. Hart stuck out his hand. "Give me those keys! Now!"

Nancy's eyes bulged. She pointed beyond Hart and yelled, "Bear!"

Hart froze. His face twitched. *Bear?* Visions of a hungry, drooling, black killing machine rammed through is mind. He gulped and slowly turned around to face the furry intruder, but there was no bear. Nothing but eerie shadows cast from the street lamp on the road. A sudden urge to stuff Nancy back in the trunk seized Hart, and he twisted around to find that Nancy, like the bear, wasn't there either. He rubbed his face briskly. *I've just been conned by a twelve-year-old detective-turned-escape-artist.*

Fuming now, Hart caught the distinct sound of sandals slapping against pavement. Nancy was on the run, heading for the Court Jester. *Great. This whole thing isn't going as Diana planned at all.* Swearing aloud, he bolted toward the noise-infested bar, hoping he could catch Nancy before she did anything stupid.

As Hart crossed the road, he heard the squeal of tires, and turned in time to catch a set of headlights bearing down on him. He clutched Diana's camera case to his side, then leaped and rolled across the gravelly shoulder as a silver sports car zoomed by him. It pulled into the bar's crowded parking lot and parked at the front, near the river. Hart's face burned. He rubbed at the bits of gravel stuck in his elbows and forearms while he approached the car, which looked like an older model Trans Am, gleaming under the light of a nearby lamp post.

The car was still running, loud music blaring through its body. Hart pounded against the window with his fist, his teeth clenched firmly. The driver, a brown-haired punk about his age, jerked in his seat, and then looked up. Hart glared at him, gesturing for him to roll down the window. The driver smirked, undid his seatbelt, rolled down the window, and then turned up the volume on his car's stereo.

Hart's face, shoulders, and neck tensed. *That's it! I'm done with having my buttons pushed!* Without hesitation, Hart clutched the front of the demented driver's white T-shirt, and hauled his ass out of his car through the window.

"W-what the hell? L-let go of me, you, you psychopath!" the driver screamed.

Grunting, Hart reached for the driver's black belt for leverage, and dragged him to the ground. "You're the one who's the psychopath! You almost ran me over back there!"

"Is there a problem, Brett?" a deep voice blurted over the loud music.

Hart looked up. Two, no, three guys, all wearing white T-shirts and faded jeans like they could've been rejects from the movie *Grease* stood behind the grounded driver. Hart's features hardened. He'd had a few good fights during his street life, and had done okay, dishing out a few nose bleeders and busted lips, but Hart had never faced these odds before. Four against one. Nope. He'd be the dark horse for sure. The driver slowly got up, wiped the dirt from his denims, and then scowled at Hart.

"No problem, guys," the driver said, one side of his mouth curling. "Now, you were saying, freak?"

Suddenly, as if coming to life, the silver Trans Am moved forward. Hart spun on his rubber soles, and took a step back. His eyes widened. There was no driver, no one in the car at all, and it was rapidly moving toward the river.

"No! No! No!" yelled the driver, while he and his band of bullies ran after the renegade vehicle. Hart's mouth dropped, watching the Trans Am go over the bank with its loud music blasting and splash into the river. Its glowing ass end stuck up in the air like a wayward mermaid hanging a moon. The engine gurgled, then sputtered, killing both the car's stereo and itself in one belch.

Angry four-letter curses trailed as Hart heard the sloshing and splutter of four bodies diving in after the submerged car. At first they shrieked, and then their teeth began to chatter. Sudden laughter emerged from behind a large pine tree. Hart wrinkled his nose. He strode over toward the tree, and there, crouched behind its massive trunk was Nancy, her forensic kit clutched underneath her dark shirt and her body jiggling uncontrollably.

Hart arched a brow. "Tell me you didn't."

Nancy snorted between laughs and shook her head. "Technically, the stick I wedged in the accelerator did it."

Clenching his teeth, Hart grabbed Nancy's arm and heaved her up. "That wasn't funny, Nancy!"

She shook her head again. "No, it was hilarious!" She snorted again.

Hart rolled his eyes. Enough was enough. He escorted Nancy around the tree and headed toward the back of the lot, away from the river to where an old GM camper was parked. A slam of the side door made Hart's eyes bulge and he froze in his tracks. Nancy smacked into the side of him, losing her balance.

"Humph! What's up with—"

Hart clamped a hand over her mouth, then maneuvered her behind an old red pickup truck. He looked directly into Nancy's eyes, brought a finger to his lips, and then pointed toward the man heading in their direction. Nancy nodded in silence as a stocky, muscular man with bushy, dark hair and a beard strode past them. He wore black denims, a charcoal muscle shirt advertising the Court Jester, and a pair of pointy-toed cowboy boots that crunched against the gravel. A colourful tattoo of a wolf ran down his sculpted right arm. He headed for the river, where the owner of the sunken Trans Am and his friends were screaming obscenities and doing their own brand of river dance.

"A-are you sure?" Nancy asked in whisper.

Hart nodded. "I'm sure of it."

Nancy smiled. "Then there's only one thing to do."

Standing, Hart peered over the truck's box and looked toward the river. Satisfied they hadn't been seen, he said, "Yeah, and what's that?"

But Nancy didn't answer. She was already hightailing over it toward the GM camper. Hart's stomach clenched. *Doesn't that kid ever listen?* Smacking the side of the truck, Hart pursued the little brown-haired bugger, dodging parked cars and potholes, until he made it to the camper and banged on the side door so hard the windows rattled. "Nancy, get your butt out here, now!"

Nancy never had a chance to answer, because at that moment Hart heard the unmistakable sound of a gun discharging from inside the camper.

14. Blackflies

"**D**id you guys hear that?" Diana yelled over the crowd of weekend warriors, her head turning toward the back of the parking lot.

"Hear what?" Brook asked, sipping on a bottle of spring water.

Diana bit her lip. She knew what she heard. She hadn't imagined it. "A gunshot, coming from over there." She pointed to where a line of pickup trucks, SUV's, and a lone GM camper were parked at the back of the Court Jester's lot.

"Diana, how could you hear anything with that noise blaring in the background? Maybe it was part of the song. Or some twit-head setting off a few firecrackers," Brook offered.

Diana shook her head. "No. It was definitely a gunshot. Go get Donovan and meet me over there. Maybe someone's hurt."

"What about Hart?"

Diana shrugged. "He's a big boy, he'll find us."

Brook nodded, then turned and swam through the crowded outside patio to where Donovan had met some of his lacrosse buddies. Diana watched her go, then turned on her black sandals and walked toward the back of the lot. Her only source of illumination was a single lamp post set in the far middle. As she maneuvered around vehicles of every sort, Diana caught the sounds of muffled screaming and splashing, as if someone were drowning in the river. Gazing over in that direction, she noticed that there seemed to be a cluster of people near the edge of the river. She rolled her eyes. *It's probably some drunken douche who decided to be the first one to swim across the river this season,* she thought. At least there were enough people around to help out. Turning back, Diana pulled her cell phone out of her back pocket, switched on her flashlight app, and scanned the area in front of her. Something she saw about ten feet away made her freeze. *Is…is that my blue camera case lying on the ground?*

Diana's throat went dry and she formed her lips into a silent scream. She cautiously took a step forward, then another, until she was standing over her case. Crouching down, she swept the beam of light around the area, catching a few footprints but nothing else. Her heart leapt in her throat. *Where the hell is Hart? Did that stocky, bushy-haired bearded man who tried to run Hart down have anything to do with this?* Her chest tightened and without thinking, Diana reached for her spare inhaler in her front pant pocket, and took a puff. Then she took a deep breath. *There. That's better. I'm clear.*

Slinging her camera case over her shoulder, Diana stood and shone the light over the area. Her red brows arched. The footprints that surrounded her case appeared to lead to the GM camper parked at the very back. Biting her lip, and hoping that Brook and Donovan would catch up soon, Diana slowly crept over to the camper, which looked like it had seen better days. Peeling decals and speckled rust spots decorated its exterior. The faded beige paint job earmarked the RV as being dated from the early eighties; its limp screens and tattered window coverings screamed for replacement.

Slinking around the side, Diana thought she saw a beam of light sweep through the inside of the camper. *That's odd.* Listening, she swore she heard the odd muffle. *Maybe Hart is in there?* Her eyes widened. *Maybe he's tied, gagged, and incapacitated!* She looked around but there was still no sign of the others, so she knew she had to do something, and fast. Diana readied herself, then yanked the camper door opened and charged in.

"Crap!" a pair of voices screamed in unison, as Diana's blinding light shone into their eyes.

Diana jumped. "Hart? But…I thought—" Then she saw who was kneeling next to him. "Nancy? What the hell!"

"Shhh!" Hart and Nancy whispered as loud as they could.

Diana clamped her mouth shut. *What's going on?* "You two better have a good explanation why, number one, Nancy is here, and number two, my camera case was left outside?" she whispered through clenched teeth.

Hart gestured for her to duck down. "One, Nancy stowed away in the trunk of your car, thinking in her own weird way that she could help us by collecting evidence, and two, I dropped your case when I saw the creep who tried to kill me come out of this camper."

Diana inclined her head. "Then why are you in here? Why didn't you call the police?"

Hart rolled his eyes and then pointed to Nancy, crouching on his left.

She grinned at her big sister and wiggled a few fingers at her. "I couldn't help it, Di, it's the investigator in me. The 'I gotta know' part that leaps at any opportunity to solve a mystery."

Diana shoved a finger in her sister's face and wagged it. "Know this! When we get home, you're going to be in so much trouble that—"

"That what? Who you gonna explain this to? Dad? Not likely, seeing as you're in the same boat....oops I mean camper, as me," Nancy said, puckering her lips like a bottom feeder.

If Diana clenched her teeth any harder she'd need dental work for sure. Her scalp prickled. *Wait. The gunshot.* She scanned the grimy mushroom-coloured floor of the RV with her cell phone and caught the gleam off the barrel of a revolver. She gulped, gesturing to the weapon. "Is...is that what I heard going off earlier?"

"Yeah," Hart said, nodding. "Nancy knocked it off the table when she broke in. It accidentally fired and the bullet went into the panel somewhere in the back. We were checking out the place when Nancy heard someone outside. She thought you were him."

Well, that's one mystery solved, Scooby, Diana thought, turning off her flashlight app and pocketing her cell phone. *Now, all we have to figure out is who owns this camper, and why does he want Hart dead?* She cleared her throat and said, "So did you guys find anything?"

Hart smiled, then gave Diana the come along sign. Together the three intruders crawled along the floor until a flimsy brown vinyl wall barrier crossed their path. Hart gripped the bottom of the barricade. "Whoever this guy is, he's playing for keeps," he said as he shoved the room divider out of the way.

Standing, Diana gasped. In the glow of soft lighting coming from a small lamp attached to the wall, she could make out a huge topographical map pinned to the wall. It was of Fairy Falls and the surrounding area. On it, a certain portion was highlighted in pink and yellow. She squinted. It looked like a substantial part of Blueberry Lake had been marked. *What's all that about?*

Below the map, a small, brittle table propped up by a solitary leg held some other interesting things. A black laptop, a silver digital camera and printer, a box of ammunition, and an empty holster, no doubt belonging to the revolver on the floor back there. An ashtray, full of half-smoked butts was placed closest to the wall. Diana's journalistic mind spun out of control. *What is Hart's connection to all this? Was this man a hired killer? And if so, who hired him?*

As the barrage of questions rambled through her head, Diana caught Nancy flipping open a small tackle box situated on the orange tweed bench next to the table, and reaching for a small camera. She quickly clicked a few shots of the map before exchanging the camera for a pair of latex gloves, which she snapped on as if she were a seasoned intern. Next she pulled out a small plastic bag and a set of tweezers, and proceeded to gather a couple of butts from the ashtray.

"Nance, what the hell are you doing?" Diana asked, frowning.

Nancy looked up. "What does it look like I'm doing? Collecting evidence, of course. There's gotta be some DNA on these babies, and where there's DNA, there's an identity."

Diana huffed. "You know better than anyone not to screw around with a crime scene."

Nancy shrugged. "Do you see any crime committed here? Nope. Just a map, a laptop, a camera, and a printer."

"And the gun and ammo?" Hart cut in.

Nancy bit her lip. "Don't you want to know who we're dealing with?"

"We? I don't recall *we* hanging upside-down in a ravine."

Diana sighed. "Unfortunately, Nance is right. We need to know the truth about this guy."

Nancy grinned. She placed the collected evidence in her kit, then moved above the computer to hit the snooze button. The screen instantly flashed on. A serene picture of Algonquin Park in all her majesty appeared as the screen saver, but Nancy ignored this and went straight to the icon on the desktop named *Blackflies*. Nancy double clicked on it, then raised her brows. "They're digital image files. There are four of them."

Hart made an odd sound, as if peanut butter was stuck the back of his throat. "Of…what?"

"Only one way to find out," Nancy said, clicking twice on the first one.

If it wasn't for the fact that Diana was gripping the end of the table, she would have fallen on her knees. A photograph of her deceased mother, all laid out in the morgue, filled the screen. Nancy, too, stared in silence, her mouth agape, her eyes wide. The grotesque morgue photo was too much. *Why? Why would some sicko keep this picture?* Diana's eyes watered, seeing her mother the way she didn't want to remember her. Pallid, stiff, waxen. Not healthy, beaming, alive. Her body tensed. She grabbed for the ammunition box in front of her and twisted, heading for the gun on the floor.

A pair of hands grasped Diana's shoulders and reeled her back into the room. The box of ammo flew out of her hands, showering bullets in every direction, hitting the walls, counter, floor, and dinner table. Hart pushed Diana down on the worn bench and gently held her face between his hands, wiping away tears as they emerged. "Take a deep breath, Diana, don't let the slime bag who did this get to you."

Breathing harshly, Nancy clicked on another image. "W-who's that?"

Both Hart and Diana looked at the screen. It was another forensic image, of another woman. Her neck was covered in purplish striations, as if she'd been strangled, her eyes were closed tight. Her colour, too, was pallid, waxen, and lifeless. Diana, trying to grab any bit of composure she could, shrugged. Hart jerked his head back and he gasped. "That's…that's *my* mother."

Diana forced herself to look at the computer screen and licked her dry lips. "Okay, Nance, what's behind door number three?"

Nancy silently obeyed her older sister. "Isn't…isn't that—"

"Archie Avery," Diana cut in. "But why? I…I don't understand."

"And the last image?" Hart asked, his tone wavering, uneven.

Nancy clicked on the fourth file. It was another morgue photo. An old man, about in his seventies, his hair a dull silver, his skin weathered and pallid, his face rigid. Diana could make out a huge bruise in the chest area, as if the man had been hit by an object with great force. Although she couldn't place his face, Diana knew, like Archie Avery, she'd seen him around Fairy Falls many times before.

Nancy fiddled with her glasses. "I know I've seen this man before. He looks really familiar."

"That's Aunt Gertie's husband, Pete. H-he died last winter," Hart said, his voice cracking. "But…I thought it was an accident? I mean, I saw it happen with my own eyes."

"You saw it?" Diana asked. "How's that possible? You weren't around here then."

"His glasses showed me." Hart set his lips in a tight, thin line. "Nancy, what else is on that computer?"

Nancy closed the file, then clicked on another icon. This one was named *Blueberries*. Like *Blackflies*, this file also contained digital images. Nancy motioned her thumb and clicked on the top one. Diana's eyes widened. Pictured was Hart's Aunt Gertie, riding around on a battered all-terrain vehicle. Hart gasped as Nancy clicked on another image. Startled, Nancy twisted around to look up at Hart, who was now white-faced, and gripping the brittle table edge for support. His face was unreadable, yet a hint of fear danced in his eyes. He swallowed hard before Diana glimpsed at the digital photo of Hart staining his great-aunt's dock.

"T-that picture is recent. It…it must have been taken shortly after your accident." Diana cupped a hand to her mouth. "Oh God, Hart, this sick pervert's been secretly stalking you and your great-aunt!"

"But why?" Nancy asked. "Nothing makes sense here. There's no connection to any of the victims—" She paused for an instant, and then snapped her fingers. "Expect for the fact that Hart's mom and uncle were related."

Hart banged on the table with such ferocity, the ashtray full of butts flew to the floor, and the computer screen instantly went blank. "Two can play at this game!" He pushed away from the table and ran toward the front of the RV.

"Hart?" Diana yelled after him, but it was too late. Hart had already picked up the revolver.

"Hart, no! Put that thing down! We'll go to the police instead. They can take care of this demented bastard!" Diana pleaded.

Hart shook his head. "The police will never get to the truth like I can."

Diana furrowed her brows as Hart whispered something to himself, then placed the gun to the middle of his forehead. He leaned back against the panel wall and let his legs slide out from under him until his bottom landed on the dirty floor.

"What's going on, Diana? What's he doing?" Nancy asked, gripping her shoulder from behind.

Diana licked her lips. How could she explain what Hart was doing when she really didn't understand it herself? She just knew it worked. She sighed and said, "Searching for answers and getting to the truth his way."

"Huh?"

Diana wiped away a trickle of sweat above her brow. This wasn't going to be an easy explanation. She pinched the bridge of her nose, and said, "Hart's a…well, he's a…you see he reads objects, or objects talk to him—"

Nancy squealed. "You mean Hart's a psychometrist? Wicked!"

Diana looked at her sideways. Nancy grinned. "Lots of crimes are solved using the help of mediums, big sis. You should stay at home and watch TV more often."

Diana rolled her eyes. Hart moaned. She looked down and her jaw dropped. His legs were jerking, his body shaking. *What the hell is that gun telling him? Can he read the future as well as the past? Does he see his great-aunt's death? His own?* Enough was enough. Kneeling down, Diana placed a hand on Hart's shoulder and gently shook him, hoping that she could bring him back from his self-induced hell.

Suddenly, Diana heard footsteps beating a path directly toward them. She dug her short nails into Hart's shoulder.

"Hart, wake up," she whispered.

Nancy peered out the front window. "Oh crap! The psycho's coming back!"

"Hey, Dude! Have you seen a red-headed chick around here?" Donovan yelled from the side of the camper.

"Great. It sounds like our backup has arrived," Diana whispered.

Now all they needed to do was to get Hart out of his trance, and fast. Diana shook his shoulder again. No response. She shook harder. Nothing. Diana positioned herself in front of Hart, so that she straddled him, then grabbed both his shoulders firmly and banged him against the wall.

"Oh, what...what happened?" Hart muttered, releasing the gun from his forehead.

"Who's in my camper?" the man shouted from outside.

"Nancy, help me. We've got to get to the back and sneak out the emergency exit," Diana whispered, trying to raise Hart.

"Hold on," Nancy said, pushing past Diana and Hart and lunging for the side door.

"What are you doing?" Diana groaned, trying to balance Hart's body.

"Buying us some time." She locked the back door and secured it with a rubber bungee cord.

At least one of us is thinking, Diana thought.

Together, both girls helped one groggy teen psychometrist to the back of the camper. Heaving Hart on the bench, Diana lifted the latch on the big window at the side and popped it open.

Bang! Bang! Bang! Diana heard the man's fist smacking against the side door, as Nancy slid out first. Next, Diana removed her camera bag from around her shoulder and tossed it outside. She took a deep breath. *Now for the hard part,* stormed through Diana's mind. She raised Hart's legs up and guided them out the window. His torso was next and proved to be more of a challenge. Grunting and huffing, she pushed as if she were giving birth.

Startled and now fully awake, Hart grabbed both Diana's arms while he teetered in and out of the window. "W-w-what's going on?"

Bang! Bang! Bang! "Let me in!" the man yelled, yanking at the door.

"Not by the hair of my chinny-chin-chin," Diana muttered. "Quick, Nancy, pull Hart through! Now!"

The stress of the moment made Diana forget one significant thing. Hart had a stranglehold of her forearms, so when he was yanked out, so was she. The two of them hit the solid ground with a whump, as Diana heard the door crash open from the inside. The man was in, and they were out.

"Hey, Di! We've been looking all over for you! Did you hear about Brett Bean's—"

"Hello? I could use a little help here!" Diana yelled, cutting him off.

"What's going on?" Brook asked, coming from behind Donovan to stand in front of the camper.

The camper's engine ignited. Choking on diesel fumes, Diana wrenched her neck as the headlights of the camper flicked on. Standing, and leaving Hart and Nancy behind, she sprinted toward Brook, waving her hands wildly in the air, motioning for her to get out of the way. Diana was about half-way when she tripped over a pothole and her ankle caved. The RV lurched forward, its tires spinning. Spitting out dirt, Diana watched helplessly as her friend screamed, then disappeared from view. Diana's chest tightened.

"Nooo!" Diana yelled. She punched the ground hard, as the RV rounded a parked truck and zoomed down the road, leaving her choking on dust and fumes.

"It's okay, Di, I got her!" Donovan propped up Brook in his arms for proof of life.

Diana smiled, gave him the thumbs up sign, and took a deep breath, feeling her chest ease. *Thank God Donovan grabbed her in time.*

"Um, Diana?" Nancy squeaked. She sounded off-key, almost fearful.

By now Diana's ankle was throbbing and her nerves were frayed. "What?"

"I-I think we have a problem," Nancy muttered, her face starting to drain of all colour.

Is she seriously kidding? In her mind, Diana could count numerous problems. She glared at Nancy. "And that is?"

Nancy gripped both hands tightly, as if strangling them. "I-I left my CSI kit in the camper. Now…" she paused, her lips quivering. "Now it's just a matter of time."

Sitting, Diana raked a few red tendrils out of her face, and shrugged. "A matter of time for what?"

Nancy started to shake. "Before we make the *Blackflies* file."

15. Pleasant Point Corporation

Hart still couldn't get the vision out of his mind. *Screams. Blood. Silence.* An overwhelming sensation of violence had been upon that gun, and it had suspended him into a type of a fear he couldn't understand, yet knew and felt, was real. Far too real.

The gun's history was blurry. In fact, it hadn't taken Hart to a particular place like Diana's mother's ring had, but instead had revealed a mish-mash of scenes, like a group of movies edited into one. It made no sense. He was propelled into a dark alley at one point, then yanked to an emergency ward the next second, and thrust into a prison after that. Hart shook his head as he picked out a garden rake leaning against the buckling wall of the green and white metal shed. He sighed. The one common factor during his short session with the gun was that it possessed an abundance of emotions it had absorbed from its owner, and this was what perplexed Hart the most. They were emotions that should never be dished onto the same plate. *Hate. Remorse. Sadness. Rage. Calm. Numbness. Fear.*

Hart scratched his head. Going to the police had been futile. After all, it had been Nancy, Diana, and himself who had broken into the camper. They were the ones who had trespassed. Hart's ears were still ringing from Constable Boyd's lecture. *'You should have phoned us the moment you recognized the man responsible for running you down! This is police business. Let us do our jobs.'* Hart winced, remembering the conversation. Even Vonnie Shipton, the bar's co-owner, had been called away from her busy establishment that night. And boy was she pissed! She argued that Diana or Hart could have approached her and she would have called for the authorities to come. Hart snorted, as he stepped out of the old, metal shed. *So much for trying to be heroes.*

As Hart walked toward the bunkie he was planning on moving into that night, he tried to wrap his head around what he had learned about this mysterious man Vonnie Shipton knew only as 'Guy'. That was it. No middle name, no last name. She paid him under the table and asked no other questions. He was only to be a seasonal worker, do his job, be gone by fall, and that was it. Hart kicked at the ground, his steel-toed work boots scattering rocks. It was as if this man wanted no identity. A blip on the radar screen of life.

Now, three weeks later, it seemed that this stranger named Guy had gotten clean away and hadn't been seen or heard of since. He had evaporated into thin air. Hart stopped. His fingers choked the rake's long, wooden handle as the image of the bearded man laughing at him, mocking him, played inside his head. A psychotic, twisted man who not only seemed to take pride in documenting his previous fatal hits—Hart's mom, Diana's mom, Archie Avery, and Pete Ellis—but who also made his intentions clear about his Aunt Gertie and himself. Hart's knuckles whitened. He felt like a moving target.

Then Hart sighed. Despite everything they had told the police that night, the crime unit's report claimed Archie Avery's death was accidental. No foul play had been evident. When Hart pressed about his great uncle, the coroner's records indicated that Pete Ellis had died of a heart bruise, directly caused by a log's wild blow originating from the log splitter, not at the hands of a madman. So those two cases were closed. As Hart continued to strangle the rake, he realized chances were getting slim of finding and convicting the psycho obviously responsible for killing his mother and Joy MacGregor. With no connection between the two murders, and little evidence to go on, these cases would continue to remain as cold as ice.

A slight buzz danced around Hart's sweaty head. He dropped the rake and waved the pesky insect away from his ears. Now that the blackflies had all but disappeared, he had to contend with yet another blood-thirsty beastie: the mosquito, Fairy Falls' national bird. He winced and blindly slapped his naked right knee. Glancing at his hand, Hart smiled. Blood dotted his scarred palm and he wiped it across his tattered cut-off jeans. He swore that if he sprayed himself with any more insect repellant, he'd be glowing by the end of the day.

At least things had returned to normal since that fateful night at The Court Jester. Hart's tutoring sessions had resumed at the high school and he'd made substantial headway. Diana had set up a filing system for him, using repetition as her primary teaching tool, and exercise books she had borrowed from the local literacy council. Now he was at level two, and feeling very pleased with himself. But with all the normalcy and tranquility that a small northern community offered, conversely came the sudden onslaught of cottagers and tourists at this time of year. Fairy Falls had now swollen to ten times the size. Hart lifted his orange T-shirt and scratched a cluster of rippling mosquito bites scattered across his stomach. He shook his head. Fairy Falls was definitely heading into a new normal.

Bending to retrieve the rake, Hart froze in mid-air, catching the hum of a car's engine getting closer. This put him on red alert. "Crap," he muttered.

Where is Aunt Gertie? He scratched his stomach again and thought for a moment. About an hour ago, she'd told him she was taking Skoka for a walk to check out some of the blueberry bushes on the south side of the property. *Blueberries.* Hart shuddered, recalling the infamous computer file. Visions of the photos taken by that creep downloaded into his mind. The grotesque morgue shots. The picture of Aunt Gertie. The photo of himself. Both being stalked, hunted like animals. Quickly, Hart reached for the yellow two-way radio hanging from his belt loop and pushed the side button, thankful for its five kilometre range.

A sudden beep squealed in reply. "Yeah?" a staticky voice asked.

"You okay, Aunt Gertie?"

"Course I am. Why?" She sounded a little annoyed.

Hart smiled. Nothing changed with her. He pushed his talk button and said, "Just checking up on you, that's all. You know, you being old and stuff."

The two-way radio screeched, then hissed. Hart thought he overheard branches snapping and Skoka barking in the background.

Then came the scream. "Ohhhh! Ya got ta help me, Hart! Help me!" This was followed by static noise.

Hart's eyes bugged. Frantically, he pushed his button. "Aunt Gertie? Aunt Gertie! Are you there? Talk to me!"

A sudden giggle erupted over the airwaves. Hart frowned, and pressed the button. "Aunt Gertie?"

"What'samatter, Hart? Did this old gal git the better of a young feller such as yur'self?"

Hart cringed as the hiss and snap of the frequency popped in his ear. He clipped the radio back onto his belt loop. *So much for caring.* The sound of the car pulling into the driveway made him jump. He turned around and listened. A slow steady smile formed across his lips. The low, powerful purr of that particular engine told Hart that it could be only one person behind the wheel. His red-headed partner in the crime of break and entering—Diana MacGregor. He walked to the top of the driveway and flagged her over.

For someone who had just finished her final exam that morning, Diana didn't look too pleased. She appeared frazzled, as if someone had keyed her car and gotten away with it. Diana shut off the engine, snatched something from the seat next to her, and swung open her door. Still favouring her injured ankle from a few weeks ago, Diana gingerly walked over to where Hart stood. The heat of the early afternoon attested to the sweat stains that pooled under the arms of her light blue polo shirt as she waved a rolled paper at him.

Hart inclined his head. "Got your exam results back already?"

"I wish that's what this was about."

"So what's up?"

"This." She unrolled the white paper.

He looked over the typed letter. *Dear Mr. MacGregor and Mr. Molnar,* it started, then Hart picked out key words he knew—*the, and, that, but, was, to, where, when,* and so on. He meshed them with new words he'd learned recently, looking for clues, skipping, reading ahead, until he got the gist of the letter. He raised his chin and smiled from ear to ear.

"Is that supposed to be some kind of offer on Avery's land?"

Diana's face lit up like a Christmas tree. She nodded and said, "I see you've been practicing your reading, Mr. Stewart. Good. And yes, an offer was made on Archie Avery's land, now that his estate has been settled."

"But…I thought you told me Avery has no family," Hart said, waving a mosquito away from his face with the back of his hand.

Diana nodded. "That's right, he doesn't. Apparently, my father's law firm is handling Archie Avery's last will and testament arrangements. That's where I got this paper." Her face reddened. "I sort of scored it off the secretary's desk and copied it. No one will ever know. Besides, I thought your great-aunt would like to know, seeing as part of Avery's land butts up to hers."

Hart stiffened. "It does?"

Diana threw him an incredulous look. "You didn't know?"

Hart shook his head and looked back down at the letter. Something familiar caught his eye, only this time it wasn't a word, but the logo in the top left corner. He pointed to it. "I've seen this somewhere before."

Diana stuck a thumb into the pocket of her cropped pants and strummed her fingers against the beige fabric. She sighed and said, "That's the other reason I wanted to show you this. The offer was made by Pleasant Point Corporation. That's their logo."

Pleasant Point Corporation? I know that name. Then Hart remembered: it was the company that wanted to build the resort development that half the town was so opposed over. His eyes widened. Now Hart knew where he had seen that logo. In his great-aunt's recycling bin, amid newspapers and flyers. Twisting on his boots, Hart's long legs carried him over the dead leaves, loose rocks, and sprouting greenery, back to the buckling shed where Aunt Gertie also kept her red recycling bin for papers, and he reached inside.

"What's going on, Hart?" Diana called out after him. "What'cha doing?"

Rummaging around the bin, Hart found what he was looking for. He pulled out a stack of letters, all typed on professional letterhead, all addressed to Gertie Ellis. The logo, a setting sun surrounding a group of towering, white pine trees, was embossed in gold foil with green and black print. It resembled the logo printed on Diana's copy, with the exception of colour. The letters looked crumpled, as if Aunt Gertie had been annoyed with the content. As Diana walked up, Hart held out the small pile of letters to her.

"I bet this makes for interesting reading," Hart said.

Taking the letters, Diana fanned through them. "It looks as if Pleasant Point has been corresponding with your great-aunt for a while. Some of these letters date back to last winter, after Pete Ellis died." Then she stopped and whistled.

"What?" Hart asked, frowning.

"Wow, they're not offering your Aunt Gertie chump change, that's for sure."

"Offering? Offering what?"

Diana perused the fine print with a finger. "Millions. They started with six figures, then moved up the money chain. Pleasant Point Corporation seems to be very interested in Gertie Ellis's large parcel of shore line and land. Land, I might add, that's adjacent to Archie Avery's property. My, isn't that a coincidence?"

Hart's eyes bugged. "The map in the RV! Remember? Part of Blueberry Lake was highlighted!"

Diana nodded. "And now we know which part it was."

Hart shook his head. "Still, there's something I don't get."

Diana looked up. "What's that?"

"Why would Aunt Gertie lie in front of the whole town?"

"Lie?" Diana arched her red brows. "Lie about what?"

"Last month Aunt Gertie had insisted that the development was just a rumour. But…but she knew damn well it wasn't if she was getting offers from them. I tell you, Di, it doesn't make any sense."

Diana shrugged, letting her eyes fall back to the letters. "She must have had her reasons to keep a cap on this, Hart."

Hart fell silent for the moment. What reasons would Aunt Gertie possibly have to hide the truth about the development? And how did all this connect to the mysterious man named Guy? Did he work for Pleasant Point? It was a possibility. Maybe this development company was behind the four deaths? After all, Diana's mother had uttered the words, *'Development. Scam. Traitor.'* Perhaps she had known Guy, and who he really worked for. But what of his mother? How did the two connect? Even now, Archie Avery's death was looking less and less like an accident, and so was his Uncle Pete's.

Diana snorted. "Oh crap, it figures! Karen Bean just happens to be the real estate agent acting on behalf of Pleasant Point."

Hart caught the slicing tremor in her tone. The seriousness of the past moments gave way and he smiled devilishly at her. "Say, Di, did that *friend* of yours get his Trans Am back on the road yet?"

Diana's mouth fell. She elbowed Hart in the gut. "If you ever insinuate that Brett Bean is a friend of mine, then you can find yourself a new tutor!"

Hart rubbed his sore belly and nodded. He never mentioned to Diana that it was her sister's fault that Brett Bean's car had taken the plunge. No way. Poor Nancy had gotten into enough trouble that night. At first from Diana, next by Constable Boyd, and then by Big Daddy Mac, himself. As a result, both girls were grounded for two weeks, with the exception of school and Diana's job. The only thing Mr. MacGregor did do was assign a detective to check out this mysterious 'Guy' who had briefly worked at the Court Jester, but so far, nothing had come up. No leads, no new information. At least that was what they'd been told.

"How's Nancy doing?" Hart asked, still rubbing his stomach. "Has she gotten anywhere in her cyber investigation?"

Diana sighed. "Not really. Although, she's made good use of her two-week sentence by using her hacking skills to check for records of 1980 GM camper models, then cross-referencing them with owners whose first or last name is Guy, but nothing panned out with that. So now she's compiling a list of names using 'Guy' look-alike mugshots, downloaded courtesy of Constable Boyd."

Hart sighed. "I wish I could do something. Even my object readings have gotten us nowhere. Your mom's ring, the gun—"

Diana put a hand on his broad shoulder. "That's not true, and you are doing something. You're making sure your great-aunt is safe."

The two-way radio squealed. Hart rolled his eyes. He snatched up his radio and pushed the talk button. "Finished laughing at me?"

There was no reply. Only squealing and static.

"What's that about?" Diana asked, handing Hart back the letters.

"She's screwing with me again," Hart said.

"Awe, isn't that special? You two are bonding," she cooed.

Hart smacked Diana on the arm with the handful of papers, then beeped his great-aunt for the second time. "This is getting old, Aunt Gertie. Oops, sorry. Didn't mean to mention the o-word again."

His radio squeaked and beeped again. This time Hart could hear Skoka barking wildly; as though something was wrong. He snorted. *What was Aunt Gertie doing to that poor dog? Sitting on him?* Before Hart had a chance to speak, a gravelly, slurred voice on the other end stopped him short. "H-h-hulph."

Hart looked at Diana, then back at his radio. He pushed the button. "Stop this now, Aunt Gertie! It's not funny anymore!"

There was a hiss, then a fizzle. The dog was still barking, sounding agitated and frantic, and then the radio went dead. Diana shook her head. "Something's not right."

Hart pursed his lips. "Okay, let's take the ATV and check it out."

It took them all of five minutes to start up the old green four-wheeler and head out toward the south side of Gertie's expansive property. The cut trail made it easy for Hart to maneuver the bulky vehicle over the rolling hills, around bulging boulders, and down deep pockets of land, but dodging the fanning, twisted branches that sprawled across the trail was another matter. Diana gripped Hart's waist with one hand while her other hand was busy with the radio, trying to signal his great-aunt, but the line had remained silent.

Hearing a dog bark, Hart braked. His butt lifted off the seat a few inches and Diana almost shoved him over the windshield. "Did you hear that?" he asked, hovering over the handlebars.

Diana swung her head around, then pointed. "Over there, past that clump of maples. Go, quick."

Spinning the tires, Hart went full throttle, gunning it over a small hill, passing the cluster of maples, and then followed the trail around a sharp bend, veering right. Startled at what he saw in front of him, Hart jerked back.

"Hart, stop!" Diana yelled.

He twisted the heavy ATV to the left, just missing his great-aunt, who was lying on her back across the uneven trial. Skoka circled her, barking furiously. Squeezing the brakes hard, Hart stopped just before smacking into the thick trunk of an old, gnarly maple tree. Diana had jumped off before he had a chance to shut off the engine and she squatted by Aunt Gertie to examine her.

"Aunt Gertie! What's wrong?" Hart yelled, running over to where she lay. He knelt down next to her. Skoka whined and tried to lick Hart's face. He batted the dog's big yellow head away, then carefully looked his great-aunt over. Her attire, black rubber boots, bulging, worn denims and a red checkered long sleeve shirt, were covered in dirt and dead leaves.

Aunt Gertie's owlish eyes were open, staring into space. Her greyish-brown hair was tucked haphazardly into a worn, off-white Tilley hat. Part of her face drooped, like her left cheek was sliding away from her eye. Then she moved her mouth as if it took considerable effort and garbled, "N-n-necckk h-h-hertt."

Hart shook his head. "What'd she say, Di? I can't understand her. It's like she's talking with mouthful of marbles."

Diana's mouth merged into a thin, straight line. She sighed, then bent down to Gertie's ear and said, "Mrs. Ellis? Can you move your left arm or leg? Just blink once, if you can't, twice if you can."

Aunt Gertie scrunched her eyes closed, then opened them. That was it. She only blinked once. "What does that mean, Di?"

Diana gently patted Gertie's shoulder, then stood and grabbed Hart by an arm. She escorted him off to the side of the trail, while Skoka romped beside them, his tail beating against his bare legs as if they were a drum skin.

"Hart," she whispered, so that only he could hear.

He caught a hint of fear in her voice. Her gaze was steady, unwavering. This spooked Hart. "What is it?"

"I think your great-aunt has had a stroke."

16. The Proposal

"Visiting hours are almost over," a young nurse with short brown hair announced, poking her head into the semi-private hospital room at the end of the hallway.

Diana looked up at the nurse from her seat next to Hart. The nurse's blue scrubs were wrinkled, signaling her shift's end. Diana cleared her throat to ask, "Could you give us just a few more minutes?"

The nurse smiled. "Sure, but no more than fifteen."

The nurse left, and Diana studied her surroundings like a practiced journalist, always observing. Mrs. Ellis's bed was farthest from the window, which didn't give much of a view since it faced the highway. The white vertical blinds looked tired, as did the flooring; a stark, marble colour worn down from ample traffic. The metal-framed bed next to Hart's great-aunt was empty, its blue linen pulled tight in military fashion, awaiting its next occupant. The white privacy curtain hanging limply between the two beds was pulled back, revealing a black night stand with a wooden top. On it rested a beige telephone and a few gossip magazines Hart had picked up for his Aunt Gertie.

Diana heard Hart sigh. He'd been silent for a while, just staring, watching over his sleeping great-aunt. She reached over and tugged on his orange sleeve, but he only grunted in response.

"Don't worry, Hart. Doctor Bennet says she's a real lucky lady, and that the stroke could have been massive, instead of mild," Diana offered.

Hart shrugged. "Massive. Mild. What's the difference? A stroke is a stroke."

"Would you rather her be disfigured and totally paralyzed?"

Hart's shoulders sagged. He shook his head. "I guess I'm just feeling sorry for myself."

"I think that's allowed." Diana nudged him with her elbow. "As long as you don't milk it."

Hart half-smiled. He reached for Diana's hand and squeezed it. "Thanks for everything you've done for me and Aunt Gertie. We both appreciate it." He squeezed her hand again, this time for longer.

Diana knew by the heat rising up her face that she was turning beet red. Hart's hand felt warm, welcoming, yet there was something else. Something more. His hand could perform unexplainable, magical feats just by holding an object, whispering to it, seducing it, until it unlocked its secret to him. She swallowed hard, and inwardly wished she possessed that kind of power, that kind of gift.

She casually glanced toward Hart, who still had a hold of her hand but was concentrating on Gertie. His free left hand reached out to touch his great-aunt's hand, avoiding the intravenous, and gently stroked her fingers. Diana's own thumb brushed up against the numerous scars that covered the inside of his palm. He had told her of the harsh winter and using cigarettes to warm his hands. *Hands that he used to help people,* she thought. *Hands that could take you away in the blink of an eye.*

"What are we gonna do, Aunt Gertie?" he muttered.

"Do?" Diana perked up. "Do about what, Hart?"

Hart, with both his hands still engaged, turned to look at Diana. There was a look of vacancy in his blue eyes, as if he was all alone. She squeezed his hand to reassure him he wasn't. "Hart?"

Hart inhaled sharply before he said, "Di, I know nothing about harvesting blueberries, and squat about making maple syrup. What if Aunt Gertie..." he paused to lick his lips. "What if she doesn't get better? What if she's stuck in a wheelchair for the rest of her life? What if—"

Diana pressed her finger to his lips. "You can 'what if' yourself to death and still come up empty, Hart. Why don't you let nature take its course and see what happens? At least you won't go crazy second-guessing the outcome, and you may be surprised by the end results."

"That's sound advice, Diana," a male voice gently intervened from behind.

Diana pulled away from Hart and turned toward the doorway. There, stood Sid Molar, leaning against the door frame, his arms filled with a basket of colourful carnations, all in bloom.

Diana smiled. "Hey, Sid, it's about time you finally showed your face! Dad left over an hour ago."

Sid shrugged. "Better late than never, kiddo. I had something I had to nail down with some clients, and before I knew it, it was eight o'clock." Then he looked up at Hart and threw him a solemn smile. "I'm sorry about your Aunt Gertie, Hart. Here—"

Hart stood and took the basket of flowers from Sid. He carefully placed them on the nightstand and knocked most of the magazines off. "Damn," he muttered under his breath.

"Not to worry, I'll get them," Sid offered.

Sid skirted around Gertie's bed. His stone grey eyes darted over Hart's great-aunt for an instant. Dressed for the greens, instead of the office, Sid sported a navy knit polo shirt and tan, pleated dockers. Expensive sunglasses were pushed back over his black, curly hair, revealing his bronze forehead and ebony brows. As Sid crouched, he brushed against the starchy sheet hanging from the bed and knocked off his sunglasses. They clattered to the floor. Diana heard him grunt, as if he had extended himself a little too much.

"How's the old gal doing?" Sid asked, as he stood and placed the magazines in a neat pile.

Hart shrugged, as if not wanting to be bothered answering the same question he'd been asked over and over again.

Diana patted his shoulder. "The doctor said he'd know better in twenty-four hours, Sid. If no feeling comes back in that time period, then Mrs. Ellis may have some paralysis in her left side. But we're keeping positive. Right, Hart?"

Hart balled his fists, then struck his thighs hard. "It's not fair! We were just getting to know each other, and now this!"

Sid propped his glasses back on his head, then sighed. "You know, Hart, you could make it easier for your great-aunt."

Hart's blue eyes widened. "Easier?" He inclined his head. "How?"

"You were just made Gertie's power of attorney. She signed the papers last week."

Hart shrugged. "So?"

Sid rubbed his clean-shaven chin. "So, now you've got the power to do the right thing for your great-aunt. Lord knows, since Pete's untimely death, I've tried to guide and counsel her in the right direction, but she's as stubborn as a—"

"Jackass," Hart muttered.

Sid smiled. "I was going to say mule. Sounds a little more respectful, don't you think?"

Hart sighed. "So then, what is the 'right thing' for Aunt Gertie?"

Gertie grumbled, then snorted, her head rolling on the pillow, like a fish fighting on a line. Then she was still.

Sid reached over and stroked Gertie's arm tenderly. "Gertie's told me of the numerous offers she's received from Pleasant Point Corporation. Maybe you should consider selling to them. The money would ensure you and your great-aunt will be set for life. She's not getting any younger, and I'm afraid that place of Gertie's has taken its toll on her. Physically and mentally." He stopped stroking Gertie's arm and looked Hart in the eyes. "Do me a favour and think about it, Hart. After all, as Gertie's power of attorney, you have the opportunity to do what's best for her."

As Hart raked his hand through his hair, Diana caught a whiff of fresh pine lingering there. He inhaled deeply before he said, "But, that's the point, Sid. What is best for Aunt Gertie? I found a stack of letters from Pleasant Point in the recycling bin, so it's obvious she doesn't want to sell."

Sid shrugged. "Then why did she keep those letters?"

"That's what we couldn't figure out," Diana said, cutting in.

"Then let me tell you why," Sid said, with a tone of conviction wavering in his voice that Diana had never heard before. "Gertie's a pack rat. Always was, always will be. My guess is that she kept them for peace of mind. Knowing there was a way out if things got tough. Tough like now, for example. Look, Hart, you don't have to be the bad guy here. Obviously Gertie wanted to take the load off your shoulders by keeping those letters so that you'd find them, and make your decision a hell of a lot easier. But, remember, a decision has to be made, and soon."

Sid straightened and grabbed for his pant pocket. Pulling out a thin black cell phone, he looked at it, nodded, and dropped it back into his pleated pocket. "A client beckons, got to go," he announced, and threw Hart a concerned look. "Phone me if you have any questions. I don't care if it's the middle of the night or early in the morning. As your great-aunt's attorney, I'm privy to all her personal matters, and I can direct you in making the best decision possible. Okay?"

Hart nodded, but the vacancy had returned to his eyes. Sid gave Hart the 'call me' sign by extending his pinky and thumb outward. Then he nodded to Diana, twisted on his brown leather loafers, and left the room whistling a tune she swore sounded like Pink Floyd's *Money*. The sudden blurt of the hospital's intercom made both her and Hart jump in unison. "Visiting hours are now over."

Diana sighed. "Looks like we gotta go, too. Come on, Hart, I'll drive you home. Skoka will be ready for some feeding and relief soon."

Hart remained silent and only nodded his reply. Standing, he reached for his faded blue baseball hat at the bottom of Gertie's bed. Her left foot kicked his hand. Hart froze. "What the—"

"H-Hart," a weak, gravelly voice cried out.

Hart backed up and looked toward his great-aunt's face. Her hazel eyes were opened, piercing and direct. Her left hand slowly slithered down the length of the rumpled blue blanket until Hart reached for it. Diana's heart thundered. Doctor Bennet had told him that if feeling in her left arm or leg didn't return within twenty-four hours then there would be a chance of partial paralysis. Not to mention the list of stroke after-shocks: incontinence, difficulty swallowing, and depression, to name a few. Diana shook her head. The thought of Gertie dragging her leg through the sugar bush or trying to pick blueberries with a useless, claw-like hand was hard to imagine. Up until this point she had been a fiercely independent woman, even after the recent death of her husband. Gertie had always played the hand she was dealt with, but this time Diana feared that she couldn't bluff her way out of this one.

For the first time, a full smile erupted on Hart's lips. "Aunt Gertie, you're okay! You...you can talk!"

A thin line of drool trickled down Gertie's bristly chin and Hart wiped it away. Her mouth moved in an awkward manner, and Diana could see she was struggling, trying to force out words, still weak from the effects of the stroke.

Hart bent his head low to whisper, "Can I get you anything, Aunt Gertie?"

Diana heard her wheeze a breath. In and out. Steady and controlled, fighting to get out what she had to say to Hart. Diana sighed. *Sid is right. That woman is stubborn. Strong-willed being a close second.* Another intake of air followed before Gertie sputtered, "Nah. I-I got Hart."

Then Gertie closed her owlish eyes, tucked her chin into her broad chest, and fell back into a deep, sedated sleep with a trace of a smile lingering on her thick lips.

17. Break and Enter

It was the brink of the July long weekend. Canada Day and America's Independence Day. School was done and the holidays had begun. Tourist season was now in full swing and Fairy Falls was alive with activity. Hart sighed and looked out over pristine Granite Lake from his position on the Stagview's patio. It was the calm before the storm and he was standing in its eye.

He took the last swig of his coffee, now cold, and winced at the aftertaste. Setting the white porcelain mug down, he reached into his apron and pulled out a dog-eared manual. As he fanned through the Driver's Handbook, he realized how badly he needed his license now. There were no more excuses. He'd have to be his great-aunt's go-fer, at least for a while. Tomorrow she'd be released from the hospital, and Hart knew he'd have the daunting task of helping change the way she lived her life. Better diet. More exercise. Stress management. These were just a few of the things the therapist had told Gertie she needed to adjust if she didn't want to have another stroke. Hart sighed again. *I feel like a parent instead of a kid.*

Looking down into the handbook, Hart stopped at the section showing the various road signs. *Stop. Yield. No Parking Anytime. No Entry. Bump Ahead.* Yup, that read pretty much how his life had been. And now, he was heading toward uncharted territory. *Winding*

Road Ahead. Watch Out for Falling Rocks. Slamming the booklet shut, Hart shoved it back into his apron pocket. At least there was one thing that the stroke hadn't taken away—Aunt Gertie could still walk, albeit with the assistance of a cane. That, and she still possessed the uncanny ability to communicate in her own words and in her own way.

Raking his hand through his tawny hair, Hart took a deep breath and blew it out. He moved his hands under his apron and hooked both thumbs into his black denim pockets. Leaning against the brick wall, he continued to look over the lake. Boat traffic had increased, and soon the whine of jet-skis and the drone of wake boats pulling boarders would take over most of the waters.

"Can I join you?"

Startled, Hart craned his neck to peer over his right shoulder. He smiled at Brook Bennet and waved her over. She held a steaming cup of tea in one hand and an apple in the other. Brook winked at him and offered him the apple. Hart snorted. "You're kidding, right?"

Brook grinned. "Actually, I have something far better to tempt you with."

"Such as?"

Brook scanned the area first before setting her cup on the table next to Hart. Brook bit into the apple while her free hand slid into the back pocket of her pleated black dress pants. She pulled out a credit card. At least that's what he thought it was.

He threw her a sideways glance. "A credit card? Hey, what a minute—identity theft. Now that's a good idea, Brook. Lately, I'm tired of being me. I say let someone else deal with my problems."

Brook rolled her eyes, swallowing the last bit of apple, and said, "You can't run away from your probs, big guy. You have to deal with them head on, or sure as damn you'll be faced with the same problems again and again until you finally overcome them, and move on with your life."

"Is that some sort of Wiccan wisdom?"

She smiled. "You could say that. Now here. And it's not a credit card, it's an electronic key."

Hart reached for the white plastic card imprinted with the Stagview's logo. He let his thumb trace its edge before he looked down at Brook. "So, are you gonna tell me why you're giving this to me, or do I guess?"

Brook smirked. "Guess."

Hart rolled his eyes. He didn't have time for this. He was due back in the kitchen in five minutes. A sudden squeal from the pool area made Hart and Brook jump. He glanced over. A boy, roughly ten-years-old had just cannon-balled a younger girl, presumably his sister, and had soaked her completely. The first of the guests had arrived. Soon this place would be a zoo, swelling with families, couples, and tourists. Hart felt a nudge and he looked down. His face flushed. Although Brook had to wear the Stagview's required attire—green blouse or polo shirt and black dress pants or skirt—he could see her lacy black push-up bra peeking through the gap at the top of her shirt. He stammered, allowing gibberish to tumble out of his mouth.

Brook's raven brows knitted. "What kind of a guess is that?"

"What's up, you two?"

Relief flooded into Hart's features as the sound of Diana's voice erased the past moment. "Nothing. Just playing a guessing game with Brook."

Diana, holding a bottle of water, downed a mouthful, before she said, "A guessing game, eh? Sounds thrilling."

"Actually, it could be thrilling if Hart finds exactly what he's looking for," Brook said.

Diana screwed the cap back on her bottle, then inclined her head, first to Brook, then to Hart. "And what is Hart looking for exactly?"

Hart caught a wariness in Diana's voice he had never heard before. *Jealousy? Suspicion?* He wasn't quite sure, so to be on the safe side, he just shrugged. Brook, however, was more animated. She grabbed the electronic key from Hart and waved it in Diana's face. "This will help Hart gain entrance into forbidden territory, so that he may use his gift of psychometry for the greater good."

"Huh?" Diana and Hart blurted in unison.

Brook sighed. "You two are thick. I'm talking about a certain condo rented out this weekend to a certain development corporation. A corporation that has a particular interest in breaking ground here in Fairy Falls. Somewhere, say, on Blueberry Lake. Any guesses now?"

Hart's mouth fell open. "Pleasant Point Corporation!"

"No!" Diana snatched the plastic key out of Brook's hand. "If Hart gets caught, he'd be fired, not to mention what they'd do to you, Brook."

"Then I'll take the full blame," Hart said, swiping the white card from Diana's clenched fist.

"Give that back! Now!" Diana demanded, jumping up after the card, but Hart held it in the air, making like the tallest limb on a tree.

"What's the big deal, Di?" Brook asked. "All Hart would have to do is wait until seven p.m. when they're out of the condo. I know this because I booked their party for supper. I'll radio him as soon as they're seated. When Hart gets my call, he lets himself in, picks up something like a pen or toothbrush, does his mumbo-jumbo thing, gets the dirty on them, and then leaves. He'd be in and out in no time. And just as a precaution, you could act as the lookout. What do you say?"

Brook's plan made sense to Hart. Suddenly, street signs danced through his head. *Parking Permitted. Walk. Green light.* He smiled. "I say yes!"

Diana's face grew redder. The stop sign was back. She pulled down her green polo shirt, which had become untucked from her black skirt to reveal a small, puckered belly button. Then she lunged for the plastic card again. "And I still say no!"

Hart held the card up higher and looked down into her flustered features. "Fine. I'll ask Donovan to be my lookout."

Brook shook her head. "No can do. He's playing lacrosse tonight."

Hart licked his lips, then sighed. *Great. Now I have to beg.* He looked down at Diana with boyish, pleading eyes, and said, "Come on, Di. Don't you want to know the truth? Think about it? Maybe I could find some link that points the finger at Pleasant Point for murdering four innocent people, our mothers included. What do you say? Are you with us or against us?"

Diana hung her head and shrugged. "With, I guess." Then she raised to head to meet Hart's powder-blue eyes. "Okay, I'll be the lookout, but I want you to promise me something, Hart."

Hart smiled, and cupped her chin. "Anything."

"Promise me you'll be careful. Promise me that you'll put a limit on the time you spend in their condo. And promise me you won't do anything *stupid.*" She accentuated the last word as if she were an old-school, strap-wielding teacher.

Hart nodded, took a step back, and held up his hand. "I promise, Di. Scout's honour."

Seemingly satisfied, Diana nodded, and as she turned to leave, Hart snorted with laughter. Her eyes darted from Hart to Brook, who was staring at Hart as if he had just lost it. Diana eyed him suspiciously. "Is something funny, Stewart?"

Hart winked, first at Brook, and then at Diana. He grabbed for his empty coffee mug sitting on the adjacent table and walked toward her. "Yes, Diana," he replied, walking past her. "I was never a boy scout."

Hart's two-way radio beeped. "Witchy-woman here. The foxes are in the hen house and ready for a feeding frenzy. All is clear. Over."

Hart shook his head. By that, she meant the Pleasant Point people were seated for dinner, and had ordered drinks and appetizers. He radioed her back. "Good thing, Witchy-woman, cause this fox is about to enter the forbidden den. Over."

Nervously, Hart slipped the plastic electronic key into the condo's door entry slot and heard it buzz. A sharp intake of air followed. *I guess it's now or never.*

Another squelch came over his radio. "Remember your promise, *Boy Scout.* Over."

Hart winced. He peered over his left shoulder to catch Diana glaring at him. She was positioned in between two parked vehicles, a blue BMW sports car and a black Lincoln Navigator, where she could keep an eye out for anyone heading towards the condo. It was her little way of helping him without helping him. Hart pushed his talk button and said, "No doubt, Girl Guide, if there's any sign of trouble, I'm blowing this cookie stand. Over."

Hart's radio popped and fizzled before Diana responded. "Cute. I wonder if you'll be this funny sitting in a jail cell. Over."

Hart rolled his eyes, then shoved his green two-way radio into his back pocket. Slowly, he turned the knob and pushed the door open. He was in. He quickly shut the door, careful not to slam it. He scanned the area with the intensity of a burglar. His blue eyes widened. *Bingo!* There, on the round wooden table near the patio doors, sat a black attaché case begging to be read by Hart's amazing psychic gift. He headed for the case as if it were a beacon in the night.

Passing empty beer bottles, a drained ice bucket, and a half-finished bottle of blue label scotch on the kitchen counter, Hart lifted the briefcase off the table and grabbed a seat on the burgundy leather couch in front of the stone fireplace adjacent to the table. His bottom sunk into the fine, soft leather, and he set the case next to him on the couch. Hart's pulse increased, and he looked around the fancy premises with the curiosity of someone who had never seen how the other half lived. He twisted toward the patio doors in time to catch a golf cart whizzing by on the rolling greens of the golf course the condo backed onto. A small garden, hosting a variety of colourful flowers and shrubs, encircled a bistro-style patio table and wicker chairs. A small barbecue shrouded with a black cover was pushed in one corner, while a tiny air conditioning unit sat across from it. The vigilant drone from the unit kept the outside noises at bay.

Hart drew his eyes back in and scanned the living room. Framed pictures of painted wildlife graced the fresh olive walls. A tall canoe-shaped bookshelf, filled to capacity with novels, stood next to a green leather recliner, and elaborate sculptures of loons, moose, deer, and bears decorated the side tables. Behind him, the kitchen gleamed with its stainless steel appliances and white marble countertops. Next to the kitchen there was a narrow hallway, presumably leading to the washroom and bedrooms. He shook his head. This place was larger, more elegant, and more expensive than Aunt Gertie's rustic, round abode, and yet there was something missing from it. Something nostalgic.

Hart sighed and looked down at the briefcase. Fanning his hands, he placed them on top of the smooth case, then pressed down and closed his eyes. Sometimes without laying an object directly onto his forehead, he could grab an impression from it, intuit the object—whatever it be—on a different level. An emotion. A thought. An intention. Something that would present a clue to who owned the item and what this person was all about. A sudden vibration stirred him onward.

Gradually, visions of a self-assured man popped into Hart's head. He went in deeper. A burly man with a receding hairline and beefy jowls. This man knew what he wanted. This man would do anything to get it. A sharp bang sounded from the hallway. Startled, Hart opened his eyes. Standing and alert now, he stepped away from the briefcase and cocked his head in the direction of the hallway. Hart swore he heard scuffling, as if a rodent was scurrying away. Beads of sweat broke out over his brow and he roughly wiped his forehead. Taking a deep breath, Hart moved toward the hallway with catlike conviction. Listening, stepping, listening, stepping; he was almost to the edge of the hallway, when the sound of heavy breathing guided him to the closet. Looking around for a weapon, Hart grabbed the closest object—a yellow kitchen broom, and then slowly reached for the closet's handle.

His two-way radio beeped wildly.

Hart jumped, fell back, and yanked the closet door open. Panic-stricken, he held out the broom in defense. He froze in mid-air, for there, staring at him with a stupid grin plastered on her face, was Nancy MacGregor. Dressed completely in black, from head to toe, she appeared more like a floundering baby seal than a sharp, undercover agent. His radio beeped again. Nancy brought a finger to her lips and shook her head. Her brown eyes, hidden behind wire-rim glasses, pleaded with Hart, like a doe about to be shot. He clenched his teeth. Throwing the broom aside, then yanking the green radio from his back pocket, Hart pushed the button, and said, "Boy Scout here. Over."

"Witchy-woman here. There's a problem. Over."

Hart sighed. Little did Brook know he was staring at one now. "Care to share? Over."

"One of the foxes has left the hen house and is heading to the den. I overheard something about forgetting his briefcase at the condo. Get out now. Over."

Hart's two-way squealed. "Girl Guide here. I don't see anyone at the moment, but I'll stay alert. Over."

Nancy threw Hart an odd look. "Witchy-woman? Boy Scout? Girl Guide? You guys have some serious codename issues."

Hart narrowed his brows. "And you have a serious snoop problem. What are you doing here, and more importantly, how did you get in?"

Nancy shrugged. "It's not hard to jimmy a patio door, Boy Scout, you just need the right tools." She flashed him her red Swiss Army knife loaded with odd-shaped accessories. "And as for what I'm doing here, check this out—"

Nancy flashed Hart a stapled, legal-size document. At the top was Pleasant Point's embossed logo, the same one he saw on the letters addressed to his Aunt Gertie. Black type filled the first page, and he looked from the letter back to Nancy. "What is it?"

She stepped out of the closet, her black knit-covered belly jiggling with excitement. "A little something that confirms what we saw in the camper that night."

Standing with a grunt, Hart eyed her annoyingly. He was getting fed up with her guessing games. "Confirms what?"

Nancy grinned smartly, then walked over to the round table and placed the document on its polished top. She flipped through the pages until she found the one she was searching for. "Here. This explains it all."

Hart strode over. His eyes fell on the page and his brows arched. "What is this?"

"A proposal for the Blueberry Hills Resort," Nancy said. "Set on five hundred acres of beautiful, rolling countryside, and providing over two thousand feet of water front. Look, there are also architectural plans attached. Plans that include a hotel, condominium buildings, shops, docks, a spa, and a huge restaurant and bar. Not to mention the seven run ski hill and chalet situated behind the proposed condos."

Hart's jaw dropped. "Where'd you find it?"

Nancy threw him a sheepish look. "I got it from inside the briefcase. It was easier to get into it than the condo."

Hart rubbed his face. *This isn't good. Not good at all.* Then something occurred to him, and he threw Nancy a sideways glance. "How'd you know about this proposal? I'm a psychic, and I didn't even know."

Nancy chewed on her bottom lip. "Actually, I didn't. You see, I was at my dad's office today 'cause we always do lunch once a week. While I was waiting for him to finish with a meeting I got bored and started wandering around. That's when I saw a big envelope on the secretary's desk. When I noticed that it was from Pleasant Point, I got curious."

Hart snorted. "And we know what that did to the cat."

"Yeah, but I bet you didn't know that the offer Pleasant Point put in on Mr. Avery's property was accepted. That's why the Pleasant Point people are in town. They've come up from the city to sign the papers."

Hart looked at the proposal again, but something didn't register with him. "This proposal…it includes my great-aunt's property. Why? She has no intention of selling to them."

"Neither did Mr. Avery, or so I've heard."

Hart's eyes widened, and he glanced back at Nancy. "Are you saying—"

"I'm saying all the fingers point to Pleasant Point," Nancy said, cutting in. "Think about it, Hart. Connect the dots. Mr. Avery's got no family, which equals no one to inherit his property. Now look at your Aunt Gertie. Her niece, your mom, is murdered, then Gertie's husband dies in a horrible 'accident'. The only ones left in the Blueberry file we found on that creep's computer are you and your great-aunt. Face it, Hart, if it wasn't for you, she'd be forced to sell her land."

Hart's mouth went dry. *Is Nancy right? Did Pleasant Point hire Guy to pick off anyone who stood in their way? Including me?* It all made sense, yet still, there was something that didn't. "But, what about your mother, Nancy? How is she linked?"

With her face rigid, Nancy shrugged. "That's the real reason why I'm here. I was hoping to find something, anything, that would connect my mom to Pleasant Point's agenda. Like a letter, or info on a laptop or cell phone, but so far I've found zip."

Hart's radio went off in a series of long beeps. Jumping, he pulled it out of his back pocket and pushed the side button. "Boy Scout here. Over."

There was no response. Hart frowned and pushed the button again. "Girl Guide? Do you read me? Over."

Still no response.

Nancy shook her head. "Something is wrong."

Hart ignored her, and pushed the button for the third time. "Come on, Girl Guide, answer me. Over."

No response. Hart had a bad feeling about this. He darted over to the couch and grabbed the briefcase. Then he looked at Nancy and said, "Quick, put that proposal back in this case. We'll go out the patio doors and circle around to where Diana is hiding. Maybe it's nothing. Maybe her radio needs recharging."

Before Nancy had time to break into the briefcase, the condo's door flew open. There, standing in the doorway, was a red-faced, heavy-set man, wearing a golf shirt, beige Bermuda shorts, and sandals with white socks. A thick cable necklace and chunky gold bracelet adorned his body in a cheap way. His thinning brown hair was slicked back over to one side. This didn't take away the fact that his gut protruded over his shorts like he had seen too many gourmet meals. Hart's view shifted from the large, green-eyed man. There, with an even redder face, stood Diana MacGregor.

"Hart?" Nancy whispered, nudging his elbow.

"What?" Hart grunted through clenched teeth.

"I thought a scout's motto was to *be prepared*."

18. Taken

"This is the dumbest, most irrational, and utterly irresponsible thing you two have ever done in your lives to date!" Mike MacGregor ranted at his two slouching daughters, seated next to each other on the brown tweed couch in the living room. He pulled at the bottom of the crew neck collar on his tan shirt and stuck his other hand in the pocket of his pressed taupe pants. A ploy, Diana figured, to keep both his hands busy.

Then her father grasped his trimmed goatee and pulled at it, while his direct, green eyes bore into both female suspects. Diana gulped. *Court is now back in session.*

"Well? Do you want to tell me what the hell were you both thinking?!" he demanded.

Diana licked her lips. *Oh, where do I begin?* If it wasn't for her, they wouldn't have gotten caught in the first place. On the other hand, if Hart had originally listened to her, he would still have a job and she wouldn't have been suspended, but she had to get caught crouching next to the blue sports car that belonged to the same man who'd rented the condo Hart had broken into. While she was watching the front, left side, and right side of the brown brick building, she'd been ambushed from behind. At least she'd given

Hart a warning signal. The problem was, he was too much of an idiot to answer her back, which in turn, busted him.

If that wasn't enough on Diana's plate of self-made misery, her younger sister had to get caught as well. Now all three of them were in deep doggy do-do. Nancy had ended up being banned from the Stagview Resort indefinitely. Diana's face burned. There was no way she was going to add fuel to her father's raging fire. She'd kindled it enough already.

This, however, didn't stop Nancy from throwing in a few dry remarks. "I guess we weren't thinking," she mumbled.

His cheeks reddened and he pointed toward the hallway. "Bed! Now! I'll deal with you in the morning."

Nancy winced and slowly got up off the couch. Her black, long-sleeve cotton shirt, now saturated in sweat, hugged her body in the most unflattering way. She turned toward the hallway and started shuffling to her bedroom as if she were a prisoner being sent to the gallows. A loud, throat-clearing noise was heard from across the room. "Nancy was only protecting your interests, Mr. MacGregor."

Twisting on his brown loafers, her father, with veins popping on his neck, glared at Hart Stewart, who was seated on the matching tweed recliner in the corner of the room. Even though the lights were dim, Diana could see that all of Hart's fingers were digging into the chair.

Her dad strode over to him. "Protecting my interests, eh? Would you care to elaborate on that one for me, Mr. Stewart?" His tone was threatening, his manner terse. Diana knew without a doubt that court was far from being adjourned.

Hart gulped in an uncomfortable manner. "W-well, Mr. MacGregor, sir, what I mean is that Nancy was there because she suspects foul play from those Pleasant Point guys. And so do I."

Diana's father knitted his sandy brows. "Do you possess any evidence to back this up?"

Hart shook his head. Her father laughed in his face. "Just as I thought. No evidence. No proof. Only mud on all our faces because of your recklessness. And thank heavens no charges were laid! You're all so damn lucky that both Sid Molnar and I were at the Stagview tonight. I left Mr. Molnar there to smooth things over while I dealt with you three. And believe me, if I find out that anyone else is involved in this mess, then—"

"I already told you, Mr. MacGregor," Hart broke in, "I went in by myself. Nancy happened to be there. No one else was involved. Diana is just an innocent bystander."

"Bystander, maybe. Innocent, I have my reservations," he said with a sneer.

"Look, I lost my job over this, and for her good deed, Diana got suspended. But I'm telling you, it wasn't for nothing. I…I felt this guy's intent, and it wasn't so honourable," Hart blurted.

Diana balked. *Uh-oh. What is Hart doing? Letting Dad in on his psychometry secret? Or setting himself up for a psycho-analysis?* Either way, Hart just opened the 'don't go there' door. She nervously pulled at her green polo shirt, as trickles of perspiration dripped down the side of her body.

"Wait…you *felt* his intent?"

"Hart's a psychometrist, Dad!" Nancy announced from the hallway.

Her farther frowned. "Hart's a…a what?"

"You know, Dad, a kind of psychic. A person who can read an object, then get a certain feeling or impression off of it," Nancy explained, waving her arms like she was batting away mosquitoes. "You should have seen Hart with that gun, he was—"

"Gun!" he blurted. "What gun?"

Now this was getting out of hand. Diana jumped up off the couch and moved in front of her father. She said, "Okay, here's the truth, Dad."

Her father's mouth fell. "You mean you've been lying to me the whole time?"

Diana rolled her eyes. *What is it with parents?* Taking a deep breath, and hoping that her asthma wouldn't kick in, she said, "No, of course not. I just didn't think you would have understood the truth."

His brows furrowed, forming an apocalyptic unibrow. "Try me."

Diana slowly nodded. "Remember when I lost mom's ring? Well, Hart was the one who found it. He told me what the ring showed him the night Mom was murdered. Dad, Mom *knew* her killer!"

Her dad snorted, then folded his arms across his chest. "So, Mr. Stewart," he said, turning to face Hart, who had shrunk down into the cushion a few inches, "would you like to tell me who killed my wife?"

Hart shrugged. "I-I wish I could, Mr. MacGregor, but he was wearing a ski mask and standing with his back to me.

An uncomfortable, heavy silence loomed in the air. Diana swallowed hard as her father's voice cracked under the pressure of the moment. "You...you were there? When my wife was getting murdered?"

Hart scratched his bottom lip. "Yes and no. I was there as a shadow. That's how it works. I can only observe, not interfere. I'm sorry. I-I know what Mrs. MacGregor went through that night. Her pain, her desperation, her—"

Her father lunged for Hart and lifted him up off the chair. He shook him furiously, like an angry child with a teddy bear. "How dare you assume how my wife felt while she was being brutally murdered!"

"Dad!" Diana screamed, reaching for her throat. "No!"

He dropped Hart to the floor, missing the coffee table by inches. He stepped back and pointed toward the front door. "Get out! Now! I don't want to see your face in this house again, and I certainly don't want to see you around my daughters. Keep your distance, and do not ever speak of my wife again. Is that clear?"

As if something explosive detonated from within, Diana's body heat rose and her skin prickled. "At least he talks about her!" Diana jumped in between her father and Hart. She balled her fists as tight as they would go and struck his chest. "What about you, Dad? You never talk about Mom! No, you're too busy selling out Fairy Falls to some stupid bigwig corporation and screwing around with that witch, Karen Bean! Mom would turn over in her grave if she saw you now!"

The stinging force of her father's open palm sent Diana tumbling over the coffee table. Stunned, she rolled onto the plush sage carpet and shook her head. Her face throbbed, burning as if fiery coals had been pressed against it. With a shaky hand, Diana lightly touched her cheek, feeling the swollen impression her father's chunky, gold bracelet had left. Hart was there in an instant to pick her up.

"I-I-I think I-I'm gonna be sick!" Nancy stammered, cupping her mouth as she bolted down the hallway.

"Oh...oh my God, what have I done?" Her father's chin trembled. "Honey, Diana, I'm...I'm so sorry, I didn't mean it."

Shaken, Diana moved to stand behind Hart. Her chest tightened and she coughed harshly. She roughly wiped her nose, which had already started to run, and she knew she was in for a bad asthma attack. She reached in her skirt pocket for her inhaler and her eyes bulged. *Where the hell is it?* She coughed again. *Think. Think. Think.* Her hands trembled. *Must be in my purse, on the kitchen table.* Wobbly, more from her father's reaction than her own bodily attack, she turned toward the kitchen with a hand pressed to her chest.

"Diana! What's wrong?" her father asked. Diana noted the panic in his broken tone and was oddly pleased by it.

Choosing to ignore her father, she continued to clutch her constricting chest and weaved toward the kitchen, wheezing and gasping each step of the way. *Screw him!* she thought. *Screw everyone!* Just as she stumbled over the ottoman, a blood-curdling scream came from the hallway, followed by the sound of glass shattering.

"Nancy?" Her father yelled. "Are you all right?"

Only the uneven sound of Diana gasping for breath was heard.

Out of the corner of her eye, Diana saw her father's face turn white. "Nancy!" he screamed, but there was still no reply.

He turned to Hart. "Take care of Diana!" Then without another word he shot down the hall, heading toward Nancy's bedroom.

Hart picked Diana up off the floor and placed her on the couch. His blue eyes met her wide open green ones. "Quick, where's your huffer or puffer or whatever you call it?"

"P-p-purse, on t-table," she managed to sputter between wheezes.

Hart sprinted into the kitchen. Within seconds he was back. Turning her purse upside-down, an assortment of make-up, pens, and a silver cell phone flew out and bounced off the spongy couch, landing everywhere. Diana noticed her inhaler go in between the two farthest cushions. Reaching for it, she wrenched it free, and stuck the yellow plastic end into her mouth. She squeezed it, and in an instant her lungs were released from their asthmatic bondage.

Hart caressed her back, rubbing it and soothing her. "Are you okay?"

Too exhausted to speak, Diana nodded, allowing his touch to soothe the beast within her.

The sound of heavy footsteps made her turn toward the dim hallway. There, leaning against the dark wall, stood her father. His breathing was unnatural, and his eyes appeared vacant, as if part of his life force had been sucked away. Despite what had happened between them, the sight of her father in this state unnerved Diana. Finding the strength needed, she stood and looked into his dull, green eyes.

"W-what's wrong, Dad?"

"N-Nancy's gone," he muttered. "Her…her door was locked, so I…I had to break in." His face turned ashen. "Diana, I-I think somebody's taken her."

Then Diana's father did something she hadn't seen him do since her mother's funeral. He dropped to his knees, covered his face, and sobbed uncontrollably.

19. Weathering the Storm

Hart batted away a mosquito buzzing around his ear, and then looked at his great-aunt sitting on the canary yellow cottage chair he had freshly painted for her over a week ago. On Aunt Gertie's lap, a pink china plate teetered precariously. A banana peel and a slice of tomato were all that was left to attest to the healthy lunch Hart had prepared for her not more than an hour before. He smiled. It was good to have her home. The place wouldn't be the same without Aunt Gertie, and whether he'd admit it or not, neither would he.

Gertie was fighting not to succumb to an afternoon nap, but Mr. Sandman appeared to be winning. Camouflaged with a bug-screen hat, her head rolled from side to side. Hart took a long swig of his cola, allowing the cool, sugary fizz to trickle down his throat, then he tugged his orange T-shirt away from his sweaty back. He hadn't told his great-aunt about losing his job. It would have been pointless. Besides, the news of Nancy MacGregor's sudden disappearance overshadowed any bit of gossip in and around Fairy Falls, and had kept Aunt Gertie's ear glued to the local radio station all morning, but so far, no new information had been announced.

Crumpling the can, Hart placed it on his empty lunch dish, then stretched, allowing the impact of last night to seep into his mind again for at least the hundredth time. It had been hell. Pure hell. Mr. MacGregor had gone into shock, and Diana, between puffs on her inhaler, pushed herself to deal with him. Again, it was the child becoming the parent scenario. Hart had his role too, dialing 9-1-1, helping with a grid and linear search around the property, and giving his statement to the police.

The truth came to light during the course of the evening when Hart mentioned the reason why Nancy ran down the hallway, and some of the police suspected that she might have run away until things cooled down between the family. This theory hadn't sat well with Hart, so without anyone's permission, he picked up a glass shard of the green vase that was found shattered all over the floor in Nancy's room, and stole into the bathroom. There, Hart sat on the toilet seat and carefully pressed the piece of vase to his forehead, hoping for a tiny glimpse as to what had happened, and possibly who had taken Nancy—if indeed she had been kidnapped. It was a gamble, and Hart was willing to chance it.

Another blood-sucking mosquito buzzed by his face, and startled Hart. He waved it away. A long yawn followed and, closing his eyes, Hart leaned back into the green canvas chair. *Talk to me,* he'd asked the glass shard, and indeed it had. *At first, he saw Nancy rushing into her bedroom, her face flushed, her body shaking. Slamming the door, she locked it. In the darkness of her room, she hadn't counted on somebody being there, waiting for her. A tall, stocky man. Bearded. Bushy-haired. He grabbed her from behind. Stifled her with his big hand. Nancy kicked. She knocked the vase off her dresser. It smashed.* Then nothing. Blackness, until Hart returned with the truth, and a suspect.

Getting the police on board with his 'tip from the universe' took some work. Hart was immediately reprimanded for tampering with evidence. Then, like most psychics, he was judged a freak and ignored. Diana had come to his aid, insisting that the police follow Hart's lead—after all, they had broken into this man's RV, perhaps he had come back looking for something Nancy had taken. After that, Hart was driven home. He managed to get three hours sleep before he took a taxi to the hospital to pick up Aunt Gertie. Blinking several times, he felt his body sinking, as if the low-slung canvas chair was a hammock. His blue cargo shorts started riding up his backside just as an abrupt snore echoed out of his mouth.

"Er, tired, Hart?"

Startled, Hart opened his eyes, sat up, and looked around. From her yellow chair, Aunt Gertie threw Hart a toothy grin behind the veil of mosquito netting. Her face was somewhat lopsided from the stroke, but her vocal slur had almost disappeared. Hart adjusted his faded baseball cap, and nodded. "Busy night, I guess."

Gertie grunted. "Busy like a bee, I'd reckon."

Busy bee was an understatement. When Aunt Gertie had her stroke, he had been given a list by the hospital staff to prepare the house for her return: installing grab bars in the bathroom, rearranging furniture, fixing any wonky deck steps, removing loose floor mats and area rugs, and filling the fridge with fresh fruits and veggies. Hart was exhausted just thinking about it. He reached for her lunch plate and placed it under his. "Did those grab bars in the shower work out for you?"

"Yeah. I 'preciate it, Hart, I do," she replied. "Not what ya expected moving up here, was it?"

Hart shrugged. "It could be worse, Aunt Gertie."

Her owlish, hazel eyes squinted in suspicion. "Such as?"

Standing, he reached over to lift the screen away from her face. "I could have lost you."

Skoka let out a succession of threatening yowls. Hart walked to the end of the deck and peered around the side. From this position, he could make out the movement of a car through the trees, as the afternoon sun flickered against its metallic body. The steady hum of the engine told Hart who was fast approaching, and he quickly hopped over the cedar rail. "Be back in a sec, Aunt Gertie," Hart shouted over his shoulder.

As Diana MacGregor's dusty Chevelle pulled into the driveway, Hart could make out her puffy eyes. His guts twisted. *What's happened? Have they found Nancy? Or worse, did they find her body?* Hart gathered his strength and walked out to meet her. She had barely shut off her engine when she threw the heavy car door open and ran into his arms. The force of their embrace surprised Hart, and Diana tucked her head into his chest, sobbing. Skoka came up from behind, wagging his thick tail, and tried to get in on the action.

"Anything?" Hart immediately regretted asking the question.

Diana's head moved back and forth. "Nothing," she whispered hoarsely.

"Are the police still looking for Guy?"

Diana shrugged. "I hope so. At least they've issued an Amber alert. Dad's at home now, but he won't rest. Sid phoned and said he'd stop by after he ran a few errands. I just had to get away from the craziness, so I left Dad with Karen Bean."

Hart noted there was a slight, cutting edge to her voice when the real estate agent's name was mentioned, so like a guy, he changed the subject. "I talked to Brook and Donovan this morning, and told them what happened. Did they get a hold of you?"

Diana, still holding tightly onto Hart, nodded. "They both wanted to cut off work to be with me, but I told them to stay at the Stagview and finish their shifts. Everything is being done that can be." Then she snorted. "You know, Brook had the audacity to remind me that everything happens for a reason and for the best. Can you believe it? A friggin' optimist till the end!"

Hart sighed and squeezed her. "Are you okay?"

Skoka whined, then pushed his big, wet nose under Diana's elbow, making Hart lose his balance. Diana attempted a giggle. She released her hold on Hart to give Skoka a pat on his large, yellow head. A sudden pang of jealousy swept over Hart in that moment. The tables had been turned and now he found himself competing with a big, goofy dog with a smelly coat and bad breath.

"Who's it, Hart?" a gravelly voice asked.

"A surprise, Aunt Gertie!" Hart announced.

Diana quickly wiped her face with a soggy tissue. "No, Hart, I'm a mess."

Hart smiled. "Mess, no. Cute, yes."

Her face reddened and she poked him in the ribs. Hart grunted, then led by Skoka, he escorted Diana around the tri-domed house toward the deck at the back. The sun sparkled off the lake, hitting Hart in the eyes, as the warm afternoon air kissed his bare arms and legs. As they walked, he caught a whiff of coconut emanating from her shiny, red hair. He noticed Diana had managed to change her clothes from her Stagview uniform to a more casual outfit, consisting of khaki cut-offs and a yellow T-shirt. The sound of her brown sandals dragging against the earth told him she was just as exhausted as he was, maybe more so.

Pasting on her best smile, Diana nodded toward Gertie as they stepped onto the deck. Still happily seated in her slanted cottage chair, she waved Diana over. Aunt Gertie reached for Diana's hand and patted it affectionately, stroking it the way only a grandmother would. She slowly pulled up a folding chair and sat down next to Aunt Gertie, who cradled Diana's hand like a nest full of eggs.

"Been tough fer ya, eh?" Aunt Gertie asked.

Diana nodded. "And I thought losing my mom was hard."

"Storms git weak, gal. Ya just need ta know how ta weather'im at their worst."

Diana grunted. "Then, I feel as if I've been in a twister and taken to Oz."

Aunt Gertie nodded. She let go of Diana's hand and gently cupped her chin. "Dor'thy got home. Y'ur sister will too."

Diana smiled. "You know, you're one smart lady, Mrs. Ellis."

Skoka whined and sniffed the air. He barked in the direction of the late Archie Avery's property. Gertie grunted. "What'smatter, boy? Smell ol' Archie's ghost, do ya?"

Hart jerked. "Aunt Gertie, that's not nice. The poor guy's dead."

Gertie shrugged. "Sorry, Hart, but the man stunk. Didn't know a bar o' soap from his arse, I say."

Diana stifled a giggle just as Skoka barked again. Hart leaned against the deck's guard rail and twisted in the direction of Avery's thickly forested land. The big Labrador's nose flared indignantly, as if he was smelling something foul. Hart stared out, not really seeing anything. Just lots of trees, bushes, boulders, and stumps. Then, he caught a movement. Or at least he thought he did. A bear, perhaps? Or maybe worse. Hart gulped, and hoped to God there were no recent Bigfoot sightings in Fairy Falls. Before he could open his mouth, Skoka shot off, barking madly toward whatever was creeping around in the bush out there.

"Skoka! Come!" Hart yelled, but the dog kept going.

"Dog's got what ya call selec'ive hearing, I say," Gertie muttered.

"Come on, Hart, I'll help you get him," Diana said, standing. "I need something that will keep my mind occupied, anyway."

Hart sighed and looked down at his great-aunt. "Maybe you should stay here with Aunt Gertie, Diana. I don't like leaving her alone, especially with what's gone on."

Gertie held up her hand, making a swishing motion. "Nun'sense. Go on, both of ya, I'll be fine. I'm 'specting someone from me lawyer's office with papers ta sign, so I won't be alone fer long."

"What papers?" Hart asked, frowning.

Gertie scrunched her face like a happy, drunken gnome. "Er, I set up a trust fund fer ya, Hart. For y'ur schooling and such. It's me gift ta ya, fer all ya done fer me."

Hart's eyes widened. *A trust fund for college? Is that what she means?* His heart warmed. Then his mind numbed. Sooner or later, he'd have to tell her about his illiteracy secret. He hoped she wouldn't be too disappointed with him. A sudden tug to his sleeve brought him back.

"Let's go, Hart, Skoka's putting a good distance between us," Diana said, pulling him in the direction where the dog had gone.

Stumbling into one another like first-graders in line, Hart led the way in his worn runners. Diana, still mindful of her recent ankle injury, carefully followed over fallen trees and uneven ground. He slowed, listening for Skoka's barking, which seemed to be coming from around Archie Avery's rustic cabin perched on a jutting cliff. Hart stopped. The distance from the cabin to the ground was quite a drop. Maybe forty, fifty feet. Remnants of yellow police tape wrapped around the broken railing flapped cautiously in an erupting breeze. Hart gulped. He shook his head in morbid reflection. The poor man must have never seen it coming.

The weathered cedar plank house stood in stoic stillness. A large, single-pane picture window, with faded orange drapes drawn, displayed the dirt of years gone by. The pitch of the roof was slight, and Hart noted many of the shingles were curled back, as if they had experienced one too many winters. It was a sad sight, really. Hart assumed it must have been a majestic house at one time, built to enjoy the view, as well as the sanctuary of the area. And now it stood empty.

"Thanks for waiting up," Diana huffed. "Did you find Skoka?"

"No, but he's stopped barking."

Diana took a deep breath. "Is that odd?"

Hart nodded. "For Skoka it is."

Diana shrugged. "Maybe he's found a bone."

Hart cringed. "By the looks of this place, maybe he's found an entire skeleton."

Diana giggled, then flicked his ear. "From what I've heard, better that than an old pair of Mr. Avery's long underwear. Look, I'll check around back and you go around the side."

Hart rubbed his ear. "Okay, but if you happen to run into Avery's ghost, throw him a bar of soap and point him toward the lake."

Diana waved him off and started to climb the steep hill that led to the back of Archie Avery's property. Hart watched her negotiate her shapely body around thick birches, drooping cedars, and protruding grey and pink boulders. Decaying pine needles carpeted the rolling grounds, which appeared to soften each step Diana took. As soon as she was out of sight, Hart snatched a deep breath, turned, and walked toward the side of the vacant cabin. Unfortunately, his path wasn't as clear as Diana's, and he had to jump the odd boulder, then break through a series of dense bushes and shrubs.

He stopped for a moment to catch himself from sliding down the slope. Grabbing onto a gnarly maple branch, Hart gained back his footing. Out of the corner of his eye, he found a set of handmade log stairs hewn into the side of the hill. Hart snorted. *Figures. I had to take the hard way.* Using the branch as leverage, he maneuvered his way toward the stairs and then snapped the twisted limb back. *There. That's way better on my feet.* Climbing the uneven stairs two at a time with his head down, he lunged up the hill like a hell-bent mountain goat, his breathing laboured, his legs wobbly. He gasped, glad to have made the top step in one piece.

Shaken and out of breath, Hart bent his head and bowed to exhaustion. Hearing a rustling coming from behind a cluster of cedars, Hart, without bothering to look up, managed to gather some strength to sputter, "S-S-Skoka? Skoka that better be you!"

A big hand came out from behind the cover of the cedars and dragged him in. Hart never looked up until it was too late. Staring down at him with a large finger pressed to his lips was the stocky, bearded, bushy-haired man known as Guy.

20. Connecting the Dots

"Skoka!" Diana yelled from the crest of the hill, but there was no bark in response. Only the rustling leaves and buzzing mosquitoes answered her.

Swearing aloud, Diana hobbled toward a huge boulder and plopped down. Her ankle throbbed and she needed a breather. Puffing harshly, Diana patted the right side of her cargo pocket, feeling the bulge of her inhaler, and a sense of calmness enveloped her.

Too many asthma attacks had plagued her lately, and she wasn't up for another one any time soon. A shadowy presence loomed in the back of her mind, as thoughts of Nancy and her whereabouts played out with nightmarish results. Visions of a shallow grave mocked her. Another morbid morgue photo haunted her. Bulging eyes, purple neck. Just like their mother. Diana's face flushed, her body tensed. Even last night, when Hart had used his psychometry to find out what had happened to her sister, he was laughed at, shunned, and swept under the rug like dirt. No wonder Hart kept his ability under wraps. When he tried to help, no one listened anyway. So why bother? She swallowed hard, knowing the truth—because Hart cared.

Diana checked her wrist-watch. It was nearing mid-afternoon. A sudden pang of guilt cut through her. *I shouldn't have left Dad. Especially with that...that gold-digging, meddlesome woman!* But she had needed to leave. Maybe, like her father, she wanted to be in the company of a peer, if only for a while. She sighed, biting the bottom of her soft, pink lip. *Or is Hart more than that to me?* True, he had become a solid, good friend like Brook and Donovan, but deeper feelings told her Hart was more on a soul level with her.

Grunting, she pushed off the cool, rough boulder, and looked around. Catching sight of a dilapidated building at the far corner from where she stood, she limped toward it. *Maybe Skoka is caught up in his own doggy fantasy world and is sniffing around over there.* As she got closer, she noticed a series of deeply embedded tire tracks that led to the leaning building, which must have been Avery's garage or workshop at one time. Her sandals made annoying sucking sounds, but she pressed on like the Girl Guide she once was. About three metres away, she spied a grimy window at the side of the garage, and headed toward it, curious as to what Archie Avery would have stored in there.

Banging the muck off her sandals, Diana wiped away a round, clean spot on the window, then pushed her face up against it. Her mouth fell open and her eyes bugged. The same GM camper that she, Nancy, and Hart had broken into six weeks before, on the Victoria Day long weekend, was parked inside. The same camper where they had found the most incriminating evidence to indict the Pleasant Point Corporation for the murders of four innocent people. And the same camper that had almost run Brook over. Her stomach churned.

Taking a deep breath and forcing herself not to panic, Diana backed away from the window, and reached into her left side pocket to retrieve her cell phone. She swiped it, clicked her contacts, pushed the saved number for home, and then waited. Nothing. Just dead static. She looked at her phone and noticed there weren't enough bars for decent cell service.

"Crap, I'm roaming," she muttered, and looked around for higher ground. A cluster of boulders was all she could find, so running over as best she could on her weak ankle, she climbed over the rocks until she stood at the highest point. The signal seemed better, so she punched in the number again. Still nothing. Now desperate, she hit all her programmed numbers until she got a weak line out. With her heart slamming against her chest, she brought the silver cell phone to her ear.

"Hello?" a barely audible voice answered, and Diana swallowed hard. *Thank God. It's Brook.*

"Brook! It's me, Diana! Now listen carefully—"

"Diana?" Brook cut in. "Speak up, girl, I can hardly hear you."

The line squawked and fizzled. "Brook! Listen! I'm at Archie Avery's place. I've found the GM camper the police are looking for! Tell my dad! Please hurry, I don't know how much time I—"

The line cut out. Diana checked her phone. The signal was gone. Rage filled her. She threw the phone and jumped up and down on her rock solid perch. She lost her balance, slipped, and fell to the moss-covered earth below, missing an emerging boulder by inches. Gripping her ankle and trying not to scream, Diana rolled back and forth, furious with herself than at that stupid piece of technology she'd thrown. This was definitely not her day.

She had to find Hart and fast. Yelling wasn't an option. It might alert that murdering bastard, who could be anywhere at this point. Searching for her cell, Diana's heart sunk when she saw it. The thin, silver phone was smashed in two, its metallic guts poking out like a biology dissection gone bad. Her chin hit her chest. *Great. Now I'm on my own. I hope Brook got the gist of my message.* She winced as she pushed herself up, and then turned to scan the area. No sign of Hart or Skoka. *That's odd.* Her shoulders tensed. *Where the hell could they be?*

Slowly, she hobbled back toward the garage. Maybe, just maybe, there was a phone in the parked RV. It was a chance she'd have to take. Picking up the pace, she tried to run, placing most of her weight on her stronger foot. There had to be a way in, other than the large double garage door at the front, so she headed for the back. Rounding the corner with her head down, and paying more attention to her re-injured ankle, Diana lifted her head just as she slammed full force into someone else.

Tumbling backward, and in panic mode, she rolled on her side and grabbed for the first weapon she could find: a thick tree branch. Struggling to stand, she whirled around to face whatever the enemy threw at her, and her eyes widened. Her chest tightened and her nose dripped.

"Diana!"

"N-N-Nance?" she sputtered, staring down into her sister's round face.

Shaking, Diana dropped her weapon and lunged for Nancy, gathering her up in her arms like a momma bear with her lost cub. Nancy was still wearing last night's outfit, which was a little ripe, but Diana didn't give a crap. Her eyes welled as she squeezed her baby sister tight, then she reached into her right cargo pocket for her inhaler. She took a quick puff, then a deep breath. There, she had gotten it in time.

Nancy pulled away and looked up into her flushed features. "Are you okay, Di?"

Composing herself, and resisting the urge to do to Nancy what she'd done to her cell phone, Diana stuffed her inhaler away and glared at her sister. "Okay? You're asking me if I'm okay? With what I've had to deal with in the past twenty-four hours, you ask me if I'm okay! Are you serious?"

Nancy's chestnut brows furrowed. "I was talking about your asthma."

"Augh!" Diana growled. "What in the frig are you doing here?"

"Looking for you," Nancy said, her eyes rolling as if her question was obtuse.

Diana's mouth fell. She was about to blast Nancy again when a grizzled male voice stopped her cold. "Nancy, did you find your sis—"

Dan Boone froze as Diana's narrowing green eyes met his earth brown ones. He straightened and inclined his head, causing his pepper-coloured ponytail to sway apprehensively, as if it were a skunk's tail on red alert. She pushed Nancy behind her. "You'd better start explaining yourself, Mr. Boone, 'cause where I stand, kidnapping is still a major felony in Canada."

A trace of a smile broke across his unshaven face. Boone crossed his arms over his fringed, buckskin coat. He leaned to one side, mimicking the garage they were standing behind, and his eyes crinkled, as if somewhat amused by Diana's accusation. This infuriated her more. "You'd better not have done anything to Hart!" she seethed, clenching her teeth in the most unflattering way.

Boone broke out in laughter. Diana's eyes widened. *What the hell is so funny?* Ignoring her ankle, and the flood of humiliation flowing through her, Diana lunged for Boone like a spider pouncing on a fly.

"Diana, no!" Nancy yelled, but it was too late. Diana had landed on her prey. Straddling Boone, and with her elbow lodged into the hollow of his throat, she caught a whiff of fresh pine and sage. Her nose flared indignantly.

"Diana, let him go," Nancy pleaded.

"Give me one good reason," Diana spat.

"B-because…you're a lot like your mother, Diana," Boone said, his voice straining under the pressure of her elbow. "A-and she went about things the right way."

Diana set her face on devour. "How dare you talk about her!"

"Diana! Let him go!" Nancy demanded.

Diana's mouth fell. "B-but, Nance, why are you siding with him?"

Nancy rolled her eyes. She stuck a finger in the air and gave Diana the 'come along' sign. "Follow me. I'll show you."

Diana pushed off of Boone, and with her legs wobbly and stomach in knots, she followed Nancy. Strong fingers wrapped around her arm, and she twisted her neck to see that Boone had a grip on her elbow. She tried to break free, but he held her firm. "You're as stubborn as your mother too, I see," he said with a grin.

Surprisingly, all his teeth were white and straight. She swallowed hard and said, "I can manage fine."

"You're limping, Diana," Boone replied, as he cradled her arm. "Support is a wonderful thing to have in life, wouldn't you agree? The problem is, most people don't acknowledge that they need it when they need it the most."

Stunned, Diana nodded vacantly, not really knowing how to respond. She allowed her gaze to switch from Boone's tanned, rough face, to his long pepper hair, pulled back in a ponytail, now adorned with dead leaves and pine needles. From the time she was young, Dan Boone had been an enigma around Fairy Falls. Some people thought he was nothing more than a bum. Others thought more on the lines of a tree-hugging trouble maker. Yet her mother always thought of Boone as a worthy opponent, and a type of respect had bloomed from their odd, often volatile, relationship. Then there were those residents of Fairy Falls who revered Boone because he pushed people to work with nature, not against it. To protect the environment, no matter what. Through her mother's eyes, Diana saw what she had seen, and a sense of enlightenment washed over her. Boone wasn't the enemy. He had never been the enemy. The only enemy in Fairy Falls was intolerance.

Diana followed her sister into the garage. Her nose flared. The air was thick with the scent of old oil and stale gas. Nancy opened the side door of the mud splattered RV and walked in. Diana swore she heard a dog whine. She stopped and looked Boone in the eye. "Where's Hart?"

"You'll see," he said, pushing her along the dusty cement floor.

Except for a few garden implements hanging on the wall, the garage was basically bare. A lone work table guarded the back wall, its top dusty and adorned with grease spots. As Boone escorted Diana to the camper, she bit her bottom lip apprehensively and opened the door.

Two big paws were planted on Diana's shoulders before she had time to think. A wet, sloppy pink tongue licked her chin and she winced, stumbling back. "Okay, okay, down, Skoka, good boy."

With all the strength she could muster, Diana pushed Skoka off and glanced around the small quarters. Her mouth dropped as soon as she saw Hart seated at the bench table, safe and sound. Next to him sat Nancy. Diana's eyes narrowed. Hart had what looked like a gold watch pressed against his forehead. It was something he did when he went into one of his psychometric trances, like he had done with the gun. His eyes were rolled back, his neck muscles twitched, and he appeared not to be here, but somewhere else. Another place. Another time.

Then, Diana caught sight of someone familiar sitting across from Hart and Nancy. Her skin tingled. A man with bushy dark hair. His shoulders were broad, stocky, and well-muscled, as if he could lift a small car off the road with no problem at all. Since his back was toward her, she couldn't see his face, but would bet her first born child that he had a beard. Slowly, Diana took a step back, then another, until she was halted by Boone's hulking form.

She swallowed hard. "Nance? What's going on?"

Skoka whined, then barked. Without thinking, Diana stroked his big, solid head, as if pacifying herself more than him. Nancy grinned, then pointed toward the big man seated across from her and said, "Di, this is Guy Royer. He's an undercover detective with the Ontario Provincial Police."

Diana stiffened. *An undercover detective? What the hell?* Guy Royer turned sideways in his seat, his bearded face set in a grin, like a Cheshire cat on steroids. Bright denim-coloured eyes twinkled back at her in the most ominous way. Wearing a red and black lumberjack shirt, black jeans, and work boots the size of Noah's Ark, he extended his huge hand toward her. "Pleased to finally meet you, Diana. Nancy's told me so much about you."

Diana blinked. "Please tell me you're not going to stop there. Please tell me why Nancy was taken from her room last night and how Mr. Boone is involved in all this. Please explain why we saw a detailed map of Blueberry Lake in this very camper. Oh, and while you're at it, please also explain why we found grotesque morgue photos of my mom, Hart's mom and great uncle, and Mr. Avery on your laptop, as well as photos of Hart and his great-aunt." She stopped, took a deep breath, then reached for her inhaler and took a quick puff. "Well?"

Guy's grin dropped. He glanced Nancy. "You're right. She is bossy."

Diana scowled at Nancy and then glared at Guy Royer. He nodded and said, "The answer to all your questions is quite simple. Blackflies and blueberries."

Diana inclined her head. "Huh?"

Boone chuckled. "Guy has always been one for using weird analogies. Has done ever since we were kids growing up in the wilds of northern Ontario."

Diana's eyes widened. "You two know each other?"

"For almost forty years," Royer said, smiling. "And what Dan means is that 'blackflies and blueberries', the name of the files you discovered on my computer, keeps things in perspective for me. The photos in them remind me that life is precious, as well as a process. One thing leads to another. Without blackflies to pollinate blueberry bushes, there can be no blooms, no fruit. In other words, we have to put up with a little grief, even down right misery, if we want to experience the good stuff, the eventual harvest. And for me, that means saving lives, before they end up on a morgue slab."

"Actually, the debate is out on whether blackflies pollinate blueberries or not, Guy. I've heard that it's just an old wives' tale," Dan added with a mischievous grin. "Bees are more likely the chief pollinators."

"Well, I'm not alone in that old belief," Guy replied, shrugging. "All I know is when there's a bumper crop of blackflies, there's a bumper crop of blueberries."

Diana shook her head. "I'm still not following—"

Royer put up his large, calloused hand. "First things first. When you broke into my RV, your sister was kind enough to leave me a calling card—her mini crime scene kit. The address on it told me where to find you, and who I was dealing with."

"And FYI, big sis, I wasn't kidnapped. I volunteered my services," Nancy blurted proudly. "Once he flashed me his badge, I knew I could help him with his investigation."

Royer rolled his eyes. "Yes. Your sister was very persistent."

Diana snorted. "The word is pushy."

Royer laughed. "You could call it that, but Nancy also has the makings of a great criminalist. She thinks outside of the box, instead of in it. That's rare for someone her age."

"Rare?" Diana inclined her head. "How so?"

"When I went through her crime kit I found some flash drives hidden under the lid. Being a detective, I was inclined to snoop. On those drives, I discovered some intriguing theories she'd come up with regarding your mother's case. Assumptions that led elsewhere. And do you know where the finger pointed?"

Diana snorted. "That's easy. Pleasant Point Corporation."

Boone grunted. "I wished it had been that easy. That's why I got Guy involved in this after Pete Ellis' death. At first, I wanted him to try and track down Catherine Stewart, but when he found out that she had been murdered on the same day and in the same way as your mother, it was too much of a coincidence. The Pleasant Point Corporation wouldn't have come into the picture if there wasn't anyone dangling a worm on the hook."

Diana turned to look up at Boone. "How do you mean?"

Boone pursed his lips. "As you know, I was one of the prime suspects, being the last person to see your mother alive. On the night she was murdered, I saw her car parked behind your father's office building and barged in on her. As I recall, we ended up getting into an argument about some damn trail system. No one else was there at the time."

Diana puffed her cheeks. "Yes. Then you left and Gertie Ellis gave you a lift, as well as a perfect alibi. So?"

"So Pleasant Point Corporation may be the whale, but there's still a shark out there," Guy Royer spoke up. "Since forensics proved the time of her death occurred after Dan left, then someone else must have paid her a visit later that night. And as you well know, only a handful of people possess a key to get in."

"And—" Boone cut in, "I know for sure that your mother locked herself in after I left. In fact, she slammed the damn door on me. I heard it click after that."

Diana shrugged. "The murderer could have broken in through a window or the back door."

"But there was no evidence to support that, Di," Nancy blurted. "No forced entry, no unlocked windows or doors, and no fresh fingerprints or footprints."

Diana swallowed hard. She didn't like where this was heading. "Are you saying that—"

"That all the dots connect to someone associated with your father's law firm," Royer broke in. "Pete Ellis and Archie Avery were clients. So is Gertie Ellis. Hart's mother, Catherine, was the only known relative of the Ellises, so therefore would stand to inherit their property once they died off. Now there's Hart, and you know what almost happened to him. Think about it. If no one was left to stand in the way, then that would leave the path clear for Pleasant Point to put down roots here."

Diana's head throbbed from the information overload. "This is insane! Who connected with my dad's firm would engineer such a heinous plan?"

Guy sighed. "We don't know yet. That's why Nancy suggested we ask Hart to intuit a watch I found lodged between two boulders near where Archie Avery landed. It's busted, but if Hart can get any hidden information from it that would help nail the killer, then I'm all in for this mumbo-jumbo psychic stuff."

Diana's stomach rolled. She knew Hart could see the truth and bring it back with him. He had done it through her mother's ring. She also knew what Royer was insinuating. So, like a lawyer's daughter, it was time for her to cross-examine. "Surely you're not thinking my father had anything to do with this?"

Guy shrugged. "Maybe. After all, he's the mayor. He'd have a lot to gain."

Diana balled her fists tight. "I won't listen to this crap! Do you hear me!"

Hart moaned. Sweat blistered across his face, and then all his facial muscles jerked in unison, as if something was wrong. Terribly wrong. Hart let out a death-rattle gasp and opened his eyes, as if he had discovered some hideous monster hiding under the bed. Shaking, he dropped the watch, then jumped up and over the bench seat. He lunged for the passenger door.

"Hart!" Diana shouted after him.

"What is it, Hart?" Guy Royer asked, standing.

"Aunt Gertie! She's in danger! Real danger!" Hart sputtered in a tone filled with terror as he shoved open the door. "T-the killer—"

"What about the killer?" Diana yelled, cutting in.

Hart turned, his face drained of all colour. "I know who it is."

21. Loose Ends

A sharp maple branch whipped across Hart's forehead, but he ignored the stinging pain. He also ignored the screams and shouts coming from behind him. There was no time to explain the details. He had to get to his great-aunt before anything happened to her. Before it was too late.

Rounding a cluster of leaning boulders, Hart's lungs were ready to explode. His mind, however, was in slow motion, going over and over what he had witnessed through the memory vibrations of the gold watch. Now everything made sense to him. Now everything was clear.

Ducking under a low-lying cedar branch, Hart busted through a line of reed-thin saplings no taller than himself, feeling like he was in the middle of a crippling jungle and running toward a wild, dark force he couldn't comprehend, but knew he had to face.

Bursts of vivid images overrode his senses, and played out for Hart again. *Archie Avery standing on his deck. He held a hammer, jimmying the rail with it. He was talking to someone behind him. Someone out of sight. Coffee was offered after he finished fixing the rail. Avery was facing the lake, still working on the rail. He was a proud man. He loved his place. He rambled on about things. The weather. The tourists. The bugs. Then, he felt it. Hart felt it. The push. A sudden jolt to his back. The sharp pain rippled across his chest as he broke through the rail. He was propelled forward and as he fell, he twisted around to capture the face of...*

Hart skidded to stop. Wrapping his arms around a bulging birch to catch himself from falling, he regained his balance, his mouth open, his breathing hard. He took a deep breath. *Good. No one in sight. I got back in time.* Pushing away from the tree, Hart hurried toward the deck where he had left Aunt Gertie. His legs, now scratched and bleeding, stung with each step he took as he got closer to the tri-domed structure. Without warning, a sharp knife appeared in his way and pressed against Hart's throat. An accompanying hand roughly grasped the back of his neck.

"Don't move, or I'll show you the right way to gut a fish, city boy," the man hissed in his ear.

Hart stiffened. "W-what do you want?"

A vicious shove to Hart's back with an elbow was all he got for an answer. With the knife's razor-sharp blade planted underneath his throat, Hart, clenching his teeth at the cutting pain, was led toward the front of Diana's car. A sensation like that of a rubber band snapping across his skin made Hart wince, and he looked down. Trickles of blood rolled down the hollow of his neck and dotted the top of his damp, orange T-shirt like a grotesque mosaic. An intense heat flushed through Hart's body.

He dug his heels in the fresh earth. "You're hurting me!"

Hart was thrown against the car's dark, green hood. It shuddered and rocked at the force. He looked up in time to catch a reflection in the tinted windshield. His torturer was wearing a ski mask, gloves, and one-piece dark overalls; the kind a mechanic would wear. The jagged blade was shoved against Hart's throat again. Shaking, Hart closed his eyes, not wanting to witness what was about to happen.

"This is nothing compared to what's waiting for you!" His captor snickered. "Now, where is she?"

Hart snapped open his eyes. "W-who?"

A nasty nudge shot through his back. "Diana MacGregor!"

Hart had to think fast. "Um, s-she's depressed. About her sister's kidnapping last night. She took a walk out in the bush. A long walk. Said she'll be hours," he lied, stammering over his tongue.

Hart received another blow to his back. "For your sake, you'd better be telling the truth!"

He heard a click. "Drop the knife, put your hands above your head, and fall to your knees! Now!"

Hart turned his head slightly to the right and spied Guy Royer, poised and ready, with a revolver in his hands. Relief flooded his entire being. Managing a meagre smile, Hart tried to push away, but he was held firmly, the knife making its point clear once again.

The cracking sound of a gun going off startled Hart. A bullet whizzed by him and hit Royer's right thigh. He grunted, going down, but that was it. No cry of pain, no swearing. A stream of blood spurted out of Guy's thigh at a phenomenal rate, and he clutched it with his free hand to apply pressure. His face contorted in pain and his breathing became heavier, but he remained in control of his emotions, despite what had just happened.

The roar of an engine accompanied by spinning tires and crunching gravel grabbed Hart's attention. He looked up in time to catch a familiar vehicle racing up the driveway, heading directly for Guy. Within ten feet of the fallen detective, the black Ford Bronco lurched to an abrupt stop, its engine sputtering as if it were a nest of angry, wet wasps. Then it died.

At first, Hart heard whinnied laughter coming from the Bronco's cab before the driver kicked open the door and stepped out. Hart's jaw dropped. *That guy could be Guy Royer's twin brother! Bushy black hair. Dark beard. Tall and stocky. What's going on?* Then it dawned on him. This was the same maniac driver who ran him off the road and left him for dead. Hart swallowed hard. *He's back to finish the job.* The Royer look-alike strode over to where Guy lay and pointed a revolver at his head. Hart heard it click again.

"Throw your weapon under the truck. Do it now!" he commanded.

Nodding, Guy obeyed his mirror image hovering over him. With a grunt he whipped his gun toward the truck, managing to lodge it underneath the front tire.

Hart's tormenter laughed, then grabbed a fistful of his tawny hair and viciously yanked on it, making Hart stumble away from the car's hood. The knife, however, stayed where it was. Skoka emerged from the bushes, growling with teeth bared and drool hanging from his mouth.

Hart's eyes widened, as the Royer look-alike quickly changed his sights from Guy to Skoka. "Nooo!" he cried.

Hart was shoved. "You best tell the mutt to sit—" the man imprisoning Hart spat "—or there'll be one less thing to feed around here."

"Skoka, sit! Sit!" Hart yelled as best he could, the knife's blade twisting into his skin, but Skoka continued to growl.

A hand emerged out of the bush in time to grab Skoka's collar. With the other hand up in the air, Boone appeared out of the cedars. "Don't shoot, I've got him."

"Stay where you are, or I finish what I started!" Royer's evil twin yelled, moving the revolver back to Guy's head.

Boone nodded. Hart could see the fear in his eyes. Fear for his friend who was slowly weakening from so much blood loss. A red puddle had formed next to Guy's leg, and he was shaking now, as if in shock. Hart clenched his teeth. Something had to be done or Guy would surely die. "Look, jackass, he's a cop! If he dies, then you'll both be cop killers! Hunted forever! On the 'Most Wanted' list! Tracked until your last breath! Do you really want that?"

The man laughed, causing the knife to jig up and down in Hart's throat. "City boy's got a point. You," he motioned towards Boone, "tie up that beast and take care of this bloody mess!"

Boone spared no time. He pulled out a piece of rope from his buckskin pocket, tied Skoka to the nearest tree, then removed a woven belt from his tan pants, knelt down, and wrapped it around Guy's bloodied thigh. He pulled tight. Guy let out a pained, guttural moan, his face now ashen and his hands dug into the earth for support. Skoka whined and then barked, with his tail furiously banging against the tree.

Cruel laughter erupted behind Hart. "Good, now get him up and walk toward the bunkie behind me." Hart's captor motioned to his pistol-waving sidekick. "Lock them in there. Make sure they can't get out. Any problems, just shoot them. Got that?"

The Royer look-alike answered with a grunt and probed at Dan to move faster.

Guy groaned. Dan pulled the belt tighter, his hands now covered with blood. "Damn it, he needs medical attention! He'll die without it!"

A shot rang out, missing Boone by inches, but he didn't recoil. He stayed focused and alert by Royer's side. The sidekick laughed. "Then you'd best press harder while you're walking. Now move!"

Dan lifted Guy, supporting him as best he could, and continued to apply pressure to Guy's wound. Taking most of the weight, Dan hobbled toward the bunkie, while the bearded henchman followed close behind, his revolver cocked and ready.

"Now, about that 'jackass' crack," the man said as he twisted the knife closer to Hart's throat.

Hart's body tensed. He'd had enough of the constant digging into his skin. Reaching up with both his hands, he grabbed onto the psycho's wrists to prevent any more bloodshed. His fingers grazed a chunky, cool object protruding underneath a sleeve, and he snatched a peek out of the corner of his eye. His eyes widened. *Sweet! A gold bracelet!* Closing his eyes, Hart allowed his fingers to do the talking. It wouldn't have the same effect as placing it on his forehead, but it was worth a try. The visions appeared.

Hart's former apartment. His old bedroom, the bed unmade, clothes on the floor. His mother standing in the doorway. She was searching for something. She didn't see the shadow looming behind her. He attacked her. Went for the throat. Her breathing thinned. She fought. It was no use. She looked across the room, into the full-length mirror, and saw her attacker. He was wearing a ski mask and staring at her. His mother's eyes connected with a pair of penetrating stone grey eyes. She made contact with the bracelet. Her eyes bulged. She knew him. Hart's jaw dropped. So did he.

Hart's eyes flew open. "S-Sid Molnar?"

He applied further pressure to Hart's throat, but Hart still had a good grip on the lawyer's wrists. "Y-y-you bastard! You're the one who murdered my mother! And I know you killed Avery! I saw it with my own eyes!"

"What do you mean you saw it?" Sid kneed Hart, hard. "Answer me!"

Hart ground his teeth and said, "I have these powers. Psychic powers. I can see things, people, events through the impressions left on any object. An object like your bracelet, for example."

"So—" Sid turned Hart's head slightly and yanked off his ski mask with one hand "—you are a lot like your mother. Pity she had to go."

Hart's throat tightened. "But…but why? What did she ever do to you?"

Sid snickered, still holding firm. "Stood in my way with making a sweet coup with Pleasant Point, that's what. I approached the development company over a year ago with a simple strategy. Pleasant Point would get first dibs on any land my clients were thinking of selling, and I, in turn, would receive fifteen percent of the sales, plus shares in the new resort."

"Selling!" Hart screamed under the pressure of the blade. "Mr. Avery loved his place too much to sell, and Aunt Gertie would never think of leaving!"

Sid dropped the ski mask and laughed brutally. "True. That's when plan 'B' came into play. If no one would willingly sell, then certain measures would need to be taken. Like getting rid of bloodlines and obstacles. Catherine Stewart was the only known link to feeble Gertie Ellis, who couldn't possibly manage this property on her own after her husband's demise, forcing her to sell. So Pete Ellis had to go. Trust me, it doesn't take a mechanical genius to booby-trap a log splitter. And senile Archie Avery, who never married or had children, was just another accident waiting to happen. Everything was planned out, set in motion. Everything to the tiniest detail. Except. For. *You*." He hissed in Hart's ear. "You should have stayed in the city where you belonged. Lost and forgotten."

Hart hoped that Nancy and Diana were hightailing it to the closest neighbour to use their phone. Of course that would constitute a lot of hightailing, seeing as the nearest person lived fifteen minutes away. Then something occurred to him. *Obstacles. Sid also mentioned obstacles.* Hart's mouth opened, and before he knew it, he blurted what he was thinking. "Development. Scam. Traitor. Now I get it."

Sid jerked. "Get what?"

"Joy MacGregor's last words. I get them. She was on to you, wasn't she?"

Sid's hot, heavy breath crawled across Hart's gritty neck. Sid cleared his throat, sounding scratchy, bitter, like steel wool rubbing against pearls. He snorted and said, "It was most unfortunate, Joy finding my development plans with Pleasant Point. In fact, I had just returned from my surprise visit with your mother when I caught her in the act. The thing is, if I hadn't forgotten that parcel on my desk, she'd still be alive today. Stupid, interfering, bitch," Sid spat. "I patiently waited behind a desk in the corner and watched her thumb through the plans. I heard the odd swear word and a couple of gasps, before she tucked my future under her arm, turned out the lights, and left. Unfortunately, she had underestimated me. I'd put too much time and money into this venture for someone to spoil it. So I went after her. Oh, I took precautions. Seeing as there was a full moon, I covered my face and moved the surveillance camera away from the parking lot. It was perfect. No complications. No witnesses."

"There's where you're wrong, slimeball," Hart blurted. "I was there. Diana's mother's ring showed me everything. I saw what you did. I heard what she said. I saw the struggle. I witnessed the murder. Then I watched you stuff her limp body into her car and drive off!"

Sid pressed the knife harder. "Like I said, city-boy, no complications, no witnesses."

Hart winced, still holding Sid's wrists tight. "What do you mean?"

"It means you and your great-aunt are going for a little ride as soon as my partner returns. Then I can finally take care of a couple of loose ends."

Hart wiggled like a worm on a hook. "No! Leave Aunt Gertie alone!" Then, seeing his chance, Hart kicked at Molnar's shin as hard as he could.

Sid yelped and released the hold he had on the knife. Hart elbowed him in the gut, twisted, and kicked the knife toward a string of thick bushes edging the driveway. Now it was just Sid and him, and Hart doubted very much that this sleazy, murdering lawyer had ever had it out on the street before.

"Move away from him, Hart! He's mine!"

Hart jerked. He twisted to his right, and there, wielding the hunting knife that had once been jammed against his throat, was Diana. She lunged for Sid, but he jumped back, stumbled, and fell to the ground.

Diana's eyes were glazed and locked on Sid. "Bastard! Murderer! I heard everything! You came to her funeral! You carried her casket!"

Sid put a hand out, his feet kicking wildly at the ground. "Wait! Stop, Diana, let me explain!"

"Explain? Explain murdering my mother because she was doing the right thing? Not even you are a good enough lawyer for that!"

"Diana! No!" Hart yelled. "Let the cops deal with him!"

"I normally would, Hart, but unfortunately—" Diana advanced closer to Sid "—we don't have the death penalty in Canada!"

She took a swipe, catching Sid's ankle. He howled and rolled back toward her Chevelle, as a thin line of blood drizzled across the earth. Now holding the knife above her head, Diana, only three feet from Molnar, set her jaw firmly and took another step closer.

"One more step and the old bat gets it!"

Hart turned. His eyes widened. Sid's sidekick, the Royer look-alike, was holding a gun to Aunt Gertie's head. The mosquito netting had been removed and thick piece of duct tape covered her mouth. She was a little wonky on her feet, but other than that, his tougher-than-nails great-aunt showed no other ill-effects. Skoka barked furiously, snarling and drooling, the rope holding him pulled taut, as far as it would go.

Diana froze. "G-Guy?"

"It's not Guy, Diana. Just a slimy double," Hart said. "He's the one who ran me off the road."

Sid snickered while he stood, using the side of the car for support. He limped over to Diana, grabbed her wrist, and gave it a vicious twist, forcing her to release the knife. It dropped with a heavy thud and he kicked it underneath the Chevelle.

"Oww!" she squealed, trying to kick Sid, to fight back. Diana clutched her chest and started to cough and wheeze. Hart bit his bottom lip. *Damn. This isn't a good time for an asthma attack.* Sid threw her to the ground and laughed wickedly.

"Seems like all the females in the MacGregor family are weak," he said, cruelly.

Hart heard a tinny whump, like something metallic had connected with a hard object. Out of the corner of his eye, he saw Sid's greasy sidekick's gun sail across the driveway and land under a clump of blueberry bushes before he stumbled to the ground face-first.

"Now what were you saying about us MacGregor girls, Molnar?" Nancy asked, smirking.

Hart smiled. Nancy's hands strangled the long handle of the shovel she had used to bring Sid's slimy accomplice down. Tossing the shovel aside, Nancy wasted no time flipping the unconscious Royer look-alike over. She reached for a handful of bushy, black hair and yanked on it hard. A cascade of long raven hair fell out. Then Nancy grasped underneath the chin and pulled up, as if it were a ripcord. The thick, rubbery piece of flesh snapped away, beard and all, to reveal Hart's would-be murderer.

"Vonnie Shipton?" Hart uttered, not believing who he was seeing.

"The one and only," Nancy said. "I figured it out when I saw the truck and put everything together. She's the only one who could pull off this kind of transformation and get away with it. After all, an ex-Hollywood make-up artist can make anyone appear to be who they want. Like a stocky drifter she knew was only going to be in town for a season, for example. Someone she could blame for her crimes who seemed sketchy already. See, even her overalls are designed to change her build from a woman's to a man's." Nancy unzipped the overalls to reveal styrofoam padding in her shoulders and chest area to bulk up her appearance. "Genius. Pure genius."

"But why would she be involved in this?" Hart asked.

Click. Hart tensed, feeling a gun's muzzle in the back of his head. He took a slow, steady breath. While Nancy had played hero, Sid had managed to dislodge the gun from under the Bronco's tire. *Great. Is anything gonna go my way?* Sid snickered, and adjusted his weight to one side, taking Hart with him.

"Let's just say Shipton wanted a piece of the action too," Sid said, slowly dragging Hart toward the truck. "And being her lawyer, I was fully aware of her financial woes, and knew her small-town establishment could never compete with Pleasant Point's upscale bar. So, like a good friend, I offered her a better, far more lucrative deal. All she had to do was provide me with her skills, and I, in turn, would provide mine. It was a perfect partnership. She would have owned a percentage of the resort's dance club, plus manage it. With all her Hollywood connections, it would have been a win-win move."

"And now it's all lose-lose for the both of you," Hart added, his teeth clenching as the gun's barrel dug in.

Sid laughed. "More like lose-win. Shipton loses. I win."

Hart stopped. "How do you mean?"

"I mean Shipton is left empty-handed, I'm not. I already took the down-payment and my lawyer's fees from Pleasant Point." Then he snorted. "Poor bastards. They still think the deal is going to go through. By this time tomorrow, I'll be in a warm, safe place, and no one will find me. Your life will guarantee that. Now, get in the truck, city boy!" Sid shoved Hart into the driver's side door.

Click. Twang! Crash!

Hart balked. With the gun still buried in the back of his head, he twisted toward the source. There, from ground level, Diana, still wheezing, held a smoking revolver at arm's length. In her other hand, she clenched her inhaler. Hart swallowed hard. She had scored Vonnie Shipton's gun from under the bushes. A bullet hole through the truck's windshield attested to Diana's ballistic skills. She cocked the gun again and took aim. This time, at Sid's head.

With a free hand, Diana took a puff from her inhaler, until her breathing steadied. Then, she licked her lips slowly, and glared at Sid. "The next one's for my mom, dirt-bag."

22. Ringing True

Sirens exploded in the distance. Diana narrowed her thin, red brows as her finger remained steady on the trigger. *Good. Brook got my message.* Her nose wrinkled. Unfortunately, she knew that noise carried through the forest. They were close, but not close enough. Sid still had the upper hand with Hart as a hostage. Yet she had one thing going that Sid didn't. She was a much better shot.

"Put the gun down, Diana, or I'll blow your boyfriend's head off!" Sid jabbed the muzzle into the back of Hart's skull.

A half-smile crept up at the corner of her mouth. Sid wouldn't waste his only ace. It wasn't in his nature, and she wasn't that stupid. "He's not my boyfriend."

Sid jerked. So did Hart. *Good. I have him where I want.* The sirens were getting closer. It was only a matter of time. *All I have to do is claim self-defence.* She silently gave thanks for Donovan's backwoods BB gun sessions during the last few summers. His lessons proved invaluable and her aim true. Now all Diana would have to do was bait Molnar. Taunt him. Get him riled up enough to turn the gun on her. But first, she needed to get rid of a couple of witnesses.

She licked her lips again and said, "Nance, take care of Mrs. Ellis. Put her in a chair on the deck, then run to the bottom of the driveway and flag the police here. I told Brook I was at Avery's, so they might go there first. Hurry."

"But, Di—"

"Do it!" Diana commanded.

"Nancy, Dan and Guy are in the bunkie," Hart broke in. "Guy's been shot. He's bleeding bad. He needs attention or he'll die!"

"Shut up!" Sid spewed, nudging Hart into the driver's door.

Twang! Pop! Fizzsh!

The shot from Diana's revolver exploded the tire on impact, making Sid jump back and away from Hart. Diana smiled. *Coward. All that's missing is the yellow streak down your back.* "Go, Nance," she said through clenched teeth.

The urgent pounding of feet against the earth told Diana that Nancy had obeyed her. The deck steps creaked, and the sound of a chair scraping across wood confirmed that Mrs. Ellis was safe, and Nancy was out of the way. *Good. Now it's just Sid and me. Hart will have to understand. After all, that sleazebag lawyer killed his mother too.* Slowly, Diana tucked away her inhaler and stood up. With her sights on Sid and her manner sure, she cocked the gun once more.

Sid laughed. "You don't have the guts."

Diana arched a brow. "Neither will you in a minute. They'll be soaking up the dirt."

"Diana, don't." Hart pleaded. "He's not worth it."

"Listen to him, Diana," Sid said, pulling Hart in front of him to create a human shield. "I wouldn't want your bad judgement to be blamed for Hart's death."

The sirens were getting louder and louder. The police were almost there. Sid led Hart around the back of the truck and down the other side, toward her car. She followed him with the revolver's barrel every step he took. Then Sid opened the Chevelle's driver's door. Her eyes widened. *Does he honestly think he's going to take my car?* Diana narrowed her brows. *Not a chance.*

"What the hell do you think you're doing, Molnar?"

"Taking your car. I highly doubt you'll be shooting up this vehicle." He gave Hart's head a nasty nudge with his gun. "Get in!"

Hart grunted. "Not until you tell Diana the truth."

Sid narrowed his dark brows. "What truth?"

"The truth about her mother's ring."

"My mother's ring? What are you talking about, Hart?" Diana asked, frowning.

"It never was meant for your mother, Diana. It was meant for someone else. Isn't that right, Sid?"

"Shut up! Shut up! Shut up!" Sid pushed the gun into Hart's back.

Diana blinked. She peered at her right hand, where her middle finger proudly displayed the glittering piece of jewelry. She licked her dry lips. As far as she knew the ring had been a gift from her father to her mother on their first wedding anniversary. *What's Hart getting at?* Still aiming the gun at Molnar, she glanced at Hart. "Then who was it meant for?"

Hart took a sharp, deep breath. "My mother."

"What?" Diana blurted, not sure she heard him correctly.

"Shut up and get in the car!" Sid raged.

"Tell her! Tell her you sold the ring to her father after my mother rejected you. I know it's the truth. Everything came together for me as soon as I touched your gold bracelet. A flash of my mother's memories surged through me. I saw a brief glimpse of the ring. It connects you to her. It connects you to Diana's mother. Mom put the truth in your bracelet for me to find. She knew about my psychic gift all along, but never said anything. She knew of your intentions. She couldn't save herself, but she knew she could save me. Tell Diana killing my mother wasn't just business! Tell her it was personal!" Hart screamed, his arms now splayed over the car's green roof like the wings of fallen hawk.

The grating noise of tires braking across gravel made Diana look up. Red and white spinning lights forced her eyes to narrow. The black and white police cruiser was followed closely by another, both blocking the end of the driveway. The back door on the first car flung open and out bolted her father, still wearing the same tan shirt and taupe pants from yesterday, now wrinkled and soaked with sweat. Even from this distance, Diana could see that his face was red. He came charging up the driveway like a raging bull out for blood. Nancy emerged from the back of the same police car. Constable Boyd managed to grab Nancy's arm before she could follow her father. She pushed Nancy behind her and drew out her revolver.

"Dad, wait! They've got guns!" Nancy shouted from behind Boyd.

He skidded to a halt and put up his hands. "Let the kids go, Sid. It's finished."

"Tell your daughter to drop her weapon, then we'll talk," Sid demanded.

Her dad nodded. "Diana, do what Sid says!"

Diana's brows narrowed. She allowed her gaze to drop from her father to the diamond and ruby ring on her right middle finger. "This ring—" she flashed it to her father, "—did you get it from *him*?" She gestured toward Sid Molnar, using the revolver as a pointer.

Her father jerked. Diana swallowed hard. *Body language is so telling.*

"Yes, but what's that got to do with any of this?" he asked in a broken voice.

Diana's throat ached. She could tell he was scared. A trait he never showed very often, if at all.

Diana didn't bother answering her father. She had just wanted confirmation, and she got it. To her, it had everything to do with the ring. *Love. Passion. Greed. Rage. Murder.* Hart's mother's love was something Sid couldn't have, or even buy. Diana adjusted her perception, and like a veil uncovering a masterpiece, she saw the true picture. She glanced at her mother's ring and grazed it gently with the tip of her thumb. *How could you have gotten so lost, Sid? You not only sold this ring, but you sold your soul as well.* Diana raised her chin. *And that's something I will never, ever do.*

A sharp intake of air shot into Diana's lungs and she exhaled. It felt fresh, and clear, and rejuvenating. And it was the first time in a long time her lungs didn't feel restricted. Guy's words returned to ring in her ears. *Life is a process.* Just like the blackflies. Just like the blueberries. She had to learn to flow with life, and not against it. Diana smiled. For her, it was over. She tossed the gun aside and said, "Hart's right. You're not worth it, Molnar."

A voice boomed over a speaker, "Drop the weapon, Molnar! Put your hands up and get on your knees. You're surrounded."

Sid's face tightened and his flushed skin stretched into a snarl. "Not worth it!" He pushed Hart aside and aimed the gun at Diana. "Why you interfering, pompous bitch!"

Before Sid had a chance to pull the trigger, two things happened. Out of the corner of her eye, Diana caught the sun's reflection bounce off a knife's blade and shine in her eyes. She blinked as Hart tackled her to the ground and covered her body with his. Over

Hart's shoulder, Diana saw Boone rise from behind the side of her car and throw the knife she'd once threatened Molnar with to strike him in his neck. A guttural squeal accompanied by a ringing gunshot echoed through her as Sid's body jerked and crumpled to the ground like a broken puppet, cut from its strings.

"Got him! We're clear!" Diana heard Constable Boyd yell.

Hart's heavy breathing brought her back. "A-are you okay?"

Diana nodded. She was too numb to do anything else.

"Good." Hart lifted his head and looked into her eyes. "I'd hate to see anything bad happen to my favourite tutor," he whispered, before kissing her gently on the lips.

"Diana!" she heard her father yell.

Startled, Hart broke their kiss. Diana smiled and stroked his cheek, feeling the soft bristles against her palm. Her heartbeat steadied, and her whole body relaxed.

"She's all right," Boone called out from the side of the car. Diana craned her neck and looked up at Boone. He winked at her. "Hart's got everything covered, MacGregor."

Footsteps beat a path toward them. The impending, shrill sound of an ambulance roared up the driveway, and Diana knew she didn't have much time to say what she wanted to Hart. So instead, she wrapped her arms around him and hugged his lean, warm body. Her nostrils flared with abundance. Heavy pine. Sweet cedar. Fresh earth. That was all Diana could smell. *Fairy Falls,* she thought. The deep, pure scent of this land was embedded in Hart. Her stomach fluttered. Whether he knew it or not, Hart belonged here. He had become one with this place, as well as with her heart.

23. Blueberries

Hart wiped the rolling sweat from the back of his gritty neck, pushed his faded baseball cap off of his forehead, and pulled at his navy cotton T-shirt. The heat of early August had produced a bumper crop of blueberries this year, and his lower back ached from the last couple of weeks of picking the sweet fruit. He surveyed the area while wiping his hands across his black shorts. The vendor next to their booth yelled at some passersby to get their attention. Hart grinned. Fairy Falls' Thursday morning Farmers' Market seemed like a circus without any clowns, except for one vendor wearing a red, fuzzy wig and rainbow suspenders.

Hart reached for a plump blueberry and tossed it into his mouth. It popped, the juice dripping down his parched throat like a welcoming summer shower. Something hard poked him in the butt and Hart turned to look down. The familiar cane prodded him again.

"Y'ur eat'n our profits, Hart! Git back ta selling!" Aunt Gertie commanded, as if she were a five-star general in a foxhole. Skoka lifted his head and barked, acting like her next in command, then yawned and put his big, yellow head back down over his folded paws, sighing with contentment.

Hart rolled his eyes and saluted his great-aunt and Skoka. Grabbing two quarts of blueberries, he moved into the growing crowd, beckoning them with the sweet smell of the freshly picked fruit, only offering a sample when he saw the look of a sale in their eyes.

"How much for a pint?"

Hart turned and smiled. Diana flashed him a wad of cash. He narrowed his eyes. *This will be an easy sale.* "For you, five bucks. Or two for eight. Now that's what I call a deal!"

Diana's brows narrowed as if she'd been taken. She stuffed the money into the back pocket of her sapphire shorts and crossed her freckled arms over her plain white top. "And that's what I call a con, considering I helped pick them. I should get a discount."

Hart sighed. No use bartering with her. She'd end up making him pay her for them. So he did what any top-notch salesman would do. He pointed to the booth and said, "I'll let you talk to the manager about that."

Diana giggled, and turned toward the sheltered booth piled with baskets of blueberries on sagging tables and homemade shelves full of maple syrup products. "Which manager?"

Hart laughed. "It doesn't matter. They're both in a cranky mood today."

A fat blueberry splattered across Hart's forehead. Aunt Gertie's thick, sugary laugh accompanied Guy Royer's hearty, loud chuckle. "Bugaboo! Good shot, Guy!"

"Thanks, partner," he drawled, knocking his cane against hers, as if he'd scored the winning goal in a sudden death hockey game.

Blueberry guts dribbled down Hart's face. "Isn't this considered job harassment?" he asked, placing the two baskets on a table to wipe his face.

Diana shrugged. "I don't know, let me ask a lawyer."

Diana whistled in the direction of a stand that sold deli meats and sausages. Mr. MacGregor waved, grabbed his purchases, and started toward them. Nancy was with him, but had decided to hang back long enough to nab more samples being sliced up for the growing crowd. She wiped her hands across the back of her denim capri pants before pulling her pink top out enough to create a small pouch to fill with freebies.

The mayor placed his bags on the ground and nodded at the pair sitting under the protection of the white canvas canopy. "Gertie. Guy. How's business, now that the paperwork on your newly formed partnership has finally gone through?"

Guy smiled, his white teeth more pronounced now that he got rid of his bushy beard. He stood, balancing himself on his left leg, and leaned on his cane. His new business attire consisted of black shorts and a silk-screened navy T-shirt with the white lettering, '*Natural Treasures*'. Aunt Gertie wore one, too. Guy offered the mayor his hand and said, "Great! I never thought that the blueberry and maple syrup business was this good. Imagine, a business that you can sink your teeth into!"

Hart rolled his eyes. At least Guy's disposition had improved. Hart didn't blame him, though. Guy had come close to losing his life. Thanks to Nancy's quick thinking, she'd released Dan and Guy from the bunkie, then scooted out the back to flag down the police. The ambulance had made it in time. Later at the hospital, Hart approached Guy about the disturbing vibrational images he'd picked up on his gun. Hart hadn't been prepared for his reaction. All Guy did was laugh, then told him to press any police revolver to his forehead. He'd probably get the same frightening, emotional reading. After all, it was part of the job. To save a life. To take a life. To serve and protect. It came with a price, no matter what the cost. And in Guy's eyes, his job was well worth it.

"Oh, Guy, before I forget—" Mr. MacGregor said, his muscles quivering under his green golf shirt "—Karen Bean wants you to stop by her office after you're done here. The deal went through on Archie Avery's property, and she's got all the paperwork ready for you to sign your life away. I'd like to be the first to officially welcome you to Fairy Falls."

Diana frowned at the mention of Karen Bean's name. Hart reached for Diana's hand and gave it a reassuring squeeze. She glanced at him sideways and squeezed back harder. Hart cringed at her strength before he leaned closer to whisper, "At least you didn't go totally red and snort fire."

"That's because I've secretly taken out a contract on Ms. Bean," Diana muttered, smirking.

Hart's cheek twitched. "Y-you're kidding, right?"

"Oh, you'll never know," Diana replied, tweaking his crooked nose. "After all, I do know people in high places around Fairy Falls. Plus, Nancy knows how to properly dispose of a body."

"Please remind me to never piss off a redhead," Hart said, planting his lips on her mouth to steal a quick kiss.

Diana giggled and smacked his butt. "Oh, you can count on that!"

"Hey, look who I found," Nancy said, coming up behind them.

Hart turned, catching Dan Boone and Constable Sara Boyd walking up.

Boone wore his trademark buckskin coat, and Constable Boyd was dressed in her uniform blues and Stetson-style hat. In her hands was a large manila envelope. She smiled at Guy and handed him the envelope. "I hoped I would see you here today. Congratulations, Detective Constable Royer, your transfer came through. You're one of us now."

Boone guffawed. "Great! Just when I thought my days of babysitting you were over." He clapped Guy on the back. "Well, take a bow, hero, you deserve it!"

Everyone cheered, except for Nancy. Instead, she let out a long, penetrating whistle. Hart winced, and a sharp beep and squealing brakes made him jump back.

"Now I know why you don't drive, bonehead!" Brook screamed from the back of a brand new candy-apple red scooter, its engine purring until it was cut. "They should take away your skateboard too!"

Donovan puffed out his cheeks and placed his hands on his denim covered thighs. "I should have dumped you back at the produce when I had the chance, Witchy-Poo."

Diana laughed. "Nice ride. Bad form."

Donovan shrugged, yanking down his purple lacrosse jersey. "Oh well, I won't have it long enough to practice with, will I?"

"Why not?" Hart inclined his head toward Donovan. "Didn't you just get it?"

"Nope." Donovan grinned. "You did."

Hart's mouth fell open. Brook giggled, her tight-fitting black tank top barely moved with her tittering. She pointed a finger at him and said, *"Mind the threefold law ye should—three times bad and three times good."*

"Allow me to translate," Donovan said, taking off his shiny black helmet. "What Witchy-Poo means is that whatever you do, good or bad, comes back to you three times. So, you done good, dude!"

"Donovan's right, Hart," Mr. MacGregor cut in, hooking his thumbs into the pockets of his beige cargo shorts. "The scooter, gear, and insurance paid up for a year is our gift to you. For all you've done, not only for me and my family, but for the town of Fairy Falls as well. We can't thank you enough."

Constable Boyd wagged a finger. "Just don't let me catch you bombing around town on it without a license or a helmet."

"Don't worry, Constable Boyd. You have my guarantee that Hart will have his license in no time," Diana said, winking at Hart. "I'll tutor him *personally*."

Hart's ears burned. He winked back and adjusted his faded blue cap. Then something dawned on him, and he took his hat off. Flipping it around, he read the embroidered words. *ALL IS ONE.* His eyes widened, now remembering what his mom had told him about these powerful, sacred words. *Now I understand, Mom, now I get it.* Hart's body tingled. *I'm connected to everyone and everything. To the tastes. The smells. The sounds. The sights. The sensations. To these people. My family.*

Smiling, Hart sifted through a quart of blueberries. Cupping a handful, he paused, feeling the positive vibrations of the fruit radiate through him. For a brief moment, he allowed the blueberries to take him on a journey deep into the bush, to where the lingering buzz of a blackfly teased him, taunted him, until it was time for Hart to return to experience more of his new life.

A life in Fairy Falls.

The End

Acknowledgements

As always, life is a team effort and a cooperative venture. Nothing is done without the help and support of others. The following people are in some way connected to the fabric of Blackflies and Blueberries, to which I am eternally grateful:

Thank you to the owner of Pandamonium Publishing House, Lacey L. Bakker, and her amazing staff, who gave this book a second chance to reach readers world-wide. A special thanks to my former editors, Justine Alley Dowsett and Robert Dowsett, who made sure that this story was in the best possible shape for publication. I've learned never to take people or situations for granted, and I truly appreciate all your support, investment, and creative expertise during our journey together.

Thank you to my mother-in-law Alice 'Toshy' Ledwith, my inspiration for creating 'Gertie Ellis'. I will always love you, and still miss you after all these years. A special thanks to Martin and Lynn Band, who supplied me with the photo of the tri-domed 'Hobbit' house on the cover, and to my first beta reader, Linda Toner Fisher, who offered some wonderful feedback to make this book better. And always, I'm so very grateful and blessed for my hubby Mike, my forever anchor.

A special shout out goes to Christine Hayton and Pamela Goldstein for whipping the tagline and blurb for this book into tip-top shape. Thank you for your expertise and camaraderie in this crazy writing business, ladies. A huge thank you goes out to my Authors Moving Forward group for their ongoing love and support, and especially to our fearless leader, Sloane Taylor who has kept this group going through her tireless passion and endless belief in all of us.

Last but not least, I want to thank all the women and men who volunteer as tutors at their local literacy counsels to help better the lives of others struggling with reading the most basic prose. You make this world a better place to live in through your kindness, generosity, dedication, and love of the written word.

About the Author

Sharon Ledwith is the author of the middle-grade/young adult time travel adventure series,
THE LAST TIMEKEEPERS, and the award-winning teen psychic mystery series, MYSTERIOUS TALES FROM FAIRY FALLS. When not writing, reading, researching, or revising, she enjoys anything arcane, ancient mysteries, and single malt scotch. Sharon lives a serene, yet busy life in a southern tourist region of Ontario, Canada, with her spoiled hubby, and two shiny red e-bikes.

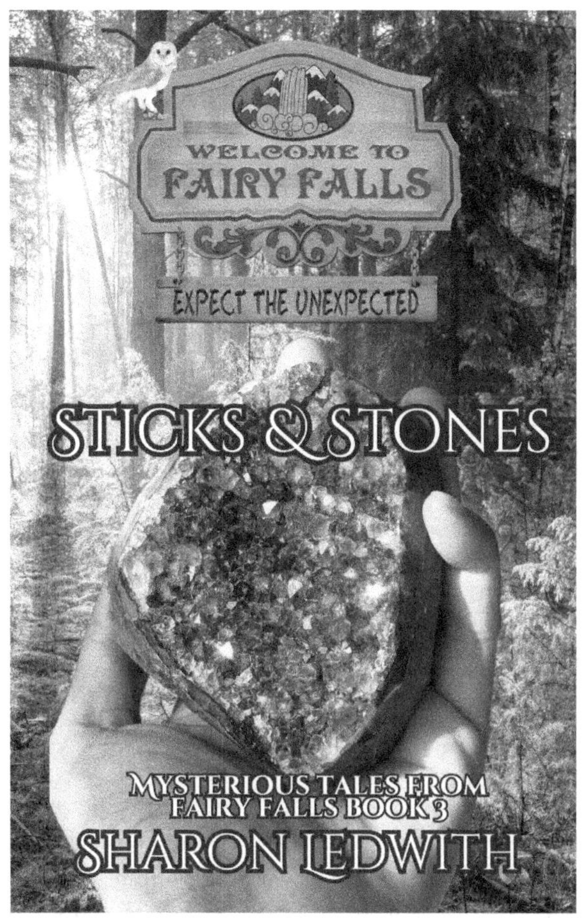

Sticks and Stones

Mysterious Tales from Fairy Falls
Book #3

1. Hard Truth

"This isn't fair! Life sucks!"

"If you think life sucks now, wait until you start shaving."

Thane Berg knitted his fair brows and looked up at his so-called father; a man who had been a stranger to him for so long it was hard to tell whether they were from the same gene pool.

Thane's eyes were light blue. His father's were dark brown. His skin was fair and freckled. His father's was tan and rough. His hair was strawberry and straight. His father's was curly and brown. Thane sighed. Nope. No resemblance, no mirror, no match. In Thane's mind, this man was not even related.

Even Philip Berg's attire couldn't be more opposite. His plumber's overalls—stained with the day's work—clung to Phil like used toilet paper. Thane cringed and tugged at his red and white striped polo-style shirt, hoping Phil had at least washed his hands before preparing tonight's supper. A red pipe wrench lay in the middle of the table, next to the salt and pepper shakers, as if it belonged there. Mom would have had a fit if he'd done that in our home. His nose wrinkled. He looked down at his bowl of mystery meat stew, and mashed what looked like potatoes and peas with his soup spoon, hoping to bring out some flavor.

"I started shaving last year," Thane mumbled.

"Last year?" Phil stifled a laugh. "Didn't you just turn fourteen in June?"

Thane's shoulders hardened. "Yup. Got your birthday card with the annual thirty pieces of silver inside." He stared at the spoon and focused on the swirling patterns etched on its handle.

But it was too late to stop the inner turmoil bubbling to the surface. The thin metal bent with ease, its wide end dipping into the stew. He glared at his father, and spat, "Maybe if you hadn't come out of the closet five years ago, you could have been there to show me how to shave!"

Phil Berg winced as if he'd been stung by a swarm of wasps, and dropped his coffee cup. It shattered across the hardwood floor, sending ceramic bits rolling every-which-way. Witnessing his father's reaction calmed Thane enough to bend the spoon back into its normal shape. He secretly smiled, thinking, *There. Anger management therapy at its best.* He'd been able to bend spoons through the power of his mind, without ever touching them, since his mother and father legally separated, and the world as he knew it, ended. At first, this spoon-bending oddity shocked him, but it also allowed him to channel his pent-up anger in a healthier, more constructive way. So, he chose to keep it under wraps from everyone in his life, even if that meant replacing some of his mother's spoons every few months.

A dog howled from outside the kitchen door, breaking his thoughts.

Phil rubbed his stubbled face. He skirted slowly around the pieces of broken cup, and opened the door. Even from his seat, Thane could see the dog's tail whipping wildly back and forth, back and forth, as if he had downed four energy drinks.

"Come here, Nobel, good boy." Phil reached out to unlatch the dog's rope from his collar, then stroked his big head.

Nobel whined, yipped, and ran straight to his food bowl. He wolfed it down as if it were his last meal.

"I want to go home, Phil," Thane stated, mashing his stew.

"You are home. And I'm Dad to you, not Phil." His voice was hard, unmoving, like he meant it.

Thane slouched. "Fairy Falls isn't my home, it's yours." He straightened. "Windsor is where I belong! If…if mom didn't go on that stupid assignment—"

"Your mother deserves that promotion, and you know it," Phil cut in. "She's a damn good journalist, and when the opportunity to go to Europe came up for her, I advised her to take it. I told her it would give you and I some much needed time together."

"Time together? I'm stuck here for a freaking year because of you! Did you even think of asking me?"

"Since I am your father, and still responsible for you, I didn't see the point."

Then, as Phil knelt down to pick up the fragments of his white mug, a sudden rage ambushed Thane. An electric jolt pierced through his body, and a stab of anger overrode his senses and infected his mind. Startled from this alien feeling, Thane inhaled fiercely, and as he did, he watched a piece of porcelain fly up and puncture Phil's right thumb.

"Oww! Son-of-a—" Phil started to curse, then stopped. Wincing, he dug the shard out and tossed it into the trash bin underneath the sink.

Shaken, Thane reached over and grabbed his can of orange pop. He guzzled it down in one gulp. Did what just happen, actually happen? Did I make that piece of cup move? Thane let out a loud, laborious belch. Hot gas bubbles burst in his nostrils. He cringed.

His father scowled. "Don't you have something to say?"

"I don't see the point."

"I beg your pardon?"

Thane belched again. This one was slightly longer. "There. Excuse me."

Phil chuckled. "I guess you and I are related after all."

Thane's face fell. "Huh?"

Phil took a deep breath, opened his mouth, and released a thunderous burp that lasted almost twenty seconds. He smacked his lips. "Whew! I can taste yesterday's lunch with that one!"

Thane smirked. "Don't you have something to say?"

"How about, 'I've missed you?'" a man blurted behind Thane.

He jumped, and twisted in his seat to find a tall man leaning against the pine door frame. He was bulkier than his father, but just as tanned. His head was clean shaven, and his eyes were a shade of leafy green. He wore a uniform of a sort—a sky blue shirt with a company name stitched on it, and a pair of dark jeans. Thane squinted to read what was embroidered on his shirt. *Cormack's Crappers and Sanitation Service*, he read, and rolled his eyes. *Nice. Classy. Fairy Falls at its finest.*

"Carter!" Phil opened his arms. "Of course I did!"

Carter grinned and strode toward Thane's father. Nobel barked, then growled. His ears went back, his hackles rose, his tail dropped, as if ready for a fight.

Carter backed off. "Whoa, where'd you get the mutt?"

"Nobel's from the Animal Shelter. Meagan, a girl who works there, says he's loyal and loves kids, so I figured he'd be a good match for Thane."

"Nobel, eh? With a name like that you'd think he'd be purebred. What is he? Husky? Doberman? Shepherd?"

Phil laughed. "All of the above I suppose, and maybe more. Whatever he is, he seems okay with it."

Thane stared at Nobel for a few moments. His mix of brown, grey, and black fur had relaxed somewhat and his ears moved forward. He sniffed, whined, then looked directly at him. The dog's light blue gaze struck Thane, penetrating him as if he were sitting there completely naked. He shuddered as Nobel let out a yip and sauntered slowly over to him. His wet, cool nose poked Thane under the arm. He licked his elbow. Thane shuddered again. *Maybe if I ignore him he'll go lay down.*

"Well, at least the dog seems to like Thane," Carter said. He held out his hand and walked toward the kitchen table. "Hey, Thane, I'm Carter Cormack, your father's—"

"Whatever," Thane cut in, attempting to suppress his feelings, his voice, his emotions. "Don't care. Don't want to know the details."

Nobel growled again. Carter withdrew his hand and backed off.

"Thane, that's rude," Phil said, frowning.

He shrugged. "At least I didn't growl at him."

Nobel wagged his tail. He nudged Thane again, but he pushed the dog away.

"It's okay, Phil, it's no big deal." Carter moved closer to him, wrapped an arm around his shoulder, and kissed his cheek. He eyed Thane, and smirked. "Your boy just needs to get used to the idea of us being in an intimate relationship."

Thane's nostrils flared. *Intimate relationship?* Intense heat flushed through his body. A strange, rattling noise behind him begged for his attention. He checked over his shoulder to find his bowl of stew vibrating on the table, as if it were in the throes of an earthquake. His jaw dropped. The bowl vibrated faster and faster until the spoon bailed, and the bowl, along with its contents, went airborne. He ducked.

Splat! The stew hit the front of Carter's shirt and rolled down the length of his pants to land on a pair of polished cowboy boots. The bowl, however, hit his prominent chin and rolled into the next room. Nobel barked. He bolted for the stew casualties strewn across the floor.

"Thane!" Phil gasped. "What were you thinking?"

"But, I...I didn't throw—" Thane stopped, thinking about his dad's coffee cup. *Or did I?*

Carter rubbed his chin, then winced. "Seems to me your kid wasn't thinking, Phil. Maybe he needs a lesson on how to respect his elders." He sneered at Thane, and advanced toward him.

Thane's eyes bugged. He jumped from his seat, grabbed the pipe wrench off the table, and stood firm. "Last time I checked this wasn't your house, septic man, so school's out for you!"

"Whoa!" Carter held up his hands. "Truce, kid! I was heading for the counter to grab some paper towels."

"Seriously, Thane, what's gotten into you?" Phil's face reddened. "You've never acted out like this before."

"It's probably a big adjustment for him, Phil," Carter offered. "Look, you need some time to sort things out with your kid, and remind him of who wears the pants in this house. I'll let myself out. Call me later." He wiped any remnants of stew off his shirt before slowly backing out of the kitchen, with one eye on Nobel, and the other on Thane. His father muttered a curse before he ran after him.

Thane strangled the wrench. Thoughts of his father and Cormack embracing out of his sight, making up like couples do, entered his mind. His mother used to be in his father's arms, not this other man, this stranger, this home-wrecker. But no. The fantasy was gone. This was Thane's reality. A broken reality. The hard truth.

Suddenly, that odd sensation returned inside him. Engulfing him, enraging him. Sweat blistered through his skin and ran down his face. What could only be described as an electric shot flowed through him again, making his hand shake and his teeth rattle. Nobel whined and Thane glanced down at his hand. The pipe wrench slowly bent backward in front of his eyes, almost melting in his grasp. Freaked, he dropped it, and stepped away. He wiped his face roughly with the back of his hand. This was no spoon. This was a heavy, solid wrench. This was not normal.

His stomach churned. *What's happening to me?*

"I'll call you tomorrow, Carter!"

Panicking, Thane lunged for the wrench and stared at it. As hurried footsteps entered the kitchen, he twirled around and hid the twisted tool behind his back. His breathing steadied as his dad leaned into the door frame much as Cormack had earlier. He crossed his muscled arms over his big chest and stared at Thane. His face was stone, his jaw set. It was the perfect poker face if they'd been playing cards. But this was far from a card game, and Thane badly needed an ace up his sleeve.

Phil raised a dark brow. "What are you hiding behind your back?"

We want to hear from you! If you enjoyed this book, please consider leaving a review online or at pandapublishing8@gmail.com.

Discussion Questions:

1. How does Hart's psychic ability shape his identity and his relationships with others? Do you think his gift is a blessing or a burden?

2. How does Hart's struggle with illiteracy affect his interactions and decisions? What does this reveal about societal perceptions of intelligence and capability?

3. How does Diana's grief over her mother's murder influence her actions and decisions throughout the story? In what ways does her grief evolve as the investigation progresses?

4. At what point do Diana and others in Fairy Falls begin to trust Hart's ability? How does skepticism play a role in their investigation?

5. The novel suggests that Fairy Falls is threatened by corruption. How do Hart and Diana's discoveries reflect larger issues of power and justice in society?

6. Psychometry is based on the idea that objects carry memories. How does this concept challenge our understanding of history, truth, and personal connection?

7. How does Hart's transition from an urban environment to a small town influence his character development? What are the differences in how people treat him in each setting?

8. How does the novel explore the difference between seeking justice and seeking revenge? Do you think Diana and Hart's motivations change throughout the story?

9. How does the town of Fairy Falls react to Hart and Diana's investigation? In what ways does the town's reaction help or hinder their search for the truth?

10. The story implies that Fairy Falls has an identity that could be lost. What do you think is the "true essence" of the town, and how do Hart and Diana work to preserve it?